Charlee LeBeau
&
The Salish Wind

c. v. gauthier

◆ FriesenPress

Suite 300 - 990 Fort St
Victoria, BC, v8v 3K2
Canada

www.friesenpress.com

Art Direction: Marty Dolan and C.V. Gauthier
Cover Design & Graphics: Marty Dolan and Cynthia Cui
Deception Map Illustration: Josephine Steeves
Cover Photo: Susanne Fauchon

TUANN ANDREWS
PUBLISHING

Steveston, British Columbia
tapublishing@shaw.ca

ISBN
978-1-5255-9293-5 (Hardcover)
978-1-5255-9292-8 (Paperback)
978-1-5255-9294-2 (eBook)

1. *YOUNG ADULT FICTION, HISTORICAL, EXPLORATION & DISCOVERY*

Legal Deposit, Library and Archives Canada, 2021
Distributed to the trade by The Ingram Book Company

For all the brave, determined
women and girls.

Deception Island

Vancouver Island

Fools Cove

N
W—E
S

Lekwungen Land

Oldwoodland Trail

North Trail

Bluff Trail

Cross Island Trail

Clamity Cove

Anguish Point

Hidden Cove

1

i

There's a freedom that comes with being dead. That's what I was thinking when I left Jake Miller's boarding house for the San Francisco docks. When you're dead, you don't have to worry about what just happened or what might happen next. All your troubles get left behind or float away. I felt so free and light, my feet barely touched the ground.

Except I wasn't really dead. I wasn't off to tend the golden horses, hitched up to them heavenly chariots that the church people liked to sing about. Nor had I been sent to clank chains through somebody's house in the wee hours of the morning. I was unburdened though, like some poor mule relieved of its heavy load after a grueling trek up a steep mountain trail. I'd read a story once about a Greek man who had to carry a boulder around on his back everywhere he went. He could never put it down. That's no way to live.

It was an hour before midnight when I left the south of town. I'd given myself double the time I needed to find the Sunshine Café on the north end, just in case I got delayed along the way. The old man across the hall from where I used to live had warned me not to arrive early or late. He had given me mysterious, detailed instructions and made me swear not to breathe a word to anyone. I'd kept my promise and didn't even tell my best friend, Jake, though it killed me not to confide in him. It was the first secret I'd kept from him in all the years I'd known him.

It was a perfect night for a secret midnight rendezvous at the docks. The sky was clear and dark, with only a sliver of a moon. Lights from house windows and street lanterns cast occasional splinters of yellow into the road. I was a wisp of a figure, an almost invisible silhouette drifting through a quiet neighborhood of San Francisco.

A sudden rustle in the hedge up ahead put weight back into my ghostly strides. I stepped behind the fat trunk of a crooked oak tree. The last thing I needed was to have a dog tear out of a yard, bark its head off, and draw attention to me.

The top of the hedge branches rocked. A hunched, cat-like figure dropped to the ground and tiptoed into the road in front of me. I didn't move. Another one joined the first. When the venture appeared safe, they paused and looked back. I grinned as a baby racoon tumbled from the hedge and scampered after them. When they had almost crossed the empty road, I continued on my way. They froze at the sight of me, eyes glowing in the dim streetlight, and then darted into the bushes. I had a little family like that once. I wished them better luck.

Jake's boarding house was on the hill near Rincon Point, south of the wharf district. With his pretty neighborhood behind me, I descended toward the yellow lights that lined the boardwalks and wharves of the bay. A mix of fear and excitement tightened around my ribs like a lady's corset. Soon, I would either step into freedom, or I would take the bait and step into a terrible trap.

I'd left Jake's house, allowing plenty of time to get across town. Traveling alone at night with a large bag slung over my back, I had to stay out of sight as much as possible. I could be taken for a night thief, grabbed and searched, beaten and robbed. I avoided busy streets and watched for anything that might spell trouble.

I hadn't even reached Market Street when men's laughter broke the stillness of the night. I ducked into some untrimmed bushes and crouched in the shadows. Three figures soon appeared, ambling up the street toward me. They stopped less than ten feet away from my hiding spot.

"Go on, boys. Shoo," I said under my breath.

But they stayed right where they'd stopped, by a path that cut through the shrubs into a yard.

They hadn't seen me and weren't in any condition to notice much more than a glass of whiskey in front of them. I lowered my bag to the ground, tucked myself deeper into the bushes, and peeked through a gap in the branches.

There were three of them, young men, maybe twenty years old. The one in the middle was flat out, stumbling drunk. His legs wobbled around under him like cooked noodles. He'd draped his arms over the shoulders of his pals and, when he lifted his head to speak, his words came out too loud. One friend clapped a hand over his trap while the other hushed him up. Then they all collapsed into a heap of snorts and giggles.

Even though I'd dressed in Jake's old clothes to disguise myself as a boy, it was too dangerous to pass by them. I'd grown taller and stronger over the past year, but I was still too scrawny and thin. A year of hard work and living hand to mouth had cut me into undernourished, lanky angles. Lucky for me, I looked nothing like a girl who'd just turned fifteen. But up close in the dark, I'd be taken for a boy, and the perfect age to be picked on.

Although posing as a boy didn't guarantee my safety, it was far better than the alternative. No girl was going to talk her way onto the crew of a sailing ship. And no girl in her right mind would be out on the streets at such a late hour. Well, the ladies of the brothels downtown would be out, but that was their work and even they didn't wander far from the familiar blocks of their employment.

I felt the clock ticking as the young men tried to pull themselves together. Drunks are annoying and unpredictable. I'd learned that the hard way, living with one for a year. It isn't easy to figure out what they're gonna do next when they don't know themselves.

The men gabbed and slurred their words and blew smoke rings into the night air. I cursed and scanned the other side of the bushes. If they didn't move soon, I'd have to cut past them through the inside yard. I prepared myself to go.

Just then, a man came out onto the front porch of the house. He held up a lantern and light flooded the yard. I was in plain view. If he turned his head a quarter turn to his left, he'd be staring right at me. I couldn't fade back into cover. Any movement would make him turn my way.

"Eddie?" the man said.

The young men stamped out their smokes and straighten themselves up.

"It's me, Pops. I'll be right in." The one in the middle was Eddie.

"Pipe down then. You boys are waking the dead."

I'm already fully awake, I thought, crouching perfectly still, trying to make myself feel invisible again.

"Please don't look this way, mister," I whispered.

The man turned away from me. He hung his lantern on a hook by the front stairs and shuffled back inside. I sighed with relief.

Eddie's friends helped him along the path to his front door. As they cut through the opening into the yard, I ducked out to the street side. My bag hooked on a branch and it snapped as I slipped through. I stopped dead.

"Here, kitty kitty," Eddie called, smacking his lips in a sloppy kissing sound.

"Wasn't that her name?" one of his friends asked. I left them snickering and guffawing in a heap in front of Eddie's porch.

4

The close encounter left me more than just annoyed by the delay. I walked on, keeping to the dirt sections, mindful of the sound my boots made on cobblestones and boardwalks. I glanced over my shoulder a dozen times or more. Every shadow cast from a tree branch was a giant arm reaching out to claw me back.

Where the hill flattened out, the landscaped streets with trees and hedges gave way to small cottages, then to inns and hotels and rooming houses. I crossed Market Street, relieved to have entered a familiar part of town.

I considered my route through the next section of the city. I didn't want to show up at the Sunshine Café in a lathering sweat, exhausted from lugging my heavy canvas bag up and down the wicked hills. The crowded, rowdy streets of downtown weren't an option. While a person carrying a sea bag wouldn't get a second look there, it was where I used to live with my no-good Uncle Jack. That was where two bad men who had lost mining shares to him had run him out of town and chased after me for them. I wasn't about to show my face anywhere near there.

The wharf district with a boardwalk that followed the water's edge was by far the shortest route, but it was even more danger-ous. The two bad men had been staying at the Nugget Hotel by the water. They had also tracked me to my job at the Livery on the wharf, and set me on the run from there, too. Even without those problems, the waterfront wasn't safe at the best of times. A random recruiter could snatch me and haul me off. There were still men around who made wages kidnapping unsuspecting boys and men and selling them off to sea against their will. I had to stay well away from the docks. That left one reasonable route to take, and that was off the water, skirting the edge of Chinatown.

I set out again, unable to shake off a sense that I wasn't alone. I checked over my shoulder, but nobody was there. I pressed on. A few blocks later, my skin itched, like I'd gotten prickles in my shirt when I'd hidden in the bushes. I stopped and looked behind me, searching for something out of the ordinary. Nothing. Three blocks more and my tingling senses got the best of me. I dropped behind a rock wall at the archway leading into Chinatown. Concealed from the street, I leaned back on my haunches, merged into the shadows and watched the street I'd just come down.

Papa always said that if something didn't feel right, it probably wasn't, and if you gave it a little room, whatever it was would show itself. Papa had been a guide for the Hudson's Bay Company in the northern territories. He'd taught me everything I knew about survival.

I counted backwards from thirty. Nothing. "Patience, Charlee," I heard Papa say. Nineteen. Eighteen. There! I hadn't imagined it. Someone was coming. Someone was sneaking along behind me!

2

i

A gentleman in dark clothing approached the Chinatown gate. A long cloak was draped over his shoulders, and a broad hat concealed all but the bottom half of a dark, bearded face. He carried a cane with an ornate head in his gloved hands. Maybe it was nothing. Maybe he just happened to be behind me and was unsure of where he was going. He walked in my direction with cautious, silent steps. I held my breath. Across from the Chinatown gate, he stopped and poked his cane into a dark doorway. He wasn't lost. He was hunting for me.

How long had he been following me? And why? No way he was some common crook seeing a chance at a quick grab. He was dressed too well and didn't act like the street thieves I'd come to know. I figured him for some kind of special investigator because he knew exactly what he was doing, like he'd trained at it for years. Nobody but my papa could follow me that close and get away with it.

He retraced his steps to pick up my trail, like a hound that'd gotten ahead of a scent. He'd caught up with me where there had been no place to turn off without being seen. He knew I was there somewhere, and he was eliminating every place I could hide. It was only a matter of time before he worked his way back to the rock wall.

Whatever he wanted with me couldn't be good and I didn't want to stick around to find out what it was. Most of all, I didn't want him to blow my rendezvous at the Sunshine Café. I had to ditch him and fast. I couldn't outrun him carrying a heavy bag, but no way would I leave my mining shares and worldly possessions behind. There was only one way out of the situation and it was right behind me.

Chinatown was full of alleys and unexpected obstacles. Its maze of cramped spaces and dead-end lanes was a nightmare for an unfamiliar traveler, even in broad daylight. It would take me a little out of my way, but I knew it like my own backyard. I doubted this gentleman had made hundreds of trips through its streets like I had. I could use that to my advantage.

Chinese men might eye me suspiciously, passing through at such a late hour. They'd track me through their streets, as they always did. They wouldn't bother me if I minded my own business. At least, they never had. I'd never pushed my luck at this late hour of the night.

Seconds ticked by like the last ones left on an unwound clock. I waited for the opportunity to make my move while massaging a sudden cramp in my shin, brought on by tense muscles in a nervous crouch. Watching this investigator, I'd determined he was on his own. It would come down to good timing and keeping my wits sharper than his. I was ready.

The investigator turned his back to look behind some stacked crates. I leaped to my feet, threw my bag over my shoulder and took off into Chinatown. He didn't call out, or holler for me to stop, which pretty much told me he wasn't official police. He lit out after me as soon as I showed myself. I had maybe twenty paces on him.

I made a quick left, aware of him gaining ground behind me. I made a right, and another left, choosing streets that had many places to exit or hide. I turned onto a main street, certain I'd thrown him off in the switchbacks. But when I looked over my shoulder, I saw him round the corner right behind me. He was reading the changes, as I would have done. He picked up on my direction using the expressions on faces, the unusual parting of a group, the exclamations of surprise, the sound of my boots echoing off the cobblestones and narrow walls. I couldn't shake him and I couldn't outrun him. I needed help.

I'd reached an area controlled by the most powerful tong in Chinatown. Ahead was a street with opium dens, seedy gambling houses, and dangerous criminals. If the man followed me in there, he'd have to deal with his own share of troubles.

I turned right and barged into the crowd. Late-night people jammed the street, drawn to the debauchery and the thrills. I was an obvious, unwelcome intruder. As I pressed my way through the smoky haze, a man came at me. He was a whole head taller than everyone. Dressed in the traditional buttoned tunic and pants worn by Chinese men, he balanced a long pole over his broad shoulders. The pole sagged from the weight of the heavy baskets on each end. People stepped out of the way of both of us. I altered my path. He matched my position. I braced myself for a hard collision, but at the last second, he stepped aside and I ducked the swing of his pole and the crushing blow of a basket coming at my head.

There was a loud commotion behind me. The tall man took it in and then scowled at me. I didn't know him, but I'd seen men like him before on the many nights I'd passed through these streets. He was a community watchman, a man chosen by the tong leadership to protect and serve. He was not someone to mess with.

"*Why jing chut,*" I said, gasping for breath. "*Hak jing.*"

I tipped my head a certain way, hoping he'd understand what I was trying to say.

He replied with a particular tip of the head back, an acknowledgment so slight that people in other parts of the city wouldn't have noticed the exchange between us.

Corrupt police, I had said to him.

He had my back, is what he'd replied.

I'd learned a few Chinese words and phrases from my friend Taitai, who had a laundry a few blocks over, but the subtle gestures I'd learned from her were even more useful. They could explain a situation in a split second. It was a whole other way of communicating when words weren't possible.

The watchman let me pass and swung his pole in behind me. The investigator would have to get past him, too. I took off while I had the chance. At the end of the lane, I looked back to see the huge watchman forcing the investigator back to where he'd entered. By the time he found another way around the block, I'd be long gone and all traces of me would have vanished.

I left Chinatown and headed for the bay, confident I was rid of him for good. I figured he'd just happened across me, took me for a naïve and petty criminal, and hoped to lure me into a protection racket. If he'd known what I was up to and where I was going, he'd have gone straight there and waited to ambush me. Nonetheless, I reminded myself to be vigilant near the Sunshine Café, on the outside chance he had a partner working with him waiting to do just that.

Although I'd vowed to stay off the wharf and approach the Sunshine Café from behind, I couldn't risk losing any more time on the unknown backstreets surrounding the north wharves. At the corner of Washington and Wharf Street, I stopped in a doorway to mop the sweat off my face and make sure the boardwalk was clear. I shifted my bag from my aching shoulder and turned north, slipping along at a steady pace. With nobody giving me a second look, and nobody in hot pursuit anymore, the light, ghostly feeling came back over me. I felt almost invisible.

Griffin's Wharf was just ahead.

Just then, the bells of a distant church chimed midnight.

"No! I'm almost there!" I broke into a fast trot.

I'd explored these streets many months earlier, when I thought the café was called The Midnight. Jake had also looked for the café one day after school, to check out its location for me. I knew where it was. I could picture it, on a cross street up from the wharf. I had to find it fast and get in the door. I turned west, away from the docks and the water. One more block to go.

The streets weren't busy, but I'd never set foot in this area after dark. I kept my head bowed, cap pulled down, bag hoisted on my shoulders like a sailor. I hurried to the place where it was supposed to be and looked around. There was no place called the Sunshine Café in sight!

As a clock in my head ticked off precious minutes past midnight, I read the shop signs in a panic. I had the old man's words in my head saying, "Don't be late!"

What would happen if I arrived late? He hadn't told me what would happen. My heart raced. The café had to be here! After all the waiting, the checking, the rehearsing, it couldn't end like this. I couldn't have made such a careless mistake. I spun around and looked frantically in all directions. Just then, a wagon across the street pulled away. Hidden behind it was a tiny café with a yellow awning.

3

i

The Sunshine Café looked different from what I expected. Its yellow awning, faded and weathered, was almost colorless in the dark street. I'd expected something brighter. Something sunnier. It was a good thing Jake had mentioned the awning. I never would have spotted the café name engraved on a small wood shingle hanging in the steamed-up front window.

I sized up the street outside the café one more time, searching for a sign of anything out of the ordinary. I looked back along the street from where I came. Nobody had paid me any mind. The old man's warnings circled like vultures in my head. My palms and armpits prickled. I took a deep breath, strode across the street and lifted the latch on the weathered door.

A little bell tinkled as I walked in. The café was small and narrow, with little tables jammed together and a counter with stools along one side. The room fell silent and every head turned to look. Black men filled the seats at the tables. The warm air carried the aroma of apple pie.

"Take the second to last stool, far end from the door," the old man had said.

The second stool was open. So were the two stools on each side of it. I hadn't even thought about what I'd do if I'd come in and found the seat taken. Lucky for me it wasn't. I made my way through the tight rows of tables, feeling the eyes of every man in the café watching me.

The customers quietly resumed what they were doing as I made my way to the stool. Complete silence would have been terrifying. Still, the hum of their voices seemed too flat. There was no laughter, not a single sound that stuck out and might cause a head to turn. I kept my eyes glued straight ahead, afraid everyone could hear my fast breathing. I slid my bag off my shoulder and placed it on the floor by the stool. I laid my cap on the counter, wiped the nervous sweat off my forehead and sat down.

A huge black man approached from behind the wooden counter. He was so big that the counter top barely reached the top of his thighs. He placed his hands down in front of me. They were the size of dinner plates.

"Late for a boy to be dining," the waiter said, his penetrating eyes searching every thread of my coat, every hair on my head for some kind of clue why I'd darkened his doorway at such an hour.

"I'd like a coffee. Black, please," I said, following the old man's exact instructions.

My voice quaked, came out quieter than I intended, but the waiter heard me clear enough. He stiffened at my request. As he lifted the pot and poured a cup of coffee into a chipped cup, his eyes swept over to the door and he motioned with his head. The bell over the door tinkled, signaling someone leaving the café.

My hands trembled when I reached for the coffee. I thought I'd spill it if I tried to drink, so I cupped my fingers around the warm mug and hung on, waiting for the next step. I didn't dare look up.

He pushed a menu over to me with a large forefinger. This was it. I politely pushed it back to him and summoned confidence to deliver my next line.

"I already know what I want. I want the Midnight Express."

"The Midnight Express," he repeated. "It's past midnight."

I looked up and swallowed hard. Nothing in his face gave away what he was thinking.

"Only a couple minutes past," I said, determined not to be deterred.

"You want that with gravy?"

Gravy! What was this about gravy? The old man didn't mention any gravy! I stared into my cup for an answer that wasn't there. Think, Charlee! Did I want gravy or not? He leaned toward me, towered over me, forced me to look up. His eyes burned a hole in my face as he waited for the right answer.

"Well?" he said.

Just then, the bell over the door tinkled again. I shot a quick glance over and saw two men come back in. One looked to the waiter behind the counter and shook his head slightly. They'd gone out to check the street. That brief interruption gave me enough time to recover.

"I want the Midnight Express," I said to the waiter. I stuck with the exact words the old man had told me to say. I'd rehearsed them every night, waiting for this day to come.

The waiter squinted at me. Then he leaned back and threw his dishcloth over a shoulder.

"Today's special. Not sure if we have any left. I'll check." He disappeared into the kitchen. The saloon-style doors slapped back and forth behind him. The café resumed the noisy buzz I'd heard when I came in.

I took a nervous sip of coffee. I sensed every pair of eyes in the place on my back. I had to look really out of place, a young whitish boy in a colored café. That part didn't bother me much since I wasn't an immediate threat to anyone. I tried to forget about feeling out of place and concentrated on the important conversation with the waiter.

I hadn't asked the old man why I had to get to the Sunshine Café right at midnight. I was running for my life at the time. I'd accepted his warning as the secret instructions I needed to find Amos Jefferson, who was the only one who could help me. I'd memorized the instructions without question, branded them into my frantic brain so I'd have them when the time came.

Was the gravy some kind of surprise test the waiter made up? Why else wouldn't the old man have told me about the gravy question? Maybe he didn't know. He'd said I had to be ready for anything and not let myself get distracted. I had to use my head.

I was half way through my coffee when the waiter returned with a bowl of hash. He plunked it on the counter in front of me with a dull thud and laid a spoon down beside it. The small bowl of steaming food smelled rich and spicy.

"If they bring food," the old man had said, "it means they're checking on you. That's good. Eat it. Means you understand."

I picked up the spoon and dipped it into the hash. I lifted a small bit to my mouth and blew on it, pretending that it might be hot, while telling my clenched stomach to calm down, cooperate, and do its job. I took a small nibble.

The waiter busied himself with dishes but had his eyeball on me the whole time. I reloaded the spoon and ate it heartily. I had to be as ordinary as possible, and that meant behaving like a hungry boy. I took another, bigger mouthful. Then another. It was delicious. Nerves buried in wonderful food, my stomach decided hunger was more important than fear. Eating something calmed me down.

"More coffee?" the big man asked as I scraped the bottom of the bowl. Another unexpected question would not throw me off.

I shook my head and pushed the bowl away from me.

"No thank you, sir. I need to see Cook." It was the last line I'd been told to say.

The muscles in his thick forearms twitched. His eyes searched me again.

"Come around then," he said. He looked again in the direction of the door.

I picked up my cap and bag. He lifted the hinged counter beside me and beckoned to me. Once I was through, he grabbed my arm, his big hand clamped around it, and steered me through the swinging doors into the back of the café. I was certain he could break my arm if he wanted to. I knew one other thing. Even if I wanted to run, it was too late for that.

The waiter shoved me straight through the kitchen, past a handful of black men and women, who gaped at me, like I was a rat that had suddenly dropped out of the ceiling. We stopped at a back room. The waiter pushed the door open with his foot. In the low light, I could tell it was the pantry and supply room.

"Sit," the man said. He flung me across the floor toward a chair beside a bin of apples. His sudden shove and the weight of my bag made me lose my balance. I stumbled and fell to my knees, clutching at the chair and knocking it over with a loud bang.

This was not going well. "Stay calm. They won't hurt you unless Cook gives the order," the old man had said.

Cook. I'd dealt with the waiter and it was no picnic so far. I had to pull myself together, brace myself for the next round of interrogation. I was on my own now. The old man said he could get me a meeting, but he couldn't guarantee anything more than that. The rest was up to me.

I turned to look back at the huge waiter blocking the door. I tried not to cower, to look as frightened and frail as I felt. At that moment, even in the poor light, I saw a flicker of something gentle on the big man's unsmiling lips.

"You pretty feeble, boy." It was easier for him to accuse me of weakness than apologize for flinging me across the room so hard.

"I'm fine. Lost my balance in the dark is all," I said defiantly, and then told myself to clam up. This conversation wasn't in the plan the old man gave me. It was a mistake to talk when it wasn't needed. Mistakes could cost me everything. The waiter stared at the floor between us. Then he shook his head as if he hadn't heard me, or wished to pretend I hadn't said a word.

"Take that chair, get comfortable. Cook's busy. You gonna have a long wait."

He went out and banged the door shut. A latch clicked from the outside. A key clattered in the lock.

I was alone in the pantry. Trapped. At the mercy of these strangers. I'd got a meeting, thanks to the old man and his instructions. But I still had to get through the man called Cook to find Amos. I hoped by the time he showed up, I hadn't missed my chance.

4

i

Half an hour dragged by in the gloomy pantry. The air was still, warm, and smelled of damp dirt and garlic. I shuffled around in my chair, shifting from one hip to the other, and fiddled with a broken button on my coat. My right leg bounced up and down like a puppet on strings. It was well past midnight now. I tried not to worry about passing time.

While waiting for Cook to come or someone to check in on me and see if I was still alive, I listened to the sounds beyond the door and tried to picture what was going on. Pots and dishes banged around in the kitchen. Nothing unusual there. How many people were out there? I'd passed seven in the back, not counting the big waiter, and fifteen in the café out front. Voices leaked through the gaps and cracks in the wooden walls, but were muffled by the time they reached me. A man gave orders while passing the pantry door. All I caught was one word—"trouble."

Trouble. That was me, all right. Or at least, that's what the rotten half of the Miller family, on the ranch where I grew up, would've said. They hated me. Mr. Miller and his son, Jake, were the good half. They liked me enough to stick up for me, unless it ruffled too many feathers. Mr. Miller even told my papa once that I had a future.

When Mr. Miller struck it rich during the California gold rush, he bought a ranch in Sonoma, north of San Francisco. He didn't know the first thing about what it took to run a big spread. So when Papa rode in with a little girl tucked behind his saddle, he was in bad need of a foreman. That was back in 1851. He offered Papa a job on the spot, and from then on, we lived and worked on the Miller ranch.

Not long after I arrived at the ranch, I became best friends with Jake Miller. At first, the only thing we had in common was we'd both lost our mamas. But we also liked what the other knew. I taught Jake to fish and track and shoot, stuff I'd learned from Papa. Jake taught me how to read and write. I caught on so fast, Mr. Miller let us do school together.

The good times didn't last long. Two years later, Mr. Miller remarried and the rotten half of the family moved in. When Mr. Miller brought his beautiful new wife and her spoiled daughter to the ranch, everything changed. The Missus, as all of us hands called her, didn't like me one bit, since I was the daughter of the poor ranch foreman and I spent all my time in an unlady-like manner working in the barns with the men and the horses. She didn't want me doing school with Jake and her daughter, Bernadette. Mr. Miller wouldn't let her boot me out. But I got moved to the back of the room where I could only sit and listen.

Bernadette, Jake's sickly and irritating new sister, was almost the same age as me. She desperately wanted to be best friends. When that didn't work out, she made it her mission to ruin my friendship with Jake. Bernadette would cause trouble, I'd be in the middle of it, and then The Missus would blame me.

Jake knew I wasn't the cause of the trouble, but he did think I had a knack for stepping in it. He shrugged off Bernadette's antics and kept his distance from The Missus. I suppose he had to adjust to their arrival on the ranch like all the rest of us. He would never admit it, but I know he steered clear of them whenever he could. The other day, I'd slipped and called his mother "The Missus" to his face. Whatever his own feelings for her were, he wouldn't abide any disrespect. So it was pretty clear where his loyalty would be, when push came to shove.

While I'd been thinking about the ranch, it had become silent outside the pantry. I got out of my chair and pressed my ear to the door. Nothing but a distant hum of muffled conversation. The kitchen sounded like it had shut down. No clanks of pots and utensils, no aromas of cooking food.

I wondered what trouble the voice outside the pantry door had been referring to. I'd been extra careful after that investigator tailed me. Some men had also gone out to make sure I wasn't followed while I was sitting at the café counter. A fresh round of panic caught in my throat and I swallowed hard. What if I was the trouble? It crossed my mind they could be hatching a plan to get rid of me.

I didn't have to examine the tiny room to know it had no windows and only one door that locked from the outside. Even if I made it out the door, a kitchen worker would probably clobber me with a fry pan on the way by. The huge waiter would crush me like a handful of grapes before I got past his counter. I had zero chance getting past all the men in the café. I felt the room get smaller and the men on the other side of the door get bigger as I waited. Sweat beaded on my forehead.

Mulling over my situation spooked my thoughts and spurred them out of control. I paced the small patch of floor between the shelves. Had the old man across the hall from Uncle's place sent me into a trap? Maybe somebody paid him for every orphan he could snare. But snare for what? To be shanghaied and taken off to sea? Uncle had warned me about that. He'd told me to never to trust anyone except for him. It was good advice in this crazy town. I'd learned that in a hurry. I'd spent the past year surviving in the worst parts of San Francisco, doing a man's job for pay that my Uncle Jack drank and gambled away.

It turned out that Uncle couldn't be trusted either. The old man took me in when I'd come home one day to find Uncle Jack gone, and two of his gambling associates after me. Uncle had relieved them of their shares in a gold mining operation, which they'd foolishly used to secure a gambling loan.

Uncle tried to find the share certificate the day he took off. He turned our place upside down, but it just happened I'd stashed it in my coat. He had to settle for stealing all my hard-earned life savings. And when the bad men somehow figured out I had the certificate, they came after me. I crafted an elaborate plan to fake my death and get rid of them. It was brilliant, I had to say so myself.

A flood of guilt came over me again. Jake still thought I was dead. He'd find out soon enough that I wasn't. I didn't mean to hurt him with my plot to get rid of the bad men, and I hoped he'd forgive me for what I'd done by the time I returned to San Francisco with my riches. He wasn't one to carry a grudge.

Where was Cook? I'd been in the pantry a very long time, hunkered down in a root cellar while a twister was bearing down on me. These people at the Sunshine Café were up to something all right, and I'd gotten myself into the middle of it. They'd sized me up like a gunslinger who'd moseyed in off the street, a big pistol hanging off each hip, a trigger-finger looking for trouble.

Maybe the words the old man taught me were part of a secret evil code. Maybe I'd be locked up in an underground vault or sacrificed in a late night ceremony. I shook my head to keep from imagining the worst. Whatever the case, it was pretty clear I meant trouble for them, or I'd unwittingly dragged it in behind me.

Muffled voices got louder outside the door. I scurried back to my chair. I straightened myself and waited for the door handle to move. There was a dull thud and a couple of boards squeaked.

Then nothing again.

To pass the time, and to keep my mind from coming up with horrible outcomes, I distracted myself by doing an inventory of supplies in the pantry. Numbers had a way of making me feel in control and alert. To the right was a pallet of goods, stacked a good fifteen hands high and tied up neatly in tarps. It looked like a new shipment. Or were these goods on their way out? Unable to identify or count anything under the wrapping, I had to leave them out of my calculations.

The shelves on my left were organized and full. The bottom shelf held eight tins of coffee, three sacks of flour, six bags of rice, and nine small barrels of something. I worked through all the shelves, calculated the sums, multiplied, divided, and played with averages and percentages. I could recall every inch of the room and its contents without ever looking around again. It was a skill I had, Papa had said to me when I was five, when I'd noticed a small hand shovel missing from its place in our shed. My mind made detailed pictures of things I saw and read.

I'd just worked out the size of the pantry in square feet, and estimated the area of the pallet of goods under the tarp, when a key turned in the lock. I hoped I was about to meet Cook. I'd know pretty fast if he was a friend or a foe.

5

i

The latch clicked. A person of average build slipped into the room and closed the door. He wore delivery clothes and didn't look to be much taller than me. His steps were so smooth and light on the floor planks, it was as if he wore slippers instead of heeled boots. He sat down on a step stool tucked in a corner behind the door, folded his arms, and leaned against the wall. I could only make out his angular jaw from under the brim of his hat.

"What's your name, son?"

A young man's voice. Not deep or scary, but he meant business. His tone was even, his words quick.

"Samuel. Sam," I said, my voice lower than his without even trying. I decided not to push my luck by adding Fitzquiddick, the full name Jake had come up with when checking out the mining shares certificate at the land office a week earlier.

"Who sent you?"

He leaned near to me, elbows on his knees, and studied my face. I glimpsed a clean-shaven face, strong cheekbones, straight nose. The whites of his eyes flashed in the lantern light. A sudden burst of nerves made my palms clammy. I croaked out an answer.

"The stationmaster on the Tender Line."

He jolted up from his elbows.

"What's his name?"

"I dunno. Never knew his name. Never told him mine neither."

"How'd you know him then?"

"I didn't know him. I was... I mean, he took me... he lived across from me at my tenement."

The questions rattled me. I wasn't prepared. I should have been thinking about what I'd be asked instead of reminiscing about growing up, tallying supplies, and measuring spaces. I knew why the old man had told me how to find the Sunshine Café. It was because I knew about the Midnight. I wouldn't say anything about that if I didn't have to.

"I need to see Cook. Are you...?"

"I'll ask the questions here," he snapped. His bossy reply made me think I'd guessed correctly. "What's your business with Cook?"

"I need him to get me to Amos Jefferson."

The man cursed under his breath and mumbled something that I took to be less than flattering.

"What's the password?"

"Password?"

He drummed his fingers on his knee. "The one the station-master gave you."

"I don't know any password! He didn't give me one. Look, I lived across from the old man is all. He hid me in his place one night. Saved my life. That's a long story that doesn't need telling right now. I had no place to go, so I told him I had to find Amos Jefferson at the Midnight. He didn't know Amos, he said, but he knew the Midnight all right, so he told me when to come to the Sunshine Café and what to say when I got here. He even made me practice what to say. He definitely didn't give me a password. He said, 'Tell Cook the stationmaster on the Tender Line sent you.' Are you Cook?"

He held up his hand for me to stop. I'd gone off, barely taking a breath. Telling a little story to gain some sympathy isn't a bad idea, but it's risky when it crosses over to loose lips and a careless rant. I reminded myself to stick to the questions asked.

The man got up and paced the room, steps so soft I could only hear the swish of his bulky coat as he moved. He was very unusual, but I couldn't put my finger on what was off. After watching him walk back and forth half a dozen times, it struck me. He was in disguise. He wasn't a delivery man at all. He didn't have the hard, choppy gait of a workman.

He stopped behind the stack of supplies, almost hidden from view, and ran a hand along the tarp cover as if it were a huge horse standing in a dark stall.

"How is it you know Amos?" he asked, finally. The gruffness was out of his voice. His words were thin, emotionless.

"I don't really know him. I mean, we met a long time ago. His sister told me if I had trouble in San Francisco to find him at the Midnight and he'd help me. Please. I don't mean anyone any trouble. I just need to find him. He's very hard to find."

"She told you about the Midnight."

It wasn't a question.

"Yes. Miss Molly Jefferson." I blurted out her name and cringed. Had I now dragged her into my trouble by mentioning her name? "She's Amos's sister…"

"Yes, I know who she is."

"You must know of the Miller ranch in Sonoma then. I used to live there. She…" I was going to say "practically raised me" but changed my mind. "She's head cook on the ranch."

"Mmmm," was all he said, and then he sat back down on the step stool and said nothing more.

I took the moment to do some thinking myself. If this man knew Miss Molly, he must have met Mr. John Miller and probably was an acquaintance of his. The more he talked, the more

I could tell he was an educated sort. I was dying to ask about Mr. Miller and the ranch, but held back. I thought it best not to aggravate the situation further and let the unusual man think things through in peace. I had already said way too much.

I put my chin in my hands and looked down at the mysterious floor that made no sound when the strange man walked on it. A bug was trying to haul a huge piece of rice past the toe of my boot. I slid my foot back to let him pass. I spent several long minutes contemplating the bug's life and how determined it was to do its job. It didn't worry that my boot might crush it flat. It didn't give up because it was too hard and too far to go. It just kept lugging that piece of rice across the floor.

"Amos can't take you back to the ranch," the man said after a very lengthy silence.

"Oh no. I don't want to go back there. I can't go back there, actually. I need Amos to take me away for a while. On the *Salish Wind*. It's not safe here for me right now."

"What about your family? Where are they?"

"Don't have any left now. I was living with my Uncle Jack here in town, but he ran off."

"Ran off! And didn't take you?"

"Nope. He's got bad men after him. 'Vigils' is what the old man called them when he saw them fixing to bust down our flimsy door. I can't go back there. They'll snatch me for ransom, or worse, use me as collateral."

"Collateral. Quite the vocabulary you've acquired." His lips pursed into a hint of a smile. His own vocabulary didn't belong to a delivery man. No, he was definitely educated. I pegged him for a gentleman in disguise. He squinted at me and continued. "Those fellows sound more like run-o-the-mill gangsters. Dare I ask, what did your uncle do to get in their bad books?"

I stuck with the old man's version of who the men were, even though I knew he'd been wrong.

"Cheated somebody, I expect. Or borrowed money he couldn't pay back. He's a professional gambler. He's a pretty slick card player except his luck went foul some time ago and he lost everything. If the Vigils catch him, they'll tar and feather him, or rip him limb from limb and hang what's left of him from the courthouse."

"Child. It's 1859. They don't do those things anymore." Then he added, more to himself, "At least not in this town."

"Oh."

"That's not to say your uncle didn't get himself in serious trouble. People with unpaid debts disappear without a trace, have unfortunate accidents. The gangs can be ruthless, if that's who he tangled with, and they've got eyes and ears all over town. You're sure the men weren't just a couple of sore losers?"

That's exactly what they were, but I had to stick with the official story or spill the beans on the mining shares that I had with me right there in the pantry.

"The old man saw them. Recognized their type. He figured they were the Vigils."

"Well, he'd know."

He got up and leaned against the door. With his build not much bigger than mine, I was pretty sure I could take him if I had to. But I didn't feel threatened. Despite the circumstances, we were having a decent, civil conversation. Plus, I thought I was making headway convincing him I needed to get to Amos.

"After Uncle took off, I hid out at the Livery."

"The big one near Long Wharf?"

"Right. I worked there all last year. Somehow the Vigils tracked me down there and I had to run. Tubby–he's the Livery boss–he helped me duck them and get away. I holed up in an abandoned boat on the south beach, waiting for the end of the month, like the stationmaster told me to, until I could come find Amos."

The man's eyes widened with my story. It was a good one for the telling, and most of it was true.

"Good Lord! How long were you there?"

"Only about a week. It's summer. It wasn't bad."

"How old are you?"

"Fourteen. I mean, turning. Soon. Just had a birthday."

He frowned. The softness drained out of his expression. I put my head down to avoid his intense gaze. Caught up in my tale of escape, I'd messed up my pretend age. He was much too sharp for mistakes. He could smell my lie like I was a frightened skunk. He paused at the door, his hand resting lightly on the latch.

"Thirteen or fourteen. Which is it then?"

The voice wasn't soft anymore. It had a scratchy rasp, the all-business edge again.

"Fourteen. Just," I said, doubling down on my deception. Fifteen was too old for me to be convincing as a boy. "Please, Cook. The old man said you'd get me to Amos. I've done everything he told me to do."

The man stared at me and smirked. "I'm not Cook."

If this wasn't Cook, who was this man I'd spilled my story to? He left the pantry and closed the door behind him.

"Wait. When can I see Cook?"

He didn't answer. He locked the door, and I was alone again. I banged a fist against the side of my head. This had not gone well. Not well at all. He'd tricked me.

6

i

Waiting for something unknown is a terrible way to be idle. It gnaws on the confidence. The imagination comes up with a list of the very worst things that could happen. My patience had run out early into the wait. There was nothing to be done about that, but I didn't have to torment myself when I didn't know what was in store.

The waiter had told me to get comfortable. He'd warned me that Cook was busy. I told myself it was nothing more or less than that. That reassurance, plus the lateness of the night, made my fear of being held captive disappear. A prisoner's restless, detached boredom replaced it. Since I'd already exhausted all the math calculations I could do, I put my imagination to work on more useful matters—like what they'd hidden under the tightly fastened tarps beside me.

The pallet was the length of a coffin, the width of two of them laid side by side. A peek through a gap on one corner revealed long wooden boxes and nothing more. Could be cheap coffins. The pine box they buried my papa in was about the same size. Then I remembered it was almost the last day of July. Papa had died one year earlier on that day.

I didn't want to go over the horror of that again. When I

dwelled on it, it dragged me into a terrible sadness. It was enough to think about the year I'd had since his passing, which had been almost as awful.

After Papa died, his brother—my Uncle Jack LeBeau—had shown up at the ranch, offering to take me in. He made out to be a rich man, who could afford to raise me well. We'd barely left the ranch when I found out he was flat broke.

The neighborhoods I'd lived in with Uncle Jack were crowded and dangerous. He kept saying we'd move back into the nice part of town as soon as his luck changed. That didn't happen. I was barely fourteen when he brought me to live in San Francisco with him. I should have been in school, but instead I had to work.

Jake had also come to San Francisco to attend school that fall. I'd imagined us living in the city and going to school, out of the critical eye of The Missus and away from the annoyance of Bernadette. But our lives couldn't have taken more different paths. His future bloomed like a spring garden. He was a promising young man, the son of a wealthy landowner. He got to attend one of the finest schools in the city. My future smoldered like scorched earth after a forest fire. I had to struggle to eat. I had to work long hours of hard labor and try not to get killed in the chaos that surrounded me.

To make matters worse, when I wrote home to the ranch, Uncle intercepted my letters. I checked the mail almost every day and nobody wrote back. I thought nobody cared about me anymore. That part was the worst. But living with Uncle and all my broken dreams was almost as bad. I couldn't show my face to Jake, even though I'd found out where he lived.

When I ended up alone, with no place to go, I pushed my pride aside and turned to him for help. I was glad I finally did, but our brief reunion was also a reminder of how his life and mine would never be the same. The future was nicely laid out for Jake. Mine was undecided, and I had to fight for every inch of it.

I could easily end up in one of them pine boxes. I had nobody looking out for me the way Jake did. They could kill me over something little, or for no reason at all. The longer the wait in the pantry, the more I liked my chances. If they meant to kill me, I'd be dead already and nailed into one of those long boxes under the tarp. Whoever was in charge had to have something else in mind.

I yawned. It was very late, and it had been a day that felt about a week long. It caught up with me. I slouched in the chair and dozed until a sound of the door opening woke me with a start.

The delivery man returned with a cup of water. I rubbed my eyes and drank it all, hoping to refresh my concentration. I meant to be sharper with questions this time.

"Thanks. I was awful thirsty," I said in a solemn, respectful tone, hoping to get us back on a better foot.

"You're welcome." The kind part of him was back. Almost reassuring. But he remained unsettled by the door this time, rather than taking the stool. "Seems you made it to the Sunshine without being followed."

"I was careful. My Papa taught me how to cover tracks."

"I'm sorry we've had to detain you like this. We mean you no harm."

"The old man—the stationmaster, I mean—he told me to trust you. He took a chance helping me and I won't let him down." I remembered the terrible thick scars around his neck, his broken voice, how he said lives were at stake and we could all be caught and killed if I made one mistake. A horrible thought struck me. "Is he all right? I hope those men didn't go after him."

Again, the penetrating stare. He remained expressionless, intensely weighing every word.

"He's fine. He sent word the day you left."

"He told you about me! Then you knew I was coming this whole time!"

"Not exactly. He told us he'd had an unexpected passenger, but we thought your chances of making it were slim. Yet here you are."

"Did Amos know I was coming?" It occurred to me that he didn't or he would have come to meet me.

"No."

I had so many questions. Before I could ask even one, the man pressed on.

"Listen now. This is extremely important. Who else knew you were coming here tonight, besides the stationmaster? The Livery boss?"

I would've asked the same question if an uninvited guest showed up in the middle of my secret operation.

"No, Tubby thinks I went to Sacramento for a job."

"Anyone else? I need the truth."

I hadn't planned on mentioning Jake, but I couldn't lie knowing what I did. They were moving runaway slaves through this café. Every detail mattered.

"Only one person knew I was coming here and I trust him with my life. He won't tell."

The man stiffened. "Who?"

"My best friend. Jake Miller." I shook my head and looked down. I was dragging every innocent person I loved into my problems.

"John's son!"

I stood up. "You know Mr. Miller?" He pointed for me to sit back down and I immediately followed the order.

"Jake Miller knows you are here." He rubbed his eyes and forehead like he'd just got a big headache. He did not like my answer.

"Yes. Jake helped me get away from... from... the Vigils. I made him swear not to tell anyone but his father, and not even to tell him until tomorrow. He'll keep his word. He doesn't know anything about the Midnight. The stationmaster made me swear

I wouldn't tell a soul and I didn't. Jake only knows about the bad men after me. All he knows is I was going to find Amos at the Sunshine Café so he could get me out of town for a while till things cool off."

He sighed. "Anyone else?"

I thought about the investigator who had followed me part way. Should I mention him? If I did, it might ruin my chances of getting to Amos. If I didn't, and he was out there, we'd all pay the price.

"An investigator tailed me, but I lost him in Chinatown," I blurted out. The delivery man straightened up. He listened intently as I gave a detailed description of the man and how I'd lost him. "I'm certain he didn't know where I was going."

"This is good information," he said, squinting at me like he wasn't sure whether he should kill me or congratulate me.

Just then, there was a light rap on the door. The man put his fingers to his lips and opened the door a crack. I couldn't make out what was said, but the voice outside the door belonged to a woman. Could this be Cook? Was Cook a woman? He stepped back and swung the door open to let the woman in.

"Sorry to drag you out so late, Mizzy. Got a boy in here named Sam. Claims to know you from the ranch."

Light from the kitchen made a silhouette out of the woman. There was something familiar about her angles. The shawl covering her head dropped to her shoulders, revealing her face. I gasped.

"Mrs. Plea," the woman cried. "It's Luke's girl. It's Charlee LeBeau!"

7

i

"Miss Molly!" I flung myself into her open arms.

"Shshsh! Don't call me that, Charolat," she whispered. "There's no Miss Molly here."

"What are you doing here? Why aren't you on the ranch?"

"Me? What about you? Everyone figured you was gone for good. I knew you wasn't. I just knew it!" She ran her hands through my short, ragged hair and frowned. "Where is that no-good uncle of yours? I swear I'll beat him like an old parlor rug."

Tears sprung from her eyes as she looked me over and gently tucked a stray piece of hair behind my ear. We hugged each other again. When her arms encircled me this time, my heart burst open with a terrible pain and I couldn't let go. Miss Molly shuddered and I choked back tears. Our shared anguish and loss flooded back in an instant. A long minute passed.

"Well, this is quite a situation," said the delivery man, who was really a woman in disguise. She'd been standing quietly to the side, watching our tearful reunion. I let go of Miss Molly and sealed off my hurt with an accusation.

"You're not a man."

"No, I am not. Unless it suits me to appear as one, which it does on this occasion. The light, or the lack of it, is definitely in my favor this evening. And it seems you are not a boy either."

The woman tilted my face into the lantern light.

"I never thought I'd see the day. I've been played at my own game, Mizzy."

I bit my lip as she scrutinized me. This was no time for talking back, raising her ire.

"I was going to tell you, Mrs. Pea," I said.

"It's Plea."

"Mrs. Plea. I mean, I obviously would have. I pretended to be a boy to get my job at the Livery, see, because a poor girl like me wouldn't have a chance in this town. I'm so used to acting like a boy—I've been doing it for a year—sometimes I forget I'm not."

"You're very good at it," she said, frowning with disapproval.

She wasn't too mad that I'd pulled a fast one over on her. I figured we were even since she'd fooled me just the same. Maybe she'd seen it that way.

"We can all drop our charades for the moment then, can't we? To be clear, you only call people by the names you're given, understood?"

"Yes. Mrs. Plea. Mizzy. Got it."

"Ma'am?" Miss Molly interjected respectfully. "This is Charlotte Lee. My Charolat. Luke always called her Charlee."

"Charlee," she repeated. "I recall."

"Are you going to give me a different name, too?" I asked.

Mrs. Plea laughed. "I think you have enough names already. Sam, wasn't it?"

She took off her broad-brimmed hat. A bun of wavy black hair was combed back tight and carefully pinned on the top of her head. Streaks of silver around her temples told me she was older than her smooth face suggested. Her elegant features and intense eyes made her striking. I imagined she could command a room of men with a single eyebrow.

"Luke's brother took her away, supposedly to attend school

here in San Francisco," Miss Molly said. "Then we were told he'd moved, taken her to Boston. I thought I'd never see her again."

"Cook told me." Mrs. Plea turned to me, her face softened with sympathy. "I knew your father, Charlee. He did some work for me now and then. He knew horses like he was one of them. I'm very sorry for your loss." Miss Molly stifled a ragged breath.

Papa's death last summer, jumping into the unbroken stallion's corral to pull the wretched Bernadette Miller to safety, was seared in my memory like it had just happened yesterday. I vowed I wouldn't go to that dark, bitter place anymore, where I'd blamed Jake's pathetic sister for the terrible accident. I had another axe to grind now, and that was with Uncle.

"I never went to Boston… or to any school." The two women gaped at me. Mrs. Plea's mouth dropped open.

"You were here the whole time?" Miss Molly asked with alarm. "Oh, my! What did Jack do to you?"

"Not much," I said, dryly. "I'm thankful for that."

"Mr. Miller said your uncle and aunt were raising you," Miss Molly said. "You were living somewhere up on Nob Hill… going to one of the best schools for a while… and then you'd moved back east…"

Her voice trailed off as I shook my head on each point. I couldn't look at her for another second or I'd bawl my eyes out. With my head forward, my nose ran. I wiped it on the back of my wrist.

"Uncle called in a favor and got me a job. I tended horses at the Livery, did some bookkeeping there on the side. It wasn't easy, but I got by. Remember you made me promise to find Amos if I had trouble? I tried, but nobody knew him, and asking around was dangerous. Then Uncle got in trouble and ran off, and now I got no place to go. If I stay, some bad men will get me." I was gasping out my story between stifled sobs.

"Are you really fourteen?" Mrs. Plea asked.

I shook my head. "That's my boy's age. I just turned fifteen."

"This boy charade is going to get harder."

"I know. Tubby finally figured it out. I couldn't keep working there much longer, even if the Vigils hadn't caught up with me."

"The Vigils!" Miss Molly exclaimed in horror. "What the Vigils want with you?"

I didn't answer. I felt wrung out. Exhausted. I rocked back and forth, hoping it would soothe me back to a place where I felt clear-headed.

"I declare, this night is one ambush short of a train wreck. Mizzy, stay here with Charlee while I go tend to matters."

"Certainly, Mrs. Plea."

"You two catch up a little. I won't be long. Time is short."

Mrs. Plea pulled her hat on over her bun, adjusted the brim over her eyes, and flipped up the collar of her jacket.

"Wait!" I said. "Where's Amos? Do I still need to talk to Cook? I have to see Cook right away."

The two women exchanged a worried look.

"Amos is Cook. One and the same. I'll leave you to handle this, Mizzy. But I warn you. She insists she has to go with him on the *Salish Wind*."

As soon as Mrs. Plea had closed the door, Miss Molly hauled the step stool over and sat down next to my chair.

"Tell me everything," she said. "And don't tell it all drawn out, like you always do 'cause we don't have much time." She squeezed my knee, gave me a weak smile, and I began.

I told her how I was no sooner off the ranch and Uncle swapped out his fancy suit for some worn out gambling clothes. By the time we made San Francisco, I knew all of his promises about a mansion and a fancy school had been lies. I had to work to help us survive. I'd lived like that for a whole year, posing as a boy so I could get a decent-paying job working with horses at the Livery, and writing letters home to Sonoma that nobody ever answered.

"I got one letter in August last year and then nothing," Miss Molly said. "My heart was broke with your papa passed and you riding off in that carriage with your Uncle Jack to heaven-knows-what. When Mr. Miller came back from town and said you'd moved to Boston, I was shocked. I couldn't believe you'd gone without saying a word."

"I sent at least a dozen letters in the fall and had to stop because I had to… because I didn't have money to spare for postage."

"Did that uncle steal our letters?"

"More likely the no-good postmaster in Portsmouth. Uncle sent me to him. Me and Jake figure he was behind it. But Uncle surely put him up to it."

"That low-down snake! To think I blamed The Missus. I thought for sure she stole them, since she practically ran you off the ranch after that run-in."

I thought of my last encounter with The Missus in the Miller courtyard where, in anger and grief, I'd pinned her hand to the ground with my boot. Obviously, everyone had heard about that. I'd gotten one thing right—I'd never be welcome on the ranch as long as she was there.

"I sent a dozen letters and didn't hear back once," I said. "Jake told me he wrote, too, but I didn't know. I thought you wanted nothing more to do with me." I could feel the tears welling up in my eyes again. Even though I knew it wasn't true, it had hurt me for so long it still felt deeply real.

"You're my child! I would never!" She threw her arms around me and rocked me.

"I'm here now, Miss Molly. I mean, Mizzy. I don't think I can get used to calling you that."

"You must. Nobody who works for Mrs. Plea uses a real name.

In my case, it's the other way around. Miss Molly was a made-up name. Mizzy was my slave name. I claimed it back. I own it now." Then Mizzy told me how she couldn't bear the ranch anymore, with Papa gone, then me, Jake off to school, and just The Missus, Bernadette, and the little Miller children left. She was so unhappy, Mr. Miller brought her to San Francisco to work for Mrs. Plea.

"I could walk the streets and imagine you here. It gave me a little peace. I always felt you hadn't left. Turns out I was right, but I wasn't looking in the right parts of town. Now. What's this nonsense of going off on the *Salish Wind*?"

I filled her in on the bad men who were after me because of Uncle. She went through all the options I'd considered, without suggesting a return to the Miller ranch, which we both knew to be out of the question, and I shot them down one by one.

"So I have to go. Just for a while. Just until those men move on and forget about me."

I was about to tell her about the mining shares when Mrs. Plea returned.

"I'm sorry I have to tear you two apart again. You must go now, Mizzy. Your ride is waiting."

Mizzy pulled me to her for one last hug. "I'll see you soon, Charolat. You listen to Mrs. Plea now, and do what she says. You're safe now, understand?" She covered her head with her shawl, nodded to Mrs. Plea, and hurried from the pantry.

8

i

"Here's what we're going to do, Charlee," Mrs. Plea said, as the door closed behind Miss Molly. "I'll be seeing Mr. Miller tomorrow. I'll speak to him about your situation. In the meantime, for tonight, I'll put you up in a safe house. You can stay there until I can arrange for you to return to Sonoma."

I stood up. "I can't go back to the ranch."

"You said you need to get out of town and I agree with that assessment."

I thought about Bernadette and The Missus and how much they hated me. The Missus would never allow me to return. She believed I wanted to kill Bernadette. Everything had changed at the ranch. And without Miss Molly there, I'd have nobody but the horses.

"It isn't my place anymore. I won't go back," I said.

She sighed. "You don't have a choice. You know too much."

What did she mean, I knew too much? I knew nothing, didn't tell anybody anything, didn't stick my nose in where it didn't belong.

"I promise I won't say a word about any of this. Ask Miss Molly."

"It's Mizzy."

"Sorry, I mean Mizzy." Every time I spoke, I made things worse. If I couldn't keep the names straight, how would she ever trust me? "Mizzy'll vouch for me. Only Jake and the stationmaster know I've come here. And Jake knows nothing about the Midnight. I swear. Not one thing. Cook has to take me with him on the *Salish Wind*. I'll be no trouble. I learn fast and I'll work hard. Please!"

Mrs. Plea listened, expressionless. I didn't even know if Cook would agree to it. It was bold of me to ask for such a thing. I slipped back into my chair and sat with the most respectful posture I could muster.

"It isn't about you, Charlee," she said, finally. "None of it is about you."

Then who was it about? Nobody else was there but me. Nobody else's life was in danger and ruins.

She fished a candy out of her pocket and removed its paper wrapping. It looked like a lemon drop, dusted with white icing sugar. She popped it into her mouth. The paper wrapper crinkled in the silent room. She was deep in thought, considering my request. I licked my dry lips.

"How rude of me. Would you like one? The air in here makes a person's mouth terribly dry."

"If you have an extra," I said.

She found a candy in another pocket and held it out to me, swirling her own around with a fair amount of unladylike smacking. I had the candy in my mouth in seconds. It was just like the ones Jake and I had swiped from a candy dish in Mr. Miller's study when we were little. Its tart lemon flavor made my mouth water.

"You've come at a difficult time, Charlee, but I will consider your request." She spoke softly now and laid a gentle hand on my knee. "It's complicated, but we'll figure this out. Can you trust me, be patient till we're done?"

I tossed the tart candy into one cheek and shrugged. "I got nowhere to go."

"Then I'll see what I can do," Mrs. Plea said, with a reassuring pat on my shoulder.

She moved to the door, then paused and looked back.

"By the way. Did you leave anything behind at the rooming house? Or at the Livery? Anything at all?"

I shook my head. "Not a thing. Not even at the beach. All I got is in my bag right here. I covered my tracks."

"Smart girl. Luke taught you well. Stay quiet now. We'll have you out of here soon."

After she'd gone, I worried about what she might have in mind for me. I could hear Uncle saying, "Don't trust anyone but me." Of all people not to trust, turns out he was at the top of the list. But what did I know then? I was a greenhorn when I first came to the city.

The first thing I learned about San Francisco when I arrived from Sonoma Valley in the summer of 1858 was that the city never slept. In the dark of night, when ranch folk were hours into their rest, this busy port city was wide awake. It isn't right, that's what I thought right off, and got the proof of it when Uncle Jack moved us into a downtown tenement. It was in a section of town where danger was never more than a few steps away, and it was most likely to come at you between dusk and dawn.

The city wasn't all bad, though. Away from the mean neighborhood I lived in with Uncle, there were some nicer sections. You had to have money for those, which Uncle didn't. I was barely fourteen. All I had was an old sock with saved ranch wages. Well, there was a small bag of gold dust that Mr. Miller had given me, but Uncle stole that. I swore I'd kill him for that alone, if it turned out he wasn't already dead, not to mention for leaving two sore miners on my tail.

I'd kept one step ahead of them, but they wouldn't give up.

To make matters worse, I'd gotten Jake involved. So I had to put a stop to it once and for all. This was the night I'd been waiting for. I meant to get out of San Francisco, go to the Fraser Canyon in British Columbia, find the mining operation, and claim my shares.

Mrs. Plea had asked me to trust her. What did I even know about her? She wouldn't suffer a fool, I was sure of that. But she had listened to what I said like it mattered. And she knew Mr. Miller. She wasn't even mad when she found out I was a girl. Truth be told, I liked her right from the start, even when I took her for a delivery man. As for Mizzy, I could feel her heart, and Papa's too, when she hugged me. She would never lead me into harm. Not ever.

Still, it was too soon to trust this Mrs. Plea with the truth about why I had to go north on the *Salish Wind* with Amos. Yes, I needed to get out of town, but that was to make sure the bad men kept believing I was dead and the shares were gone. Soon, they'd move on to their next get-rich-quick scheme. They'd seen my face only once in a dark lane. Before long, they'd forget what I looked like, too.

When Jake told me that Amos worked on the *Salish Wind* and it sailed to Victoria on merchant business, it seemed like a tremendous stroke of luck. That's where I had to go to claim my gold mine company. But there was more to this merchant run than supplies to a new gold mining town. Outside of the pantry walls, something secret and important was going on. I'd barged right into the middle of it. I had undoubtedly caused problems with my unexpected arrival.

With the candy gone, my mouth felt even more sticky and dry than it had before. I fumbled around in my bag for my canteen but my hands wouldn't cooperate. I forgot what I was looking for.

All the excitement had made me very sleepy. My head jerked as I fought to stay awake, waiting for Mrs. Plea to return. I tried the counting game but lost my place. Numbers and supplies tumbled around in my head.

I can't say how much time passed. I dreamed I was on the ranch again, sitting across from Mizzy, writing in my book. Papa was there, too, enjoying a big slab of apple pie. Birds in the nearby oaks chirped along, and the whinny of one of my horse friends reminded me of good things in much better days. Suddenly, ominous grey clouds filled the sky. Papa was lying in the corral and Bernadette, on the back of Thunder, had run him down. "You killed him," I yelled at her, and then she wasn't the rider, I was, and I was trampling her into the ground, urging Thunder to charge, digging my spurs into his sides in a blind rage.

I woke up. The corral vanished and I was sitting in a dimly lit room. I couldn't get my eyes to focus or my limbs to move. I recognized the blurred outlines of two men from the diner. I remembered! I was in the pantry at the Sunshine Café.

They pulled a burlap bag over my head. It smelled of something familiar but I couldn't name it. My neck wobbled as they lifted me and carried me out like a sack of potatoes. I was so numb I could barely stay awake.

Help! Mizzy! Mrs. Plea! I'm being kidnapped! They couldn't hear me. The words tore around in my head and crashed in the back of my throat as I plunged into darkness.

9

i

I opened my eyes into pitch black. The bed I lay in enclosed me on the sides and swung in the air when I tried to move. I felt for its edges. Woven rope. A hammock. But hanging where? My fingers searched the air around me for something solid to grasp. Empty space one way, but a curved wooden wall was within easy reach on my left.

My thoughts were a jumble of puzzle pieces, fragments of a broken picture: Jake peering down from an upstairs window; a row of street lanterns strung along the wharf; a little silver bell tinkling above a yellow door; the striking face of a mysterious woman, dressed in black hat, coat, and trousers.

The unusual sound of water lapping near my left ear snapped me out of my recollection. I fought the ropes and sat up, banging my forehead on some kind of low beam right above my head.

"Dang it all," I muttered, wincing from the blow. What was this blackness? It closed me in like a coffin.

"Ahoy, Charlee," a man whispered from the darkness to my right. "Thought you were going to sleep the whole way out of the harbor, miss the pretty sights."

I hadn't imagined it. I was on a boat.

"Who are you? Where are we?" I demanded loudly.

"Shshsh! Voices carry on the water. It's me, Charlee. Mizzy's brother."

"Amos!" I stifled a holler into a hoarse reply.

"It's Cook. Call me Cook."

I wriggled onto my side and groped in the direction of his voice. I caught nothing but air. He had moved away. I strained my ears to track him. There was a soft shuffle across a hard floor, the click of a metal latch, then the sound of rushing water. A blast of cool sea air swept through the stuffy warmth and odor of oiled wood and onions.

Then I remembered the supply room! I'd fallen asleep in the back of the Sunshine Café. Two men from the diner had put a sack over my head and carried me away.

"You people kidnapped me!" I whispered the accusation at where I guessed Amos was standing.

"*You people?* I won't take that the wrong way and get our arrangement off to a foul start. You weren't kidnapped. We just stowed you with the onions and spuds for a while. You smell like a pot roast, come to think of it." He chuckled under his breath, a quiet little laugh that instantly reminded me of Miss Molly.

"Very funny. I could have walked aboard on my own."

His clothing rustled as he moved closer. I got a whiff of tobacco and soap.

"Not a chance. Not even the elusive Charlee LeBeau could sneak aboard unnoticed. You almost cost us our mission. We had to make sure you hadn't left a trail. Besides, I hear you begged Mrs. Plea for me to bring you along."

"I didn't beg. I was persuasive."

He laughed again.

"Oooeee! She said you were a fancy talker." I smiled into the dark. So I had won her over. I sat up awkwardly in the rope bed, careful not to knock my head on the beam again. "I'll be honest. No way I wanted to bring a girl on board. But what Mrs. Plea says goes."

"You didn't have to knock me out. I thought I'd been tricked, snatched by gangsters or caught by the Vigils or something."

"The Vigils. Now that's funny. Like they'd be after you. Anyway, you had a nice nap. No harm done."

"What's the mission, Cook? Are we on our way north? Is Mrs. Plea here?"

"You got a lot of questions. Mrs. Plea? She doesn't sail. You'll know soon enough what's going on."

"Can we at least light a candle? I can't see a thing in here."

"Not yet." I felt his hands on my arm. "Come on, I'll help you down you can look outside. Pay attention now. We're in the back of the galley. Your hammock is about four feet off the floor. Roll over, throw a leg out, hang onto the rope edge like it's a horse's mane. Just like dismounting bareback."

I untangled myself from the ropes. Cook guided me as I tipped out of the hammock into the dark. My boots clunked onto the angled floor. Teetering around with every movement of the boat, I found the back of Cook's shirt and steadied myself. I could sense his size, both bigger and taller than me. I shuffled along behind him toward a faint glow outlined by a small, square opening in the low ceiling. He slid something across the floor.

"Stand on this box." He helped me step up and I poked my head out through the open hatch. "Look behind the wind. We're sailing out of San Francisco Bay," he said from below, holding my legs.

The view was spectacular. Above us, past a huge billowing white sail, the sky was jeweled with a million stars. Water rippled and frothed as it gushed past the hull of the boat. Across the black water, a thin row of fading lights marked San Francisco, already nothing more than a faint string of pretty beads. I took a deep breath and pushed my whipping hair out of my eyes and mouth.

"A sight for sore eyes, ain't it?" Cook said.

It was strange and beautiful. Also terrifying. My fingers tightened on the edges of the hatch opening. I imagined the rocking boat was my horse, Magic, and I was riding him over the rolling hills of the Miller ranch on a starlit night. We galloped over the dark water in silence until the lights of the city fizzled into the sea behind us.

"City just disappeared," I said. My knees rattled. I'd never been away from land.

"Come down and close that hatch. It's mighty brisk with the wind funneling in."

I'd been gripping the square opening to keep my balance. My ice-cold hands fumbled with the unusual cover. Cook tapped my leg, which I took to mean I should get out of the way and let him do it. I stepped down from the box and grabbed his shirt. I felt him stretch beside me. He could touch the ceiling with nothing to stand on.

With the hatch closed, Cook lit a lantern and hung it from an overhead beam. Cook was taller than me by a foot or more. In these cramped quarters, he slouched a little so his head wouldn't hit parts of the ceiling. He looked so much like Miss Molly. His cheekbones were the same and he moved his hands like her.

The kitchen of the boat took shape behind him. It was as wide as Uncle Jack's last rented room, but three times as long. It was full of things, all neatly attached to something or stowed in tight little compartments. One side had a narrow counter with chopping blocks and knives hanging on a rack. A cast iron stove stood next to it. Its legs were buried into a deep bed of sand and a big black chimney pipe poked up through the roof. Well-used pots and pans were tucked in bins and dangled from the ceiling, swinging with the motion of the boat. The other side had a built-in table and bench. Drawers and cupboards filled every wood wall. At the narrow end were two hammocks across from each other. One of them had my bag beneath it on the floor. A narrow door at the far end led into a pantry, packed to the ceiling with provisions.

"Let's get a few things sorted out," Cook said. "That's your bunk, mine's the other. Stow your stuff underneath."

As he spoke, he pointed with the middle finger of his right hand. His forefinger was nothing more than a stump. I'd forgotten about that finger. I'd noticed it when we'd first met, seven years ago, when he was still a gangly teenager. He kept his hand in his pocket a lot then, as if he was ashamed of people seeing it.

"Back of the pantry is a crate over a bucket where you can relieve yourself. If you drop anchor, take the bucket up top and empty it overboard. Otherwise, put the cover on. Wash water and basin are back there, too. Dirty water goes into the bucket."

"Good to know."

"And empty downwind... unless you're fixin' to wear it all."

I scrunched my nose at the unpleasant thought.

"Work starts 5:00 a.m. sharp. We aim for regular meals but it depends on conditions. When you're not working in the galley, you're working on deck, on assigned watch or in that hammock. Any questions?"

"No, I think you covered it. Thanks."

Cook lowered himself onto the bench behind the table.

"Now then. Everyone on this ship works for Mr. Miller, including you, starting today."

"And we're on the *Salish Wind*." I wobbled my way over to the table and spilled into a seat across from him.

"That's right," he said with surprise.

"Jake told me. He said you worked for him, and Mr. Miller's merchant boats take supplies to the British colonies."

"Ah. Not the entire story though. You'll learn more over the coming days. For now, we're getting away from the coast. Then we'll turn and head for Vancouver Island."

"Are we going near the gold mines?" I seized the chance to

get more information about the mining certificate I'd nearly got killed over.

Cook chuckled. "Not that far. Fort Victoria is across the water from them."

The teacher hadn't covered these places in our geography lessons at the Miller ranch. Nothing was marked north of the Oregon Territory. The old map he used called it all America and made it seem like nobody lived there. I knew that was wrong.

"The mining up here is near the coast, right?" I asked.

"Not exactly. Coal is on the coast. But most of the miners are after gold, in the Fraser River Canyon."

"Have you been there?"

"One time. Never again. It was brutal."

"Oh."

Cook changed the subject before I could come up with another question. "You saw Mizzy at the Sunshine."

"Yeah, we got to visit for a few minutes. She looked tired."

"This past year took a toll. I'm glad she got to see you. Almost broke her when she thought she'd lost you, too."

"I felt the same," I said, loosening my bandana to ward off a wave of smothering grief.

Cook eyed my stable clothes and riding boots. "It's a wicked sail north. Not warm like what you're used to. You'll need proper sea gear." He threw me a pair of black rubber boots. "Get those cowboy boots off. They're dangerous."

"I got a good wool coat I bought off a sailor," I offered as I yanked off my boots and tossed them on the floor by my duffle bag.

"Put 'em away. Nothing gets left adrift or underfoot."

I saluted him and he rolled his eyes. "I hope this kitchen can use a good horse groomer 'cause it's all I know."

"It's called a galley. Mrs. Plea told me I have to teach you."

"Is she your boss, too?"

"She is, for the mission part…"

"I'm gonna be a boss like her one day, Amos."

"Funny. She said that exact thing." His smile faded and he patted my arm. "Listen. Don't call me Amos. It's Cook, all right? And Mizzy."

I yawned and rubbed my eyes with clammy palms.

"Cook and Mizzy."

Cook puttered around the galley, humming a tune Mizzy used to sing while working in her cookhouse. I closed my eyes and let the music carry me back to that happy place.

I slumped forward, laid my head on the table and fell asleep.

10

i

A loud bang woke me with a start. I lifted my head from the table. It felt heavy as a blacksmith's anvil. The boat lurched from side to side. Cook was puttering around the galley, unconcerned.

"Ah. You're awake."

"I feel horrible." I rubbed my face. Resting my head on the wood table had given me a stiff neck and a numb cheek. "What was in that candy Mrs. Plea gave me?"

"A little something to make you sleep. It wore off long ago."

"You sure about that?" I closed my eyes. Cook shrugged and rummaged in a nearby cupboard.

"Ever been on a boat before?" he asked, putting some cheese and bread in front of me on the table. The sight of it made my stomach heave. I looked away.

"Me and Jake built rafts, floated them on the river. Hardly the same thing." There was another loud thump from below our feet. I clutched the table. "Does it always bang around and rock like this?"

"We're hitting a bit of chop off the point. This here is nothing. Wait till we run in a high sea. You'll understand why everything's tied down, why we have edges on tables and holes to keep cups and pots from sliding around."

I straightened up in a panic. This was nothing, this pitching and banging and rolling? What if the boat flipped over and sank? The streets of San Francisco, with its drunks and thieves, stray dogs and gangsters suddenly seemed much safer. Sour liquid gurgled and burned in the back of my throat. I swallowed hard.

"It'll take you a few days to get used to it. There's a slop bucket right there when you have to vomit," Cook said, grinning and pointing with a small knife. "I'll go over your jobs tomorrow."

He bit into a piece of stinky cheese. The stench of it hit my nose. Drool flooded my mouth. My stomach heaved and I dove for the pail in the corner.

I spent the rest of the night and half of the next day in my hammock. In between fits of sleep, I threw up more times than I could count. Men spoke in low voices and Cook was among them. They spoke of winds and waves and knots and meals. Nothing was a complete story. It was all fragments of things, like what happens in dreams.

I'd always imagined the sea to be flat. I mean, not flat like we'd sail off the edges or anything. I knew my science. But flat enough that I figured being in a boat would be much like riding down a road. Looking out across the bay, with the solid wooden wharf beneath my feet, I'd never imagined the water had gigantic mountains and valleys. As soon as we left the harbor and reached open water, the motion of the boat became wild. We rose and tipped, teetered and plunged, and my stomach heaved. The ship creaked and banged through the night, each hour more violent than the last. Finally, too weak to care, I surrendered to what I imagined was certain death in a soggy wooden coffin on the sea.

By daylight the next day, I had nothing left in me. I was like the people I'd seen, alone in some back alley, sick and ready to die.

Cook poked me. "Good news, Chuck. Storm's passed."

I cracked open my dry eyelids and groaned. He was standing

beside my hammock, all cheerful like a Sunday morning preacher.

"Is that my name now?" I said, voice raspy and hoarse.

"Seems fitting. But no."

Sunshine flooded the cabin through the roof hatches and stabbed my eyes with daylight.

"Drink this." He nudged me with a cup. My mouth was as parched as a desert, but I didn't want to drink. I didn't want to swallow anything and have it come right back up again.

I pushed it away with a limp arm.

"Don't want it."

"Drink. You need liquid. It'll make you better. Promise."

My throat felt like I'd swallowed a bag of sand. I couldn't remember ever feeling worse. Cook pressed the cup to my lips. It smelled of mint and metal. I took a tiny sip.

"I'm going to die, aren't I?" I said, clenching his arm with a weak hand.

"You aren't dying."

"How do you know? If I've caught the fever, tell me the truth. My mama died from it, too."

"The fever!" Cook said, and burst out laughing. He unwound my clenched fingers from his sleeve. "Charlee, you just plain seasick."

"Seasick?"

"Yep, seasick."

I took another sip of the mint tea. It stayed down, soothed my throat. I hoped it would calm my turbulent belly.

"We hit a nasty squall heading out of the bay last night. It was tough going. All the passengers were sick, not just you. I fed the crew hard tack and water for breakfast. Too rough to even brew a batch of coffee."

"What's hard tack?"

"Dry biscuits. We keep 'em in stores for when it's too rough to cook. Fills the gullet in a pinch." His eyes darted around, charting the cabin walls. "See now? She's riding real smooth and steady." I noticed the boat wasn't lurching, climbing, and falling anymore, but it still rolled from side to side, back and forth. He gave my leg a reassuring pat and tucked a blanket around me. "Sleep it off while you can, which won't be for long. This ain't no holiday cruise."

"How long does seasick last?" I moaned.

"Usually a couple of days. First day's the worst. You should be able to drag yourself through the rest of it soon."

I guzzled the rest of the warm tea and lay back in the hammock with the empty cup on my chest, relieved to know that death wasn't on my doorstep.

"Cabin boy! Look alive! You got work to do!" Cook's voice yanked me out of a happy dream. I'd been riding horses with Jake, racing a herd of mustangs across the golden fields of the Miller ranch.

Cook stood at the chopping counter, rattling pans and mixing things in bowls. I stretched my stiff limbs and massaged a cramp out of my shoulder.

"What time is it?"

"Half past three. It's time for you to get up, move around with the ship. You any good at peeling?"

He set a bin of potatoes on the table along with a knife and a big cup of black coffee.

"I feel a lot better, thanks for asking," I replied, tipping myself out of my bunk.

Cook snorted. The sickness I thought would kill me was no big deal to a seasoned sailor like him. "Get going then. We're making stew." My stomach did a little roll at the mention of food. "Look up and around as you work or you'll get queasy all over again."

I peeled potatoes and chopped carrots and onions. Cook hung over the big oven and stove, making flat bread and tending to several pots at once. As he put together the meal, he explained what he was doing and showed me how to stoke the stove.

By the time he rang the bell at six, I could barely keep up with his orders. I sat back, finally a little hungry myself, and watched wide-eyed as a dozen people formed a line and shuffled by the galley door. Cook ladled stew into their bowls, topped it with pieces of bread, and filled their mugs with coffee.

Some people brought a pan. "For how many?" Cook asked, and he gave each person a fair number of servings for their group.

"Are the passengers all your kind?" I said to Cook as the last person in line left the galley.

He dropped his ladle into the pot with such a loud clank I jumped. He untied his dirty apron and tossed it on the counter.

"What's that supposed to mean?"

"The passengers. I mean, they're all colored. Like you."

"And what about it?"

"I, well, there's nothing about it. It's just an observation. Don't get all mad."

"An observation. Well, maybe I shouldn't have agreed to bring 'your kind' along. Most sailors agree, girls don't belong at sea. I should've made Mrs. Plea take you with her, shove you in a housekeeping job befitting the weaker sex."

We stared each other down like gunfighters.

"Housekeeping! Well, thanks for sparing me from that. I'm grateful you kidnapped me, being a poor waif of a girl that nobody wants and who really can't do much other than tend to horses. Never mind I don't know where I am or what this stupid mission is you and that Mrs. Plea are all so secret about. You drugged me, I retched half the night and day, peeled vegetables until my hands look like prunes, and I'm trying my best to ride this bucking bronco of a boat. I just made an observation and you get all huffy and mean."

I picked up a handful of potato peels and flung them at his chest.

If I were Cook, I'd have clocked me one for lipping him off, never mind throwing scraps at him. His chest heaved as he carefully picked potato peels off his vest. He shook his head and squinted at me.

"Oooeee! You's a feisty one, just like you always was."

"Don't make fun of me."

"Well, you should hear yourself. 'I just made an observation.' Oooeee… that's some kind of fancy talk."

"I have a right to know what's going on."

The corners of a faint smile vanished. His lips formed a tight, hard line.

"A right? You have a right? That's a mighty high horse you riding, girl. You listen up. You think you got rights? You got no rights. You're lucky you look mostly white like your Papa and figured out how to get by as a boy."

He didn't raise his voice, but what he said struck me like a bucket of ice water. The cold, bare-naked truth wasn't spoken like that. Not ever.

"I didn't mean those kind of rights."

But I had. I'd spoken of black people like they were others, different and separate from me.

"Then watch your words. This 'your kind' talk, I've heard it my whole life from folks who think they're better. I know your papa and Mizzy didn't teach you that."

I cringed at the insult. It didn't stop me from retaliating. "You just put me down for being a girl. How's that any different?"

He glared at me and said nothing more. I looked away from his judging stare, down at the wooden floor under his feet.

Wasn't it the same thing? Of course it wasn't. Mizzy had let a few things slip about her early life as a slave. Even when she skimmed past the ugly bits, which was most of it, I found her stories horrifying. Cook, her little brother, had been there, too. I couldn't fathom the things they'd seen and been through. Mizzy, who I'd known as Miss Molly since the day we met, was so much more than my child's eyes had understood. During our short reunion in the pantry, she told me Mizzy had been her slave name. "I claimed it back. I own it now," she'd said proudly, as she made fists and pressed them over her heart.

As for me, I'd nearly got myself killed over shares in some stupid gold mining company that wasn't even on a map. That's what I'd fought to own.

"I'm a fool," I blurted out.

"Impulsive, maybe. But not a fool," Cook said. He shoved a bucket and mop at me. "Swab the floor." He didn't look at me as he left the galley.

11

i

As I washed the galley floor, I thought long and hard on what Cook had said. I'd heard those words before and knew they weren't innocent. It took me back to winter, when I'd made friends with the woman who owned a laundry on the edge of Chinatown in San Francisco. A difficult customer had come in to Taitai's laundry one Sunday afternoon when I was there doing some extra work for her. "You people," the man had said, complaining loudly about wrinkles he claimed Taitai had left in his freshly-ironed shirts. There were no wrinkles. His laundry was perfect. I'd wrapped his bright white starched shirts myself in the brown parcel paper Taitai used to keep laundered clothing pristine. "You people," he'd said, jabbing a pointed finger at her face, because she was an immigrant and Chinese. He didn't mean "you women" even though that was another way he could've made her seem less valuable or worthy.

What I'd done wasn't nearly as bad, and I hadn't done it on purpose neither. But Cook wasn't about to let me get away with one bit of it. He'd called me out on my careless words because I knew better.

When Cook returned to the galley, he kept his back to me and made himself busy measuring flour and ingredients into a bowl. I caught his profile as he moved about. His jaw was set, his face pulled tight in concentration. I could feel the hurt hiding beneath his blank expression. I'd hid my own feelings the same way many times.

"Cook."

He didn't answer.

"I didn't mean those words, the way they sounded." I rolled my eyes at myself. That sounded like a lame excuse if I ever heard one. I knew what needed saying. Why was it so hard?

"I'm sorry, Cook."

His pinched forehead slowly softened. He stopped slapping the batter around his bowl, placed it on the counter and stared at length into its beige depths.

"I accept your apology. And I apologize back for what I said about girls. Just muddied up the pond, throwing that in there."

Cook filled two bowls with stew and set them on the table. Mine was mostly gravy, which seemed unfair until he pointed out that my stomach would appreciate a lighter load.

I approached the topic of the passengers again, with more care.

"All the black passengers surprised me when they showed up for supper. I had no idea there were so many."

"You only saw half of 'em tonight. The rest are still in cargo, most still pretty seasick down there."

"Will they get to come up?"

"Of course. They are free."

Cook told me more while we ate.

The *Salish Wind*, he said, was one of two merchant schooners built for Mr. Miller's coastal business. The twin sister ship, called the *Sonoma Wind*, was loading back in San Francisco harbor and would follow us in a few days.

"Does the *Sonoma Wind* have secret passengers, too?"

"Not this time. We mix it up. Passengers aside, Mr. Miller's two ships haul goods between San Francisco and Fort Victoria during the spring and summer."

Fort Victoria was a booming city in a British colony, full of American miners who'd gone north after hearing of another gold rush. They desperately needed supplies in the town and out on the claims. Mr. Miller's merchant schooners carried food, clothing, and other provisions. More importantly, the *Salish Wind* was loaded to the gunnels with tools and mining equipment. Cook had launched into a full lesson on the shipping business.

"Cook," I said, interrupting a fairly boring description of how we'd load cut lumber for the trip back. "The people. Who are the people and where are we taking them?"

"Oh, I thought you knew. They're undocumented. Runaway slaves, like me and Mizzy once were. We're taking them to the British colonies, to homestead and start a new life."

"Undocumented?"

Cook confessed he was part of a railroad, even though this railroad didn't have any trains or tracks. It was a network of secret routes across America that helped black people escape slavery and get to a place where they could be free. He was part smuggler and part sailor.

"How many are there?"

"Hundreds of routes and they're always changing."

"I mean how many people?"

"This trip? Two dozen."

"And you snuck them all aboard? How?"

"Used the *Sonoma Wind* for distraction. Set her adrift, fixin' to smash into a brand spanking new clipper anchored nearby. A jewel floating in the harbor made a perfect decoy. In the commotion, with everyone running to catch the loose boat and avoid a collision, we quietly got everyone aboard."

"Clever."

"That's Mrs. Plea. Anyway, that's why you see so many of... my kind."

He poked himself in the chest on the last two words with his spoon. Still injured from our fight.

"Mrs. Plea could have told me what was going on."

"At the café? With two dozen souls slipping aboard right under the noses of harbor snitches? The *Salish Wind* was almost ready to sail when you showed up. There was no turning back for these folks."

"Then it was smart of y'all to drug me up and throw me in with the provisions," I said dryly.

He ignored my sarcasm. "Yes, it was. Twenty-four fugitive negroes without papers had to stay hidden, half suffocated under tarps and in containers while we checked out one sassy know-it-all with too much information who showed up outta nowhere when we were about to haul anchor."

I gasped as what Cook said sunk in. I hadn't understood what I'd caused, the danger I'd put people in.

"We gave you something to keep you quiet while loading the last of the supplies," Cook said. "To keep everybody safe, so everything would go as planned." He mopped up the last of his stew with a crust of bread and crammed it in his mouth. "Eat up now. You'll need your strength."

The weight of my sudden understanding crushed what little appetite I had.

"I almost messed things up."

"Nah. But you helped drive the last spike in the tie. This is our last railroad this year."

Thanks to me, some people were going to find out that the boat to freedom would no longer sail.

"I didn't know."

"It's not your fault. The operation is… complicated. Too risky to do any more."

This was way bigger than a handful of people fleeing from slave states. Mr. Miller had to know he had fugitives aboard his boat. These were his workers. Cook, Mrs. Plea, Mizzy, the crew—they risked everything to help these people. I'd endangered them all, showing up as I did. I'd been up to my neck in it the moment I'd asked for the Midnight Express at the Sunshine Café.

Cook pulled his biscuits from the oven and we cleaned up the galley in silence. As I worked, I tottered around. My stomach had settled a lot, but my thoughts churned like butter. It wasn't about me at all, just like Mrs. Plea had said. I'd been so caught up in my own personal mission—to go after my mining shares and claim my riches—I'd failed to see what was happening around me.

Lost in my thoughts, and feeling a huge dose of guilt, I followed Cook's lead as he showed me how to prepare for morning. We'd almost finished when heavy thumps on the galley ladder signaled company coming.

Cook squeezed my arm. "You're Charlee, ship's boy."

I nodded and immediately slipped into my familiar role.

"Ahoy, mates!" A burly man filled the galley door and swaggered inside. He was a real sailor, a weathered seafarer type like I'd read about in my storybooks. He wore a billowing white shirt, dark fitted pants held up by a woven belt, and a brimmed hat pulled down over his tied-back black hair. A real gold earring dangled off his left earlobe. One thing didn't fit the tough, swashbuckling image though. This sailor had a disagreeable-looking white dog tucked under his arm.

"Evening, Kuno. How's she blowin'?" Cook said.

"Steady as she goes," he replied, and they exchanged a few more bits of sailing small talk that seemed mostly to do with weather and the ship's course.

Cook yanked me forward. "Meet Charlee, my new helper. Charlee, this is First Mate Kuno."

"And Second Officer, Mr. Bubba Jones, if you please, sir," Kuno said, ruffling the dog's scraggly ears, one of which had a piece missing.

They were an intimidating pair. Although I remembered to put extra strength into my handshake, my fingers were swallowed by Kuno's massive palm. Mr. Jones bared his teeth and I stepped back quickly.

"Don't take no offense from Mr. Jones here, son. He usually bites people so I think a growl means he fancies you."

"They let you bring a dog on a sailing ship?" I said. Mr. Jones took exception to my remark and glared at me.

"Sure. We don't let him steer though." He burst into a laugh, which was as big as the rest of him.

Cook produced a dish of food scraps he'd set aside. "You'll never be forgotten on this ship, Mr. Jones."

Kuno beamed and put the dog and the bowl on the floor. Mr. Jones smacked away at the contents with considerable pleasure.

"You look almost seaworthy, Charlee. Cook shown you the ropes yet?"

"Just the galley." I wasn't sure I was ready to tackle the top deck. I chewed on the inside of my lip.

"I think he's done studying that bucket yonder," Cook said.

The two men chuckled and Kuno slapped me on the back. Had I not seen it coming, it might have knocked me clean into the pantry.

"You and the boy are on first night watch, Cookie. A little air'll do him good. It's a pretty night." He tucked his dog back under his arm. "Mr. Jones thanks you for the lovely meal, gentlemen. See you up top."

I waited until Kuno's boots thumped onto the deck over our heads.

"None of the crew knows about me?" I asked.

"Why would they? Girls aren't sailors."

"Girls don't work at liveries either. Until they do."

"From what I hear, girls just mend and dust." He nudged me with an elbow and I slugged him on the shoulder. My knuckles throbbed like I'd punched a rock wall.

"It's windy up top. Get your coat. Put that city cap away if you're fond of it. We don't go back for what goes overboard." He tossed me a beanie cap, like the ones the sailors wore.

I wondered if that ship rule applied to people, too. I'd bought my pea coat on the wharf in San Francisco. It had belonged to a boy who had been lost at sea on his first voyage. I didn't know the boy's story, but I could imagine the terror of going overboard and seeing the ship sail away. My fingers trembled and I fumbled with the buttons.

I vowed to pay careful attention. I followed Cook out of the galley and up the short, steep ladder to the weather deck.

12

i

A cutting wind greeted us as we poked our heads out of the forward hatch and onto the main deck. Two huge masts towered into the sky, their sails full and taut with wind. Behind me, two smaller triangular sails swooped out to the pointed bow. We were in full sail, flying over the smooth water with incredible ease. Against the pinks and blues of the evening sky, it was a breathtaking and magical sight. I stretched my arms up and filled my lungs with fresh, salty, evening air.

"Shoot, we missed sunset," Cook said, flipping up his collar. "Look at that gorgeous sky."

Golden light outlined a patch of dark clouds drifting above the horizon. Overhead, the clear sky had turned a translucent indigo, a watery contrast to the deep grey waters stretching out in every direction.

"It's beautiful," I said.

"Out here, away from land, that big bright burning ball plops into the water, she sizzles and spits and sputters like pork rind in hot oil, and then she vanishes, leaving a trace of light and a smoky trail."

"That's mighty poetic... in a deep-fried kinda way."

Cook grinned. "We'll catch her tomorrow. You'll see."

"Mateys!" Kuno hollered from behind a huge steering wheel on a raised platform at the back of the boat. He descended a narrow set of wooden stairs and lumbered toward us, Mr. Jones still tucked into his armpit.

The fur on Mr. Jones's head slicked back as he faced into the wind. His eyes were closed and his ears flapped out behind him like a pair of white flags.

"Does that dog ever go anywhere on his own legs?" I asked, before Kuno was within earshot.

"Why would he when he gets a free ride everywhere?"

Kuno walked around the ship with us, pointing out its modern design and elegant features. I memorized the names he used for things and interrupted him more than once to ask what he meant by some sailing term. He informed me that as ship's boy, I'd be called out of the galley and put into service whenever extra hands were needed. Just as I was thinking I'd be too weak and small to be of much use on deck, he said sometimes there are situations that call for a nimble sailor. I followed his gaze to the rope ladders that ascended the main mast and felt my stomach drop to my feet.

We toured bow to stern, up the starboard side, past the two huge masts angling high into the night air, back down the port side and finished up in front of what they called the quarter-deck. A wizened old sailor named Drak had taken the wheel for Kuno. I waved at him and was pretty sure he scowled back in acknowledgement.

"You've got free run of the ship except for two places," Kuno said. "Crew don't go into the captain's quarters, there under the bridge, and you don't go down into the main cargo hold."

"Where the passengers are hiding," I said.

Kuno raised an eyebrow at Cook who shrugged and said, "He knows."

"They aren't hiding no more," Kuno said. "Thank the gods,

67

that trouble's past. But that's their quarters down there amongst the cargo. We crew don't need to go tramping around through their accommodations."

After Kuno excused himself to resume his duties, Cook and I took a seat on the deck in a spot out of the wind. He put his head back and looked up into the billowing sails.

"I got a question, Cook."

"You got a lot of those. But sure. Ask away."

"Why'd you agree to bring me? It wouldn't have taken much to convince Mrs. Plea that stowing me aboard was a bad idea."

"I said that. And not 'cause you're a girl. I thought it was too risky and too hard. She told me your whole story, how you had your uncle's loan sharks after you and no place to go. It didn't leave us with many options. Besides…"

He let the words trail off into the wind.

"Besides what?"

"Besides, Mizzy wrote me last year after you left the ranch. She had a bad feeling when you left with your uncle. Mr. Miller and Jake had already looked for you, told her you had moved and were gone for good. She didn't believe it, said something was wrong, said you had to be there somewheres. She begged me to look again. So I did, before going east with Mrs. Plea last winter. Nobody'd seen you. But I tracked your uncle down. I never told Mizzy that part."

"You saw Uncle Jack?"

"Caught up with him outside one of them all-night gambling halls. After some persuasion, he confessed he'd shipped you off to school in Boston, in the company of a Miss Buffy something. Some rich lady friend. I wrote it down."

"Lady friend? Is that what he called her? She's supposed to be my aunt, but I never met her. He probably made her up, too."

"He swore you'd gone east. He said, by your own wishes."

"I never left."

Charlee LeBeau & The Salish Wind

"Not a soul I talked to had seen hide nor hair of a young girl. Didn't occur to me to ask about a boy."

"I sent letters home. Me and Jake figure Uncle got his postmaster pal to steal them."

"What a louse! He's a mighty slick liar, that uncle of yours. Even when I threatened to bust him in the head, he stuck with his story. I should've tailed him home. I thought he'd told the truth. Jake hadn't seen you. Thought for sure if you were in town, he would've seen you."

How different the past year of my life might have been if Cook had gone that extra step. Or if I had swallowed my pride and turned to Jake for help sooner.

"You probably would have found me."

"I should have found you," he said, shaking his head.

Two male passengers appeared at the main cargo hatch. One of them gestured to Cook that he wanted to speak to him. Cook acknowledged him with a wave, stood up and I followed without giving it a thought.

"No, you wait here," he said. It was an order, cold and without explanation. I shrunk back down out of the wind as Cook walked away, a little hurt by his tone.

Why didn't he want me to hear their conversation? He made it pretty clear the meeting was none of my business. People behaving all secret-like usually means they have something to hide. I kept an eye on them, careful not to stare or draw attention.

Just then, Kuno rang the ship's bell eight times. This signaled the end of the dogwatch at eight o'clock and the beginning of our night watch.

Lantern light shone onto the deck as the Captain emerged from his quarters. I'd pictured a brute of a man with a big facial scar and a sword on his hip and maybe even a wooden leg. Of course, all I had to go on was what I'd read and he was nothing like what I'd imagined. He was a frail man with unremarkable

69

features. His white shirt added to his already pale complexion. His plain black trousers made his legs look like scarecrow sticks stuffed into black boots.

The Captain's appearance had broken up the meeting of Cook and the passengers. The passengers had quietly drifted away, barely noticeable as they casually took in the view, and took in some fresh air before going below. Cook returned to my side, as if he'd been there the whole time.

"What's going on?" I said.

"No questions," Cook replied.

Why didn't they want the Captain to see them talking? That's all I wanted to know. He wouldn't let me ask. Two crew men appeared from below deck. They both glared at me as they passed by.

"What's the matter with them?" I asked Cook.

"Just seeing the odd little cabin boy for the first time," he replied. I followed Cook to our watch post as Kuno and Drak handed the ship over to the unfriendly sailors. Cook pulled out his pouch of tobacco.

I held out a palm. "Roll me one."

"You aren't smoking," he replied, all big brother and bossy like.

"All the men smoke. You said it yourself. I look like an odd cabin boy. I can't stick out."

"Just keep your head down." But when I kept my hand out waiting, he slapped the smoke he'd rolled into it with a scowl and said, "Don't inhale then."

I sighed. "It's not like it's my first time. I learned so I'd fit in around the Livery. I smoked if somebody offered me one, which wasn't often because the other hands couldn't afford to be that generous. I couldn't afford to waste money buying my own."

I lit the smoke and took a long, angry drag. The tobacco was wicked strong, not like the lighter stuff the men around the stables smoked. My chest burned like I'd sucked in a bucket of hot coals. I tried to hold back but the pain was awful. I hacked the smoke out of my lungs in a loud blue cloud.

Cook chuckled and clapped me on the back. I elbowed him away.

"Don't you dare laugh at me, Amos Jefferson," I sputtered. My eyes watered. I stifled the desire to cough out loud and cleared my irritated throat. "That's some… mean… tobacco… you got there."

"It's French. I told you not to inhale. And you're not to call me Amos, remember?"

We leaned against the bulkhead in silence. After a while, I took another cautious puff, held it in my mouth and blew it out like a pro.

"There you go. That's better," he said.

"Sorry I snapped at you, said your name. Nobody heard."

"All right."

"I get a little ornery sometimes. Living with Uncle and working at the Livery was no picnic. It took me over half a year to track you down. It wears me down, pretending to be a boy, looking over my shoulder all the time."

"I don't know. You seem to come by it honestly."

"What's that supposed to mean?"

"It's a compliment. You handle yourself better than many men." He glanced over at the Captain. "If anything, you should try to be less extraordinary."

It was a compliment, and I felt proud that Cook saw me in such a good light.

"Do what you do, and keep it ordinary. We are an ordinary merchant crew on an ordinary coastal run."

"I get it." The entire mission out of San Francisco depended on not attracting attention.

"By the end of summer, it'll be over and done. Truth is, men don't notice much unless they're clobbered over the head with it."

"I worry they'll find out."

"Keep up with your work and you'll be fine. Don't smoke too much."

"All right." I stubbed out my smoke on the bottom of my boot and tucked it into my vest pocket.

13

i

The bad seasickness left me after the first two days, but it took me two more to feel at ease and able to handle a tipping floor. By the afternoon of the fifth day at sea, I marched a huge sack of onions across the sloped galley floor without hanging on or losing my balance.

"You got your sea legs now, matey," Cook said, with a mock salute.

"Sea legs and arms, you mean." I heaved the sack onto the table with a thud.

So many things in my life had been heavy. Leather saddles, heavy harnesses, big wooden barn doors, shovels of wet manure, full buckets of oats. Now I could add cast iron pots, sacks of milled flour and vegetables, barrels of fresh water, coils of thick ropes and wet canvas sails to the list.

"At least Kuno won't send you up a mast to reef a sail in a pitching sea."

"You two said that to scare me."

"No, we didn't. That's the work. But luckily, not for you, cabin boy. You'll keep your feet on deck. Captain's orders."

"I'm grateful for my low station in life," I said.

Cook chuckled. "Wait till you have to tend boiling pots in a squall. Nothin' about being at sea is easy. Now chop a dozen of those onions and huck 'em in the pot. Unless that cleaver is too heavy for the lady."

I pointed the end of the blade at him, flicked the sharp edge with my thumb and threatened him with a string of pirate talk. Cook played along and begged me not to make him walk the plank. Then I remembered pointing a knife one year earlier. It had been tiny compared to this hefty blade, but it was no laughing matter. It was just over a year ago. When Papa died.

Cook nudged my shoulder as we set to work making supper for the crew and passengers. He must have known the story. Mizzy would have told him what had happened on the ranch, how I'd cut off all my hair and waved the knife around, how I blamed Jake's sister, Bernadette, for the tragic accident and threatened to kill her. I couldn't remember saying that, but Jake had told me after that I did. I was relieved that Cook didn't press me to talk about it, and unlike others, wasn't quick to pass judgment. To shake off a sad mood that threatened to swamp me, I got him talking about the particulars of a recipe. The pride he took in his work, and my enthusiasm for it, pushed the horrible memories overboard.

Since passing through the squall outside of San Francisco harbor, the wind had been strong and even, pressing the taut sails as we zigged and zagged into the northerly winds at a determined pace. The sea carried us one way and then the other, up on a swell, dipping over into a trough, rolling side to side in between. The ship rode steady across the hills and valleys of deep green waters, through the frothing white waves. If I imagined myself riding on the Miller ranch, the constant motion didn't bother me too much. The sea was kind of like a wild horse, and a million times bigger and stronger.

I'd fallen into Cook's fair weather routine and it was no picnic. Up at 5:00 a.m. and straight to work preparing breakfast and lunch and baking while the stove was hot. With lunch over and the clean-up complete, we'd report to the main deck to work. Then it was back to the galley to prepare supper.

After evening clean-up, we'd brew coffee for the overnight crew and finally take a quick break. Then we'd sit by the light of a lantern, have a cup ourselves, until it was time to take our turn on the night watch. I'd get my writing book out while Cook would hum and picked out some mournful tunes on a small guitar. He played better than most I'd heard who had ten fingers. Sometimes he'd read or make some notes in a book he kept on a shelf by his hammock.

"Did you go to school in San Francisco?" I asked him one night as he carefully wrote in his book with neat handwriting. Mizzy could read and write a little, but he was so much better. He'd obviously been up to more than cooking since he'd left the ranch.

"Not a regular school, if that's what you mean. Blacks weren't allowed. I learned with a handful of other colored folk in a church basement. Mrs. Plea wouldn't hire me if I didn't learn to read and write. She told me, words reveal thoughts and actions. If I worked for her, she said, I had to learn their power and become very good at using them."

On our sixth day at sea, while on a long tack into a favorable wind, we were given an unexpected afternoon break on deck. Cook produced a pack of playing cards. I screwed up my nose at the sight of them and drew a book out of my coat pocket. He enticed the two unfriendly sailors to join him for a game.

After half-watching Cook string together a couple of feeble wins, I couldn't resist the temptation to take him on, particularly since trying to read with the rolling motion of the boat made my head fuzzy all over again.

Unlike Uncle, these men played cards for fun. They didn't

have his serious intensity, his impatience, his greedy focus. They laughed and joked around and teased each other as much as they paid attention to the game. I saw an opportunity to earn some quick cash and asked them to deal me in. After winning three hands in a row and a decent stack of coins, the other sailors bowed out and returned to work. Cook hung in for one last game.

"It can't just be luck," he said, tossing his cards down as I raked in the coins he'd lost in the last hand. "You're good."

"For a girl, you mean?"

"I mean, you are good. You just earned a lot of respect with those boys."

I smiled. "Maybe they'll be less suspicious of the odd cabin boy now."

"How'd you get so good?"

"Uncle made me learn the hard way."

"How's that?"

"He made me play for my allowance. If I lost, I'd go hungry. Losing is a great teacher. That's what he told me, though he never seemed to heed the lesson himself."

"He teach you all that fancy talk, too?"

"No," I said, offended by the idea that Uncle had taught me anything more than how to gamble. "He'd use a hundred words to say something that needed ten. He was a smooth talker though."

I stopped short of saying he was a liar and a thief. I'd already surprised myself by blurting out as much as I had. Uncle ran off to save his own neck. He left me to fend for myself against pretty nasty odds. For all I knew, the bad men had caught up with him and killed him. Or maybe he thought my chances were better without him. I'd probably never know why he left me behind. He was my only blood, Papa's brother. I didn't want to speak poorly of him, in spite of what he'd done.

Cook laid some tobacco onto a thin wisp of paper, his long fingers tucking stray strands into place as he made a skinny roll. Bending out of the wind to light a match, he lit the end, his cheeks hollowing as he dragged heavily on the smoke.

"How'd you lose that finger?" I asked.

He took his time deciding to answer. "Kitchen accident."

"Nice try. You'd lost it before you and Mizzy came to the ranch, before you were a cook. I remember." I pictured him offering me a glass of buttermilk, a stump on his hand where a forefinger should have been.

He scowled and looked away.

"Tell me the truth. I'm not a child anymore."

"The truth doesn't set you free, Charlee, in case that's what you think being grown up is all about. The truth can be hard and violent and unforgiving. Difficult to live with sometimes." The muscles in his cheek clenched as he spoke.

"Lies don't make it better."

"Not lying."

"Then it's omission and that's just as bad."

"O-mission. Where you get such big words and ideas?"

"I read a lot. It means 'leaving things out on purpose.' It's worse because it robs others of the truth and punishes the person who keeps the silence over and over and over."

Cook opened his mouth to speak, but nothing came out. He studied me, a strange, quizzical expression stuck on his face.

"Silence does punish. You're right. But sometimes silence beats letting all the horror out. Understand?"

He didn't have to say anything more. I knew where he and Mizzy had come from. That missing finger was a reminder of some past hell.

"How far are we from land?" I asked, changing the subject. An invisible mist of salty spray prickled my face as I looked out across the churning water. It stretched in every direction with nothing else in sight but miles of sky.

"Reckon two hundred mile or so." A cool gust whipped the

smoke from his lips as he spoke. A shiver of cold alarm ran up the back of my wool sweater and I wrapped my arms around me in a chilling hug.

"Two hundred miles!" We were days away from land. Alone on the vast, unpredictable sea. At the mercy of nature. "Why so far?"

"Can't sail tight to the coast. This boat can take any kind of wind and water, but her wooden hull wouldn't win a battle against unmarked shallows. Wind and tides want to push us back and onto land. And land spells fog hiding a nasty shore. It's safer in the open water."

"We must be halfway to China."

Cook laughed. "Passengers be mighty disappointed if we was." He pointed his cigarette at the eastern horizon. "We're really just a spit off the coast. It's a mighty big sea."

The wind suddenly felt very cold. "Feels like winter." I shivered and tucked my hands inside my sleeves.

"Soon a sweater won't be enough. Northerlies carry a bite."

Cook butted his smoke out in a little metal box he carried in his pocket. He got up and offered me a hand.

"I can manage," I hissed, checking to see if anyone had noticed. "Don't treat me special."

"Aye. Then head down and get the stove fired up. I'll be along in a bit."

At the stairs leading down to the galley, I looked back to see what Cook was doing. He paused at the main hatch, looked in the direction of the Captain's quarters, and then disappeared below.

14

i

On day seven of our journey, we awoke to a sea of green glass. Not a trace of wind blew from any direction. The boat stood completely still upon the flat water. After lunch clean-up, Kuno assigned me the humble job of scrubbing decks with a brush and pail. The rest of the crew had other jobs cleaning the ship, repairing sails and weatherproofing gear.

Late in the afternoon, when I had all the salt scrubbed off the mid-ship deck, and my hands and knees were raw from the work, Kuno told me to knock off for a short rest. I found a quiet place out on the deck to read.

The sun glared through a pale haze of blue and white streaks. A huge orange ring circled the sun, which seemed to get a lot of attention from the Captain, Kuno, and Mr. Jones, who were examining the sky from the bridge. Mid-ship, passengers lounged in bits of shade. Paddy and Lu Chan, the two sailors I'd beaten at cards, mended canvas sails and checked riggings and lines. I picked a spot away from them all and lost myself in my book.

Sometime later, a shadow fell across my page. I looked up, squinting to make out who stood between me and the blazing sun. Polished boots, pressed trousers. I lost the upper portion of the figure in the glare, except for the shape of his hat.

"Captain!" I leaped to my feet. My book slid from my lap and plopped to the deck.

"As you were." He spoke with a strong accent. Cook said he'd sailed around Cape Horn all the way from England.

I stood straight as a post awaiting instructions, hardly at ease and not a bit relaxed. I bowed my head, certain I was in some kind of trouble for lounging about.

"I'm sorry, sir." I wasn't sure how sinful reading was in the Captain's mind, other than I had been doing it in plain view of the rest of the working crew. But Kuno had told me to take a break.

"What are you reading?" His voice was soft, almost musical. I looked up. I'd expected harsh words for my laziness and folly.

"Excuse me, sir?"

"I should like to know the title," he said, pointing to the book, flopped open, pages face up on the deck.

My book. He was curious about my book.

"*Uncle Tom's Cabin*. By Mrs. Harriet Stowe."

"You don't say."

I thought I caught him smirk. I was reading a book about slaves. Uncle had told me not to flash it around because some white folks didn't like it. It was controversial, he'd said.

"Our cook's helper can read and has a taste for… for literature."

"Have you read it then, sir?" I said, relieved he seemed more amused than perturbed.

"I have." He picked up my book, sat down on a storage box, and motioned for me to do the same. At the same level, I could see sky blue eyes squinting at me from a pale, beardless face. He wasn't the type to be a captain. He should be bigger, tougher, more seasoned, like Kuno.

He flipped the pages with delicate hands. "I should like to hear your opinion of it once you have finished."

"Oh, I finished it a long time ago, sir. I've read it many

times through."

"You find it that inspiring?"

"Well, it is, but it's more because I don't have any other books handy. Except for *The Swiss Family Robinson* and I've read that as many times as this one."

"This is not a book I'd expect a youngster to choose."

"It's Mr. Miller's. From his library. I didn't steal it or anything. It's just on loan from him." I didn't want to mention that I'd had it for so long it was as good as stolen.

"How extraordinary! Miller has a knack for seeing gold where others see only rock."

"Sir?"

The Captain chuckled and shook his head. "Tell me. What struck you about this book?"

The question caught me off guard. It had been a long time since I'd sat in school. Even then, nobody ever asked my opinion on something I read except for Jake.

"Well... Tom reminds me of Papa, my own father, with how he works hard and cares about others. Never selfish or complaining. A good man, and loyal, too. Even when other people treat him awful. Tom, I mean. And it's the truth. The book. What it shows."

Silly schoolgirl babble. Nervous and shallow. Not a complete sentence anywhere to be found. I paused, willing my thoughts to descend and anchor on a solid bottom. The Captain frowned, like he was trying to sort out what I was saying. I made a second attempt.

"I believe it is a call to arms," I continued. "If we stand by and let others be treated badly, we're no better than slave masters," I said. "It is immoral to do so. Complicit."

The Captain lurched as my words caught. His mouth opened ever so slightly as if he was going to speak but nothing came out. He looked away then, past me to some troubled horizon. His brows pulled together. His eyes darkened like gathering storm clouds.

My skin crawled as if I'd sat down on a nest of ants. I willed myself not to scratch. I'd forgotten my place again, said too much. Why couldn't I just answer politely? Why couldn't I come up with a simple answer befitting a ship's boy?

"You seem sure of this," he said at last, with a deep frown that didn't look like it was meant for me.

I wasn't sure of anything, I wanted to say, but made myself keep my mouth shut.

I followed his gaze to the group of passengers, sitting together on the quarterdeck. Cook was there with them, playing his guitar. A man sang a line and the others answered with a low chorus. It was beautiful, the way the music floated up over our heads, into the still sails, and rolled out across the water.

I wondered what they had gone through to get to this place. Had they been on the run? Like Mizzy and Cook, had they escaped with only their lives, with unlucky friends and family left behind or captured and killed? I didn't know how many hard miles they'd traveled to reach the *Salish Wind*. I didn't know them at all. But I knew that song. It was one Mizzy sang many times over. It was full of sadness, yet also seemed filled with hope.

I looked back at the Captain. He'd been studying me while I was lost in thought. He stood up and I took this as a cue to do the same. He wiped his brow with a white linen handkerchief and looked up at the sun, an angry eyeball staring down upon us.

"I better get to the galley, sir," I said, shifting from one foot to the other and back.

"Mrs. Plea was right about you," he said, handing me back my book. "You are much more than meets the eye."

He tipped his head. "Dismissed." I turned to leave. At the stairs to the galley, he called out. "Boy!"

Cursing to myself, I paused. I'd almost made a clean break.

"I have several fine books in my cabin. I'll select one for you. You'd enjoy something new to read, I would think."

He didn't wait for a reply. He walked along the deck, hands

clasped behind him, surveying everything, pausing to examine a winch that a sailor had polished. He did not stop to speak to the passengers, gathered away from the crew. They stopped singing as he passed by, like they'd been doing something wrong.

"No, please continue," I heard him order. The people started to sing again, one by one, voices joining in, but it wasn't the same. The tune was no longer rich and full.

Why did they stop? Why did he tell them to keep going? Why did they start because he asked them to? I looked down at the book in my hand and was struck by something it had taught me. Even with some good people doing some good things, the world was still a broken place.

The Captain stepped into the galley just before supper later that same day. Cook and I were in a flurry of last-minute preparations, bumping and dumping, filling bowls and dishes, elbow to elbow, sweat pouring off our heads in rivers.

"Captain!" Cook put down a tray of hot biscuits and straightened up, nearly banging his head on the ceiling.

"Carry on, good fellow. I've just brought a book down for your helper."

I wiped my hands on my apron. Cook's eyes widened. The Captain didn't make deliveries, let alone set foot in the ship's kitchen.

"I took the liberty of selecting a splendid new publication by Mr. Walt Whitman. Have you read any poetry?"

"No, sir. Just children's rhymes. A few limericks and such."

"Ah, not surprised. Miller isn't fond of poetry," he said with amusement, and I wondered how Mr. Miller had ever come to hire this peculiar man to command one of his sailing ships.

My fingers played with the hem of my apron as the Captain spoke. The smell of something burning hit my nostrils. Cook was oddly unmoving beside me. He kicked my foot below the table out of the Captain's sight.

"Thank you, sir," I said, jolted into action. I took the book from him.

"You must tell me which passage you enjoy most." He turned and left as abruptly as he'd appeared.

Cook pulled a pot off the stove and cursed under his breath.

"You two and your chatter nearly ruined our gravy!"

I tossed the book into my hammock and got back to work.

We cleaned up fast that night and got up on deck a good twenty minutes ahead of our watch. I began reading the Captain's book while Cook smoked in the fresh air. The Captain passed by us twice on his rounds, but thankfully did not stop to make conversation. Cook nudged me in the ribs and whistled softly.

"Oooeee. Captain is fond of the new cabin boy," he whispered.

"He is not," I shot back.

"I seen that look. He fancies you all right."

"He saw me reading. That's all." A familiar knot tightened in my belly.

"He knows you're a girl. Mrs. Plea told him. He's intrigued. Got his eye on you."

I remembered the Captain's piercing look earlier that afternoon. He had looked right into me, past my protective cover. He'd opened my pages without asking.

"He knows I'm fond of books," I insisted. "Besides, he's old and creepy."

"Too starched for you, I agree." Cook blew smoke into the night air and chuckled, amused by my protest.

I stuck the book in my jacket like it was evidence of a crime. "Wanna play a quick game of cards? I'm looking to get rich fast."

15

i

It was shortly past midnight, at the end of our watch, when I finally crawled into my hammock, exhausted from another long day. Instead of falling asleep, I tossed around, preoccupied with what Cook had said. How could that Captain fancy me? I'd chopped my hair short in a ragged cut and all my clothes were for boys and men. I was an orphan case, supposedly taken aboard until Mr. Miller and Mrs. Plea could figure out what to do with me. He was a naval officer, probably twice my age, and well-educated. He wasn't much to look at without his uniform. Papa would have joked about that. He would have said the Captain was behind the kitchen door when good looks got handed out.

Cook had to be wrong, but why did he take such an interest in me then? Surely he wasn't that starved for a discussion on books. Maybe I'd return the poetry and tell him I couldn't follow it. But then he might try to teach me! I didn't want to offend him, but I didn't want him tracking me around the boat neither. I tossed around, unable to come up with a good plan.

I was sick and tired of pretending to be a boy. I didn't even care if the crew found out. This Captain wouldn't keelhaul me or do whatever the laws of the sea said he should do. That wasn't the problem. Cook had said a new cabin boy wouldn't get a second look whereas a cabin girl surely would. It had something to do with the ship's log and port registers and such. They couldn't have anything look unusual on the manifest. They couldn't risk some port official spotting something odd and deciding to come aboard and snoop around. I decided I'd steer right clear of that Captain and deal with the poetry book when I had to.

The *Salish Wind* sat for two long days in the beating sun with not a whiff of wind to even ripple the water. We drifted southeast with the ocean currents, far off course and in the direction of the treacherous Oregon coast. The sailors ran out of jobs to fill their time. All the painting, mending, swabbing and repairing was caught up and done twice by the middle of the second day.

Meals broke up the monotony. Cooking was easy in the flat conditions and Cook showed off his skill. The only hard part was the muggy air, made worse in the galley by the heat of the stove. Even with the hatches open, the air was smothering below deck.

Everyone talked about food—the fresh biscuits at breakfast stuffed with sizzled pork, how Cook made the best coffee they'd ever tasted, the delicious potatoes, gravy and beef for lunch, the salted fish with rice and turnips, with a sweet pudding pie for dessert at supper. The two main conversations on deck were the weather and the last meal. Waiting makes little things important.

When meals were served, people ate quickly at the tables between the galley and the crew's quarters and returned to the deck as soon as they finished. Cook took pleasure in preparing good food. I never told him in case it went to his head, but he was almost as good at it as Mizzy. I told him she'd be proud and he liked that. We got many a compliment on those calm days.

On the second evening of calm, I was reading Whitman's poems while Cook worked out the meal plan for the next day. Kuno came through the doorway with Mr. Jones tucked under his arm.

"Aloha, Amigos. She's cooling down up top."

"Is it then?" Cook glanced up at the open hatch overhead. "Nothing moving down here yet. Still hot as Hades."

"Capan says weather's gonna change by morning. I agrees with him, but sooner, by my accounts."

"I'm ready for it to turn, get a move on here. We'll be floating into some dog port at this rate," Cook said.

"Nah, lots of room yet, since we took her out so far."

"Plenty o' stores at least. Could sit a week and still have leftovers."

"Aye." Kuno scanned the galley for the familiar pan. "What can you spare tonight for our loyal seaman, Mr. Jones?"

Every night Kuno showed up and asked the same question. Every night we put together a small bowl of tasty scraps for Mr. Jones. Tonight's feast was beef trimmings, turnips, potatoes and gravy. I put the bowl of food on the floor and in less than a minute Mr. Jones had eaten the works. He licked his chops in gratitude. But when I reached for the empty bowl, he shrank away from me.

"Don't take it personal," said Kuno. "Bubba had to fend for himself before I found him. He don't take to most people." He dumped Mr. Jones into my hammock. "You rest here for a while, Bubba. You'll be in good hands."

Mr. Jones didn't care for the arrangement. I bunched my blanket into a round nest for him to lie on, but he sat stiffly beside it in protest.

Cook stirred some whiskey into a mug of water. "A wee shot o' grog for the night shift?"

"Aye." Kuno knocked the contents back in a couple of large swallows. "Me and Mr. Jones appreciate your kindness. We'll batten the hatches 'fore midnight, mark my words," he said, and he left the galley.

Cook and I took our usual stations for the eight to midnight watch, even though there was little to look for in the calm. The sun sank into the water, colored the most dazzling and unusual shades of gold and purple, and a waxing moon rose on the opposite horizon, casting shimmering silver streaks across the black water.

The air had thinned and had a freshness to it. Not long after dark, the riggings quivered. Kuno's prediction was right. All of us sprang to work, hauling on lanyards and setting the sails. Within minutes, a brisk wind was upon us, whipping up a cool mist from the waves cutting along the bow. Once the ship was underway, the Captain sent all but the night shift to their quarters. The temperature dropped, we secured the hatches, the boat heeled, and we sailed close into the wind.

By midnight, we'd sailed into another world. Rain started pouring down and the winds blew harder and harder by the hour. The sea was enormous, with waves as big as hills and valleys low between them. On deck, nothing looked familiar. Water splashed over everything. The crew, dressed in grey slickers, hung on to get around. Passengers were nowhere in sight, ordered to stay below.

"Get sick again, you know where the bucket is," Cook said, as we made our way down the steep, slanted stairs that led to the galley.

"I won't get sick," I said.

I vowed to myself I wouldn't repeat the embarrassing display from the first days on board. My nerves were rattled, but my legs remained steady.

"How will we make breakfast in the morning?" I asked Cook.

"We won't. It's all stores in a storm. Hard tack. Coffee, if we can use the stove and manage boiling water, till we're through it."

I didn't get more than a few minutes of sleep that night. In the worst of the storm, seawater washed over the deck and threw water down the stove chimney, nearly dousing the remaining coals of our fire. Lanterns swung around so wild I thought the oil would tip out of them. Water leaked in the closed hatch and trickled like a small waterfall to the floor.

"We're sinking!" I yelled to Cook over the crash of another wave.

"That bit of water?" He tugged my beanie down over my ears and handed me a mop.

I grabbed the counter to steady myself as another wave pitched me toward the hot cast iron stove.

"Mind yourself," he said, catching the back of my shirt. "That's how cooks get burned."

I lodged a pail under the steps to catch the incoming water and sopped up the wet patches beneath my rubber boots. Cook didn't seem worried in the least. He knew ships like the best of them. I tried to think of things I could be grateful for. For one, I hadn't thrown up. I'd never been through a big storm on the water, and it terrified me so bad I almost forgot about my stomach. Seeing Cook handle it like another day at work gave me quite a lot of comfort. In spite of being tossed around like farm animals in a twister, I was pretty good on my legs. But I couldn't get past the terror of being at the mercy of the sea.

"When it settles down enough, we'll put water on. The boys up top will be mighty cold and wet," Cook said.

He whistled and stoked the stove, keeping it lit and ready to be fired back up into service. I eyed it with concern. It was a hot weapon that could slide across the galley and brand me, its hot iron sizzling my flesh and pinning me into a painful death. Then I noticed the huge leg bolts tightened right into the floor. It wasn't going anywhere. Still, if the boat pitched badly, its metal guard rails had no chance of keeping a steaming pot from spilling or flying onto the floor.

Within the hour, the roar of the wind and water died down. The boat no longer smashed us through the waves and we struck a choppy but more even course. Cook and I mopped up the last of the water. When he was sure the storm had passed, he gave me a nod. I made coffee while he put sloshing water in a tall porridge pot.

Cook cracked open the galley hatch, revealing the grey light of dawn. A gash of icy wind blasted in, but no streams of seawater followed from the deck. Mr. Jones, who had slept in my hammock the entire night, sniffed at the fresh air flooding the galley and then went back to sleep.

The forward hatch was opened next, which signaled to the crew on deck that the galley was back in service. The aroma of brewed coffee soon filled the air. Kuno appeared within minutes, empty mug in hand, seawater still dripping from his rain slicker. Without giving it a second thought, I fished Mr. Jones out of my hammock.

Kuno anxiously relieved me of his unpredictable mutt. Dragged from sleep, Mr. Jones grunted his displeasure, but otherwise wasn't the least bit concerned with my handoff.

"He slept through the whole thing," I said. "The one time I got a few minutes to lie down, he wouldn't let me. He hogged the whole end of my hammock."

"I shoulda warned you. He won't share a sack with anyone."

"Well, I wasn't having any of that. I couldn't keep my eyes open so I crawled in anyways. He barely let me stretch my legs out, but he agreed to share."

"I think Bubba's finally made himself a new friend."

His big toothy smile was as bright as the morning sun that streamed in through the hatch above his shoulders. Mr. Jones yawned, clearly bored with my report. I decided not to push my luck and attempt a farewell scratch behind his ragged ear. He had a reputation to uphold and I wasn't sure he'd take kindly to it, even if he had decided to tolerate me.

16

i

We sailed for another week in unremarkable weather, the boat beating into the wind with sails full and taut, the seas moody but predictable. Each day was much the same—long hours standing in the galley, back-breaking work on deck and fighting to stay awake during the night watch. I slept barely five hours each night.

On our last day at sea, just before lunch, the bell on deck rang calling all hands. Cook and I dropped what we were doing and raced to our stations. Since Cook was strong, he hauled sails. They assigned me to the bottom of the main mast, where I had to coil or pay out the thick, heavy lines attached to the mainsail.

"Land ho!" a sailor called out.

As I looked out across the water, two powerful hands suddenly grabbed me and yanked me into the air.

"Charlee! Watch out!"

The ship lurched and came about as Kuno put my feet back on the deck away from the coils. The rope where I'd been standing shot off the deck like a streak of lightning. Had he not lifted me out of the way, I would have been struck by it, or tangled in it and thrown.

Kuno was back on the bridge before I realized what one minor mistake might have cost me. I'd been shown, warned about my hands and feet getting caught. One split second of careless distraction might have ended it for me.

Kuno ordered the crew to heave to, which I'd learned meant we were going to drop our sails and hold position. We'd spun around to face south, like we were ready to head home. Soon, all but one jib maneuvered us in the light breeze. With our slower movement, the waves rolled beneath us, lifting us up and then pushing us down and away from land.

"What are we waiting for?" I asked Cook, who joined me on deck once the ship was in position.

"Tide and weather. We're entering Fuca Strait. She's a whole lot o' trouble if you sail her under the wrong conditions. We've come up on her high side early in the day. We'll wait for the tide to turn and the westerlies to blow, and ride the flood tide in."

"Water's awful rough." I eyed the waves colliding and frothing ahead of the boat.

"Entrance to this strait churns on a good day." Cook pointed at the northeast horizon. "See that bank of fog sitting over there?" A thin white ribbon strung across the water, an outline of blue land rising above it. A few distant, snowy peaks gleamed in the morning sun. "Captain'll be looking for that to burn off so he can sail in with a clear view. There's a lot of unmarked hazards in these parts."

"Like the coastline on the way up."

"Exactly. You're a fast learner, sailor."

I dismissed his compliment with a half-smile. He had missed Kuno's quick action to save me from myself only minutes before.

"Will the passengers get off in Fort Victoria?" I asked.

"Yep. They're getting homesteads on a nearby island from the governor."

"For how much?"

"Free, to start."

"Free!"

"The land isn't cleared. It'll be tough getting it started, but the group of 'em will help each other."

Back home, Jake had talked about the government selling cheap parcels of land to attract new settlers. This British colony was giving land away to American settlers for nothing.

"What's that land there?" I pointed at the faded blue outline of a distant shore on our starboard side.

"That's America. Thataway," he said, pointing back at the foggy coastline off our port side, "is British territory. The two governments have been scrapping over the border between 'em like a couple of mountain cats. Victoria's much like San Fran in the early days, chock full of Californians, most of 'em here for another crack at gold up the Fraser River. That's over on the far coast, east of Vancouver Island. Can't see it from here."

I thought about the mining certificate tucked away in my bag in the galley. Cook seemed to know quite a lot about the territories and I needed information.

"So... how do you get to a Fraser River gold mine from Victoria?"

"Depends where it is. All the spots are far-flung, hard to get to because the land is so mean. These boys get a big shock, the ones who come here expecting to pick gold like a patch of ripe strawberries. It takes the better part of a day to get across the water, up into the mouth of the Fraser River."

"A whole day?"

"Best part of one. Some canoe over, if you please. From there, they steam up river to Fort Yale. After that, it can take weeks to get into a claim because travel is bad and all the close spots are long picked over. Rugged, brutal land like you never seen. Most miners work the summer and clear out. Two months from now, Victoria will be full of 'em as they get out before the snow flies."

"They wait for spring in Victoria?"

"Yep. Like even right now, nobody new is heading in. It's too late in the season."

"But it's only August!"

"I was in there last year. Left Fort Vic mid-July for the north canyon. Didn't get back out until early September. Was worried I'd have to spend winter in there."

"What happened?"

"Remember what I said about this here border? Brits and Americans are fighting in there, too, over who owns what. Plus the Indians are mad. Can't blame 'em, everybody tearing up their backyard without asking. It's a right mess. I won't go back any time soon."

"Wouldn't you like a chance at gold?"

"Gold!" he snorted. "This here isn't the Sierras where you could shovel up gold from a creek bed and haul it out on horse-back year-round. This place is cruel. You gotta dig and you gotta sift through piles of rock and gravel and you gotta mule it out. Most of the year, if the weather doesn't get ya, the bugs will. No thank you."

I turned away so Cook wouldn't spot the disappointment surely written all over my face. I'd come all the way from San Francisco for this? Getting my gold out of the Fraser sounded impossible. It was all placer mining, which required equipment and hard labor. I hadn't come north expecting to set foot on my claim and stuff my bags full of gold. But I had expected to track down my business partner. From what Cook told me, there was a good chance the other owner was over in the canyon, far away, in a place I couldn't even get to.

"Is the land office for the Fraser in Fort Vic?" I asked, with as little enthusiasm as possible.

Cook narrowed his eyes. I pretended not to notice.

"It is. Why?"

"Just curious."

"Curious. Why do I think there's more to this?"

"Oh, I had an idea for a story."

I could have been writing a story, but I wasn't. I didn't want to be dishonest with Cook but it was too soon to tell him about my mining shares when I didn't have the facts straight myself.

"Mr. Miller's got an operation in the canyon."

"He does? Where?"

"In Yale, which is as far as boats can go up river. Miners pass through to their claims. He's got half a dozen busted men working for him, fellas who hoped to find gold and came up empty-fisted. He brings up big equipment, to get gold out, build roads and such. His men make a good, steady salary doing that work, but it's tough in that lawless town. They can have it. I'll take my seaman's wages and my peaceful life on the water. A lot of men went in, ain't never come out."

I half-listened to Cook. My mind had raced in another direction. Mr. Miller knew the place! He could be my ally. He could help me claim my shares. And to think I'd just left him behind in San Francisco because I didn't want him involved. Jake had been right about asking him for help. Why didn't he tell me his father had his business right in Yale?

"Mr. Miller's winding down his operation for the season. We'll take his men back to San Fran with us on our last sail back in September. They'll have lots of interesting tales you can work into your story."

"My what? Oh yeah. That'll be great!"

Mr. Miller was smart at business. After striking it rich in California, he'd obviously taken his knowledge to the new gold rush territories. He'd help me find my mine if I could prove it was real. I could trust him, no doubt about that. I'd even make a deal with him, give him a small cut of profits for helping me.

The mining region was difficult to reach and the company had only a numbered title. I gloated a little knowing the two sad sack miners who had tried to steal the share certificate didn't have a hope of ever finding the place. With me supposedly dead, and the share certificate burned up along with me, they'd probably already forgotten about their misfortune and moved on. As for me, getting rich would require a lot more patience than I'd bargained for. Jake always said patience wasn't my strong suit, but this was adult business and I'd have to learn. The mining shares were in my hands. I intended to manage affairs for myself going forward. I thought of Mrs. Plea and her calm, confident manner. I'd be like her.

Kuno barked out orders and we returned to our stations. This time, I paid attention to the ropes and didn't let my mind wander. The schooner returned to full sail and cut through the water to the opening of the strait due southeast. A steady wind off our beam pushed us along at a good speed. The warm sun still wasn't enough to overcome the cold air. I buttoned up my coat and shoved my freezing hands in my pockets.

After a couple of hours riding the wind and a flood tide, the ship tacked to keep a steady course away from both shores. The channel was many miles wide and plenty deep, but dangers loomed on both sides.

"Looky there, Charlee," Cook said, taking my arm at the top of the stairs as we returned to work in the galley. Off to our left, a white light blinked through the distant mist. I'd never seen anything like it before. "That's the new lighthouse on Deception Island."

"Deception Island. What's with the bleak name?"

"I guess it's what early explorers thought of the place. That lighthouse will save many a ship from getting destroyed on hidden reefs. Captain knows to keep her a couple of miles off our beam."

Just then, the boat changed course to starboard as if it had been listening to Cook and warned by the island lighthouse.

"Is that where the homesteaders are going?"

Cook laughed. "Not that desolate place. Animals don't even live there, from what I hear. The homesteaders are going to a pretty island on the inside passage, not far from Victoria."

"What's that one called?"

"Locals call it Chuan. The British call it Admiral Island."

"Some big shot military man decided it needed a new name, I suppose?"

"No doubt."

The lighthouse blinked another time before it was swallowed up by the thick sea mist clinging to the distant shoreline. I searched the horizon east of Vancouver Island. Somewhere ahead, behind the coastline and in those big mountains, was gold that belonged to me. It would take some work, but I'd claim it one day soon. Then I'd be rich.

17

i

We arrived in Fort Victoria as the sun dropped behind a distant band of forest and cast evening shadows across the bay.

"Look at those canoes! They're amazing!" I said to Cook as two needle-nosed long boats paddled out to a giant ship anchored beside us near the harbor entrance.

"That's the local Salish people. They trade in the port, live over on the north side of the bay."

He pointed to a shore across from the town. Smoke from a sprawling settlement drifted in wispy patches over the flat roofs of wooden houses. Other long-nosed canoes rested on the muddy shore. Fishnets and drying racks were piled away from the water's edge.

The inner harbor was jammed with boats of all sizes, mostly sailboats but a few small steamships and the occasional rowboat running around between them. Although many boats flew the Stars and Stripes, an equal number flew a flag Cook said was for the Colony of British Columbia.

From the deck of the schooner, Fort Victoria seemed pretty small. At the end of the inside harbor, a cluster of buildings marked the main townsite. On the edges of the little city, the buildings were spread apart and surrounded by what looked like new farm fields. The land had been ruthlessly torn up and turned over. Burning stumps, rock piles and tilled dirt stretched out over the flat land, with only a few trees left behind like sad, gnarly scarecrows. In the far distance, trees of the remaining forest waited in a quiet, brave line. I felt the beauty and the sadness all at once.

As the crew prepared the rowboat, passengers milled around on deck, the excitement of arrival creating a buzz among them. Excited smiles fell away when the Captain announced all must stay aboard for proper clearance. They stood back, shoulders slumped with disappointment, as he and two crewmen set off for shore.

"The Captain has to meet with the governor, get their land papers," Cook said, as if he'd read my mind.

"What about us? When do we get to go ashore? I gotta get off of this thing and get my head right," I said.

"Sorry. Captain says you're not to leave the ship."

"What? He can't stop me!"

"Yes, he can. He has his orders. And he says you stay onboard. Besides, we have a big day of work tomorrow."

"More work?" A string of words unbefitting my decent upbringing slipped out of my mouth. Cook sighed, half amused, half disgusted.

"Look. Even Kuno isn't going ashore. I remind you, this is what you signed up for."

I scowled. I had signed up for this. But I was also exhausted and desperate to get off the ship onto solid ground.

Not far from us, Kuno was holding court with the passengers. They peppered him with questions and he explained what was going on, cool as a sea cucumber, Mr. Jones tucked under his left arm like a sack of flour.

Cook slung a heavy but reassuring arm over my shoulders and drew me into his armpit. "Look, I'll talk to the Captain, see if he'll let you go ashore when we're done with cargo."

I ducked out of his hug. "And you'll take me, right?"

Cook rubbed my hair with his knuckles and didn't answer.

The Captain returned to the ship well after dark. Cook spotted the bobbing lantern on the approaching rowboat while we lounged out on the deck, free of night watch duty for the first time in two weeks. Once aboard, the Captain met with each passenger following the order of the alphabet. I was called upon to record their particulars in my best handwriting.

Cook and I sat with the passengers well into the night, the excitement building with every land certificate carried out of the Captain's cabin. The deck became a joyful place—with clapping and singing as each new landowner emerged, waving his papers in the air. Kuno handed around mugs of grog to toast a new beginning.

When I descended the stairs to the galley just before midnight, I left the joy that didn't belong to me on deck with the new settlers. Heaviness gushed into the empty place that remained. I was happy for them but couldn't ignore how my own future was still so weighted and uncertain.

After breakfast the next morning, Cook went off to talk to the passengers. My presence was required on deck to assist Kuno and the crew as they artfully maneuvered the *Salish Wind* into the smaller part of the bay. Using wind, tide and a steam tug, we eventually tied up at a pier in front of a lumber operation.

The shore was just steps away. If the Captain wouldn't let me go, I could always sneak off. But if I got caught, I'd be in big trouble. Insubordination, Cook called it. I'd probably be put in chains or something. I wondered if the *Salish Wind* had a dungeon somewhere down in the main hold.

The passengers prepared to disembark. They'd spend a day in the town purchasing supplies before catching a steamer for their homesteads on Admiral Island the next morning. The Captain held a stiff and formal farewell ceremony for them, and they politely endured his unnecessary speech. At least he didn't drag it out. As the passengers left, I wished them "good luck" or "safe journey." I even threw in a "Lord be with you" because the event called for some such reverence and protection, and Mizzy would have suggested that, if she'd been there.

Their good fortune reminded me of my own disappointment. Never mind I couldn't go after my gold on this trip. I'd be lucky to be allowed off the ship. I slipped away from the farewell gathering to think. Cook found me an hour later, propped up against a pile of ropes, stewing over my problems in the late morning sun.

"Listen, Charlee. I have something to tell you." I braced myself for more bad news. "I'm going with the passengers to Chuan tomorrow."

I sat up. "And I'm going, too, right?"

"No. You have to crew back to San Fran."

"So that's what you've been off secretly plotting this whole time. Good of you to let me know."

"It's no secret. I'm helping them get set up."

I looked away in disgust. "Are you getting a piece of land, too?"

"No. Why are you so mad?"

"I'm not mad!" I said, raising my voice. "Who's going to run the galley?"

"Drak. He's fine. He's got at least two recipes that don't turn meat into shoe leather."

His attempt at humor fell flat. I fumed. "It took me the best part of a year to find you and now you're leaving me."

"You'll see me the next trip back up! Captain'll keep you on as long as Mr. Miller agrees. I gave you a shining report and the Captain likes you. It'll be the last run of the season and we'll sail back together. In the meantime, you can crew and make good money. Then Mrs. Plea can help arrange school for you in the fall. She knows people."

He threw every good reason he could think of at me, trying to sell his announcement as good news. I shook my head.

"I wanna go with you."

"You can't."

"Everyone decides everything for me. Nobody ever asks me what I want."

I protested even though staying aboard was better for me. If I could go ashore while in port, I'd find the land office. Then I'd be ready to talk to Mr. Miller about my claim as soon as the *Salish Wind* got back to San Francisco. Still, I wished grownups would stop arranging things for me.

"Look, it's only three weeks. I'll be back in the galley annoying you before you know it. Besides, Mizzy's back home. You'll get to stay with her for a few days on the turnaround."

He'd got me good on that one. He knew how much that would mean to both of us. I uncrossed my arms but held on to a disagreeable pout so it wouldn't look like he'd won me over with his smart little reasons.

"Three weeks?"

"Weather cooperating, three weeks."

"Drak's the cranky one, right?"

Cook tipped his head at the hunched over sailor smoking a pipe by the main mast. I sighed. He was the unsmiling, miserable fellow who reeked of garlic and sounded mad when he spoke.

"He's pretty long in the tooth for the sea, even on these short offshore runs," Cook said. "Fell off a mast some years ago, landed on his back. Should have finished him. Nobody hires a broken sailor."

"Except for Mr. Miller," I said.

"Except for Mr. Miller," he repeated. "Drak's gruff, his English is bad, but he's smart and trustworthy. He's a good man."

"And a rotten cook," I added.

"Get him to make coffee my way and you'll be the ship's

hero," Cook said as we went below to prepare lunch.

We spent the rest of the day unloading empty boxes and barrels, and loading fresh stores for the return trip.

"Why so much for the trip back?" I asked Cook as we wiped our sweat and guzzled water after lugging half a dozen small barrels into the pantry.

"What's that?" He looked away.

"I'm saying, seems like a lot o' stores with no passengers to feed on the way back."

"Ah. We always carry extra."

"Yeah. But for a whole blinking posse?" I muttered, as I followed him up the stairs for another load.

Luckily, supper that night was easy fare. With all the passengers gone and the crew taking advantage of daylight hours to load, we laid out a platter of smoked fish with cheese, apples, and biscuits. The crew helped themselves when they had time.

With no additional work assigned and nothing left to do in the stuffy galley below, I grabbed the chance to read on deck. It was a beautiful evening with a warm, woody breeze coming off the land, carrying the scent of fresh cut timber. The warmth of the summer day lingered in the protected harbor.

I'd barely made myself comfortable when I heard Kuno holler, "*Sonoma*, ho!" The crew echoed his call. Mr. Miller's other schooner had sailed into view from behind a point of land. I joined Cook on the mid-deck as the ship drop its sails and chose a deep-water spot in the harbor close to us.

"They made excellent time," Cook said. The *Sonoma Wind* had left two days behind us.

As soon as they were anchored, four men boarded their rowboat and headed our way. The captain of the other ship sat in the bow seat facing us. He was easy to identify in his blue waistcoat. Three crew members in the boat faced away from us. Two of them did all the rowing. The third man was a spare.

I shielded my eyes in the blinding glare of the setting sun, watched the boat pass through the dark shadows cast by anchored ships, through the amber glow of evening light that had settled over the water. Suddenly, a beam of sunlight struck the boat, illuminating the sailors. I rubbed my eyes to make sure I wasn't mistaken. The spare crewman's hair glowed an unmistakable orange and gold.

"No. Don't tell me…" I muttered.

"Is that who I think it is?" Cook asked.

"Jake!" I called out. He spun around as the boat drew alongside.

"Ahoy, Charlee!" he replied, grinning and waving. He tried to stand, but a crewman stopped him. The next pull on the oars caused him to topple into the bottom of the boat. I giggled as he struggled to get himself back onto his bench. He threw up his hands at his clumsiness and straightened a make-believe tie. I shook my head at his charming, carefree antics. The warmth of an entire summer was in his smile.

"What the devil is he doing here?" Cook grumbled.

"He followed me, I guess."

The reality of the situation wiped the smile from my face. Jake should not have come. His presence was a problem, and one I would surely be blamed for.

18

i

We took our places at the stern, behind the Captain and Kuno, to greet the landing party from our sister ship. The Captain welcomed our visitors aboard with another small, rambling speech. The business of rank and order was tedious at the best of times. I widened my eyes at Jake, dying to pepper him with questions. He pursed his lips, trying not to smile, like his arrival at Fort Victoria was no big deal.

Formalities dispensed with, the Captain led the guest officer away to his quarters, leaving the rowboat crew to mingle. Cook steered Jake away and we walked him out of earshot.

"You are an unexpected surprise, sir," Cook said.

"I know," Jake whispered. "Turns out I got to come along after all, Charlee."

I stood in front of him, arms crossed, shaking my head. "Let's start there, shall we, Jake? What on earth are you doing here?"

"I told you I could get on Father's boat if I wanted."

"And I told you not to come."

"I didn't. Not with you anyhow," he said indignantly.

"Whoa, you two," Cook interrupted. "Sit down. Take a breath. Now, Jake. Start from the beginning."

Jake recounted the events of the weekend after the *Salish*

Wind had left port. As soon as we were gone, Mrs. Plea told Mr. Miller what had happened. Worried that the bad men might go after Jake, they hauled him out of bed before dawn the next morning. Jake told them about the burning boat and how I'd tricked the bad men into thinking I was dead. They decided he should stay with Mizzy for a few days, just to be safe.

"But school wasn't over," I said. "No way they'd let you come."

"Right you are. So I stowed away and came anyhow."

"Oh no! You ran away?"

"Well, I didn't ask permission, if that's what you mean. It's Father's boat, so what are they gonna do?"

I tapped my fingers on my elbow, livid. "I can't believe it. This is a nightmare."

"Well, it ain't good," Cook said. He shook his head. We both knew that Jake had made things worse for me.

"What did the Captain say when you showed yourself?"

"He was real mad. I told him I'd work and it was just for one trip and I'd make sure he didn't get fired. We had perfect sailing weather, the crew said. We saw pods of killer whales and dolphins!"

"Of course you did," I said. I was pretty sure they provided him with all the comforts of a wealthy, paying passenger. The captain of the *Sonoma Wind* would be doing everything to make sure the boss's eldest son was given the best care, under the circumstances.

My journey, on the other hand, was memorable because of gale force winds, wild seas, water crashing over the deck and pouring in hatches, mops and ropes and endless buckets of nasty human waste thrown overboard.

"Okay, listen up," Cook said. "I'm going to find out what's up. We usually sail back together when we're here at the same time. And I'll find out what's to be done with you."

Jake chimed in, "I was already told. I'm only allowed over

to the *Salish Wind* while we are in port and only when my work is done."

I'd been banking on a chance to go ashore and look into the mining certificate at the land office. It was a hard sell even before Jake showed up. Now it would be impossible to get permission.

I was about to launch into a complaint about that when Cook held up his hand.

"I already know what you're going to say. I'll see what I can do." And with that, he left us alone.

I lit in to Jake as soon as Cook was out of earshot.

"I can't believe you've been so reckless."

"Me? What about you? Blowing up that boat and burning it to the ground. I thought you were dead! Who's the reckless one?"

"That was accidental. Besides, I explained it all in my letter."

"Yea, but I spent a whole night not knowing. That was pretty thoughtless, wouldn't you say?"

I'd never seen Jake so angry. It wasn't like him.

"I'm sorry. I didn't plan it that way. But that doesn't matter now. Do you realize what you've done, running off after me like this?"

"I thought you'd admire my sense of adventure," he said. His tone was hard and cold.

"This isn't a game, Jake."

"I know. Since I'm here now, let's not waste precious time arguing about things. Tell me what you found out about the mining company."

I filled him in on the Fraser Canyon gold mines, how hard it was to get to them, and how it was too late to even try to get in this year.

"You were right about talking to your father. Which reminds me. Cook says his company works out of Yale, right in the thick of the gold rush."

"I saw that place on the map in the San Francisco land office."

"Why didn't you tell me your father's company was there?"

"I did."

"No, you did not. You said he had business here. In Victoria. It's a whole different thing that he also does business over there in the canyon. It's almost like two different countries, they're so far apart."

He shrugged. "I didn't know. Father doesn't say much and I don't ask. So now what?"

"I want to go to the land office but I'm not supposed to go ashore. Not safe for a girl." I rolled my eyes before continuing. "Cook said he'd ask the Captain for permission."

"I'll get permission to go, too."

"No, you will not. You've probably ruined my chance already, just being here. Don't mess this up, too."

Jake scowled.

The two captains appeared on deck, which meant it was time for the visitors to return to their ship. I walked Jake back to the stern.

"At least let me help you plan your daring escapade," Jake said.

"Sure," I replied.

To Jake, my life was one big, exciting adventure. He observed it from a place of comfort and security. He would never know the dark and scary corners of my uncertain world.

"What's going to happen with Jake?" Cook said, after the rowboat had departed and we were back in the galley having coffee at the table.

"Nothing. He's going back to San Francisco. I'm guessing his father will be more frightened than angry."

"And then Mr. Miller will talk to the headmaster at the school and fix it all up, right?"

"Right."

We both sat in the weight of that moment, seeing how easy it was for something to be set right, if you had the money and the right color of skin.

"I'm going to let you in on a secret," Cook began. "Nobody else knows except the Captain and Kuno."

"Not much of a secret then, if half the crew's in on it."

"Listen, wiseacre. In the back of the pantry, where we loaded the new provisions? We've got gold in some of the barrels."

I fumbled my coffee cup but caught it before it spilled in my lap. "Gold! We're hauling gold?"

"Shshsh! You wanna tell all of Victoria?" Nobody had heard me but Cook still turned his ear to the door. "You're sailing back to San Fran with gold from Mr. Miller's mining company."

I thought about my own mining shares in those far-away mountains and my voice trembled. "How much gold?"

"Don't know exactly. Say sixty pounds. Probably worth twenty-five thousand or so."

"Twenty-five thousand dollars!"

A small fortune was stashed somewhere right beside me in the galley! If my gold mine made that kind of money, I really would be rich like Mr. Miller. I could buy a bunch of ranches.

"There's more. Mr. Miller is a partner."

"In what?" I'd been mulling over the exciting possibility of becoming a ranch owner when he added this twist.

"In the Midnight Express. It's Mrs. Plea's operation. Mr. Miller is a benefactor. They fund the railroad, as we call it. Usually the *Salish Wind* isn't part of the line, but the governor here on Vancouver Island offered to help. They say he's a colored man himself."

"The governor?"

And then it struck me. The governor, Mr. Miller, the *Salish Wind*, Mrs. Plea, the Sunshine Café, the old man that lived across from me in the tenement. They were all connected.

Mr. Miller was a very wealthy man and a respected

businessman. He had more money than he knew what to do with and had always been generous with it. Jake had told me his father was fiercely opposed to slavery. It wasn't at all surprising he was using some of his money in the fight for freedom.

"Who knows about the railroad? I mean, Mizzy must know then?"

"Oh, she knows. Your papa, too."

"Papa knew!"

"Yep. Mr. Miller keeps his family out of it. The Missus don't know at all, which is good because she's got a mouth on her like a river during spring runoff. Look, even after you tapped into the line, what could you have told anyone about it if you'd been caught?"

"I wasn't going to get caught."

"But say you did. An old man told you a bunch of mumbo jumbo about what to order at a café? Even if they'd beaten the name Amos out of you, nobody knows anyone by the name of Amos."

"Wait. I asked down at the docks, when I first went looking for you. Your name made them go pale as a bucket of milk."

"Not my name. You said you asked about the Midnight."

"Oh."

"That's what set 'em off. Folks got eyes and ears, but they shut 'em up when there's any mention of the Midnight. As for the *Salish Wind*, she's just a merchant ship, no different from hundreds of others working the port. Folks only know what they need to and nothing more. That's how it works."

"No wonder Mrs. Plea locked me up."

"She had to. You'd come through the line."

"Because the old man that lived across the hall helped me. I hope those men didn't go after him."

"He relocated the day you left."

I thought about the old man packing up his unmatched

dishes, his patchwork quilt and pillows. He'd made a cozy little home in that drafty, rodent-infested dump, something Uncle had never done. Thanks to me, he had to move and start all over somewhere.

"The Sunshine Café is just a café. Nothing to see there at all and nobody knows anything."

"I can't believe Papa didn't tell me. He never kept secrets from me." As soon as I said it, I realized I wanted to believe that, but it wasn't the truth at all. He'd kept lots of things from me. About my mama. About Uncle Jack. About Mizzy.

"You have to keep those you love safe. Mizzy knew because of me. We kept in touch but had to be extremely careful."

"So that's why you never visited."

"Yep. As for your papa, he was what we call a watchman. He looked out for Mr. Miller, kept his ear to the ground for him so he'd know what was going down. I'm sure you get why your papa didn't tell you."

"Is that why Mr. Miller hasn't told Jake?"

"Exactly why."

"You can count on me to keep the secret. I'd like to join Mrs. Plea's operation. I could be a watchman like Papa. Or a messenger even."

Cook grabbed my shoulder and gave it a firm squeeze.

"See the gold gets to San Francisco, sailor. That's your first railroad assignment."

"I will. I promise."

19

i

Early the next morning, Cook packed a small bag by the light of the galley lantern. The boat taking the passengers to Admiral Island was leaving early, which meant he'd be gone well before breakfast and daylight. I peered at him through the web of ropes that made my hammock.

It was only for a few weeks. One round trip to San Francisco and he'd be back with me in the galley. Even though I understood why he had to go, I didn't want him to. In spite of how hard the sailing trip had been, and how tired I was from it, I'd felt I could get through it with Cook nearby.

I dressed and dumped myself out of my hammock.

"Need a hand packing?"

"Nah. Not much to take."

The dread of being left behind was momentarily relieved by what he'd packed. If he really meant to be gone longer than a few weeks, he would have taken more than a few personal items and his guitar.

"Don't let Drak wreck the place. I don't want to come back and find all my wooden spoons snapped into kindling."

"From stirring his coffee," I added.

Cook ruffled my hair and shook his head. "Lord help y'all."

We were making small talk, joking around to keep things light. That's what people do when they feel their hearts getting heavy and they can't bear the weight of saying goodbye. I thought then that Cook might miss me as much as I was going to miss him.

"I'll make a project out of Drak. Good thing I like a challenge." We climbed the stairs to the deck. "Cook… about the mission."

"No more talk about that."

"One question. It's important."

He sighed and held up his remaining forefinger. "One."

"Jake can't know about the Midnight or the gold, right?"

"Right. I know you're close, but you can't tell him."

I replied with a solemn nod. "Did you ask the Captain, about letting me go ashore?"

"That's two questions," he teased, and I slugged him in the ribs. He pretended to be winded. "Matter of fact, I did. He doesn't like it, you being precious cargo and all."

I made a sour face and Cook grinned with amusement.

"I suggested Kuno could take you. No way Jake goes though. He's thinking on it. Talk to him later. Pretty sure you can win him over."

The harbor before dawn was abandoned, the waters still and black. As Cook left the dock and disappeared into the shoreline shadows, I felt nervous and unsettled, abandoned on the ship.

"Don't you fret." Kuno had come up behind me, Mr. Jones as ever tucked into his armpit. He'd seen me hanging over the gunwale, staring into the dark. "Mr. Jones here tells me he's gonna keep his eye on you till Cookie gets back. Ain't that right, Bubba?"

I could have sworn Mr. Jones winked at me just then, but it was probably just a bit of his curly brow getting in his left eye. Kuno said I was officially assigned to them until Cook returned. That gave my spirit a big lift. They were my new friends. It wouldn't be so bad.

While I'd been seeing Cook off, Drak had moved in and started on breakfast. When I returned to the galley, he grumbled something that was either "good morning" or "get going," I wasn't sure which. I tied my apron and set to work.

Drak made coffee like he was mixing a batch of plaster. I knew it would be awful before I even tasted it. He added so much water into the pot for the breakfast porridge, I figured we'd be able to drink it from a cup. When I tried to ladle some of the excess water out, he rapped my interfering hand with a wooden spoon. I threw up my hands up and stepped away. Our meals would be mighty grim if he didn't let me pitch in.

With Cook gone, galley work was going to be tedious. Cook chatted, sang, joked around and told stories to make the time pass. Drak was silent but for grunts whenever he exerted himself. His bushy black eyebrows formed an unruly hedge on his forehead. His beard was mostly grey, thin and uneven. A long red scar ran from the bottom of his right ear into the collar of his shirt.

I figured I'd make the best of the situation and attempted a little conversation. He interrupted me with a gnarly, wagging finger.

"I Russian. English, no good."

I shrugged. "I Californian. Russian, plo-ka."

His mouth cracked into a wrinkled laugh, showing a black crescent of stubbled, broken and missing teeth.

"Plo-ka!" Laughter sent him into a wretched coughing fit, which ended several minutes later with a horrible slimy ball of something being horked from the back of his throat and gobbed into a nearby saucepan.

By mid-morning, our main hold was full and the mid-deck loaded with milled timber. The *Sonoma Wind* had been brought in from the outer harbor and was docked on the other side of the pier. With low tide, the smell of salt and seaweed filled the air, a welcome change from the heavy stench of oily masts and grease. I waved to Jake, who'd been unloading supplies along with his crew. "Lunch!" he hollered back, mimicking eating out of a bowl.

I followed his movements for a few minutes as he worked. His back had become longer and broader since leaving the ranch, his torso a better match for the gangly legs he'd had a year earlier. Papa would have said getting away from his bookwork for a spell would do him a world of good. I thought so myself. He seemed to enjoy the physical work.

Back on the *Salish Wind*, Drak toiled in the heat of the late morning alongside Paddy and Lu Chan, the two healthy crewmen half his age. I'd never noticed how hard he worked before, how determined he was to do his fair share. Although he struggled to keep up with his mates, he could still outdo a landlubber like me with one wiry arm tied behind his back.

I knew then why Cook chose him to take over in the galley. He would get three weeks away from constant hard labor. As he puffed and grunted while stowing some thick ropes, I could see he needed it.

Cook was a lot like Mizzy that way. He'd take care of someone without letting on that's what he'd done. I overheard him tell Drak that the galley needed him because the younger men were splendid sailors but didn't know their arses from a griddle. Mizzy wouldn't have used those words, but she'd have done the same thing. She'd have chosen the terrible cook, one demanding shift away from an early grave.

Lu Chan, the crewman who worked the riggings high above the deck, scaled the wood stacks like a nimble goat, a long poker-like tool balanced across his palms. He rolled the last of some smaller posts into place between two low stacks of long plank lumber. Kuno and Paddy lashed the timber to the deck with ropes and chains. Nothing could shift when we were under sail or at the mercy of rolling seas.

Hunched over to catch his breath, Drak mopped his dripping brow on a dirty kerchief. Kuno tapped his shoulder. Saved by his new galley assignment, he flapped a hand at me and disappeared below. I took the cue to follow.

"Helloooo?" Jake's familiar voice called from the top of the stairs just before lunch. "Yo, Charlee!"

"In the galley," I called back, quickly drying off a handful of wet utensils and stuffing them back into a compartment.

"Go," Drak said. He waved a wooden spoon at me.

"Da?" I pointed to the stairs.

"Da! Go!" he repeated, and shooed me out with the flick of a linen towel.

I collided with Jake right outside the galley entrance. We hugged each other awkwardly for a moment, then stepped back and complained that the other should mind where they were going.

"Wait. What's for lunch?" Jake said as I led him up the steps to the deck.

"Trust me. You want to eat on the *Sonoma*. Drak's got some cold oily rice dish with weird spices going on in there. He ain't Cook."

"That reminds me. I saw Cook leave this morning. Where's he off to?"

Can't tell him about the Midnight, I reminded myself.

"He's doing some business for your father."

I explained about the new galley arrangements. It was now my job to make sure Drak didn't poison the crew until we returned to Victoria and picked up Cook on the last run of the season.

"You're the kitchen expert? Wait'll Miss Molly hears." I waited while Jake enjoyed a hearty laugh at my expense.

"Mizzy. She goes by Mizzy now."

"Oh yeah. She told me. You all have different names in the underground."

"What are you talking about, Jake?"

How did he know about the underground? Who'd told him? Not Mizzy. No way.

"You know what I'm talking about." He looked around to be sure nobody was listening. "I didn't let on to Cook, but they told me about the mission after you'd gone. I made them tell me."

I'd been listening with my mouth hanging open. He knew. But how much had they told him? I couldn't talk about it. I gave my word.

"So what now?" I asked, a safe question that allowed him to take the conversation any direction he liked. He didn't seem to think his revelation was a big deal and moved on.

"They've got me lined up for a full day of deck work. My punishment, I guess. I've got to get back. What about you?"

"I still have to get permission to go ashore."

"Well, get on it. I've done the homework for you," he whispered, brushing a bit of lint off his trousers like a know-it-all.

"You found out about the land office?"

"Address and everything," he said over his shoulder. "See you later."

Jake crossed the dock back to the *Sonoma Wind*. I needed to talk to the Captain right away!

20

i

"He'll see ya now," Kuno said, eyeing the book tucked under my arm with curiosity. He waved me through the open door leading into the Captain's quarters.

"Ah, splendid! Close the door and have a seat. I shall be with you in a moment," the Captain said, glancing up from behind a large wooden table. I closed the door quietly, against my better judgment, and took a seat in a single wooden chair opposite him.

His cabin wasn't what I'd pictured at all. I'd imagined a massive oak desk containing important papers, shelves of books on every wall, fancy-legged furniture upholstered in red and green and gold. His furnishings were plain, old and rather worn. They gave off an odd musty smell in the closed quarters. Navigational charts, open books and papers covered the surface of his table, topped off with a sextant, a ruler, and another calculating tool I didn't recognize.

He finished writing a few lines in a large, leather-bound book and returned his pen to a decorative holder. I waited for him to set the course for our conversation. I was much better at navigating myself when I had a hint of a direction.

"Now then. I see you have brought my poetry book."

"Yessir."

"Were you able to read some of it then?"

"Oh yes. I read all of it, sir."

He raised his eyebrows. "Well! Then I would enjoy hearing your opinion of Mr. Whitman's work."

My stomach dropped. This felt like a teacher's trap, like he didn't believe I'd read the book and wanted to catch me pretending I had. I hesitated. I wanted to say that the poet's words sounded very much like a white man who was used to having everything go his way. But I couldn't say that to him.

"The form surprised me, sir. I mean, I expected lines to rhyme, and more order in the verses and such. He puts words wherever he pleases. I didn't think that was allowed."

The Captain's eyes widened. "Funny you should mention his form. Whitman's received much criticism for it. It's called free verse. It's very controversial."

He squinted and tapped his lips, as if he couldn't figure out how I'd come up with this observation. The cabin was getting hotter by the second. It reminded me of school on the Miller ranch, where I sat in the back of the stuffy parlor and was required to keep opinions to myself.

"I mean, it didn't bother me, the uneven lines and messy verses."

"But did you enjoy his subject matter?"

I cringed. The Captain was bent on having a literary discussion.

"Well, some of it was hard going. I didn't get all of it other than he's big on freedom and independence and stuff."

"Yes."

"I liked the 'Poem of the Road' the best... even though he's inviting the whole world to go with him and that seems like it would be a mighty crowded trip if they all agreed."

The Captain burst out laughing. I laid the book down on his table and stared at the floor.

"That may be the most honest, albeit unconventional, review

I've heard of the man. You've cut right to the heart of it, I dare say."

I looked up to meet his pale, smiling eyes.

The Captain picked up his poetry book and walked it over to a shelf with wooden slats, designed to keep books from flying off when under sail. He ran his hands over the spines of his precious collection, straightened up volumes out of line with the others, and carefully slid the book into its place.

"Now I see the secret of the making of the best persons," he said in his best speech-giving voice.

It was a line from "Poem of the Road." My memory instantly took me to the verse. I could picture the exact spot on the page, the position of the lines, every word in order.

"It is to grow in the open air, and to eat and sleep with the earth," I said.

He spun around.

"You've memorized it! How extraordinary!"

He stared at me now, not like an object of unusual curiosity, but like something magical and unexplained. I hadn't memorized all of it, just the parts I liked. I thought it best to keep quiet or he'd have me reciting lines all day. All I wanted was to be allowed off the ship.

"It would be hypocritical of me to endorse Mr. Whitman's ideas and then bar you from the smallest experience of a new world.

"Sir?"

"Kuno says you wish to have shore leave."

"Yessir."

"The situation, as I'm sure you are aware, is… delicate. Mrs. Plea entreated me to keep you safe." His eyes were moving over me now, searching for obvious girl details. I squirmed under his gaze, hoping he couldn't find any.

"You may go ashore," he said, with stern authority. "You

must stay with Kuno at all times. Tomorrow afternoon only, as I cannot spare him any other time."

"Thank you, Captain!" He opened the cabin door and gestured for me to leave. I couldn't wait to tell Jake.

Our Captain wasn't a bad sort, really. He was a little odd, not the type you'd expect to command a merchant vessel, but one could do a lot worse than having to report to a man with a fondness for poetry.

By mid-afternoon the next day, our ship was fully loaded. Kuno gave the hard-working crew the rest of the day off. The weather was perfect for a walkabout, with blue sky, sunshine, and a fresh breeze.

I'd been loitering on the floating dock between the two schooners waiting for Kuno when Jake appeared.

"You're not coming," I said.

"Yup. I am. Captain already arranged it with your officers."

He could tell I wasn't happy.

"C'mon, Charlee. Since I'm here, let me help."

He could help, but I didn't appreciate him deciding for both of us that he should come and organizing it behind my back.

Kuno climbed down from the *Salish Wind*.

"You two stick close to me. Captains' orders," Kuno said.

I'd put my ranch boots back on for the occasion, and they echoed on the boards of the pier as we walked to the beach. As soon as I set foot on the slimy shore, I discovered boots weren't the best choice for tide puddles, sucking sand, slippery rocks and seaweed. Even worse, the familiar roll of the sea was still in my body. I turned my head too fast and lost my balance.

Kuno chuckled as Jake pulled me to my feet. "Sea legs go both ways, mate. It's why sailors never pick fights in port. They swing and fall over and the landlubber never has to throw a single punch."

"You're making that up," Jake said, laughing.

"I might be. Or I could be talking from experience. You never know. Now. What sights suit your fancy? There's a couple of them quaint British shops up the way. There's the Hudson's Bay for more practical things. Fan Tan Alley is good if you're hungry. There's outdoor vendors around the wharf if you want to barter with the locals. Adult establishments are off limits for you two, goes without sayin'."

Jake jumped in. "I'd like to go to the government house."

"The what?" Kuno's cheerful expression soured.

"The land office." Jake handed Kuno the address. "I study property rights. Thought maybe I could speak to someone for my research."

Kuno scratched his head. "That sounds like a swell time. What about you, Charlee? What do you wanna see?"

Jake flashed me a conspiring look.

"I don't mind if we go to that place for Jake. We should do that first, in case it closes. I'm happy to poke around after, maybe buy a souvenir or two."

"All right. We'll go do Jake's thing and walk around a little. On the way back, we'll buy a fresh salmon. I'm giving Drak the night off."

"Great idea," I said. "One less greasy meal with mystery ingredients."

"Stay close now. No wandering."

Kuno marched off, with Jake and I mouthing words to each other behind him. I slipped the mining certificate to Jake and he shoved it into his pocket.

As we walked, Kuno gave us a history lesson on the town. Only a year earlier, Victoria was nothing more than a little Hudson's Bay Company post with a few hundred employees living along the harbor. When news of gold reached San Francisco, miners loaded on steamers and came north by the thousands. The governor made them come to Fort Victoria to get licenses to mine. So, in the space of a year, the town had become a sprawling mess of slapped-together public houses and tent shanties, most of which were filled with gold-digging American men.

We left the docks and walked up a dirt lane. The wood buildings on both sides looked like they'd been built in a hurry. Ordinary and unpainted, they provided a roof and walls around whatever operation was needed. The aroma of fresh baking replaced the fishy odor of the low-tide mud flats at the water's edge. We passed a big hardware store, a couple of hotels and saloons, a boat repair shop, and a gun and tackle store.

We turned onto a wide street where brick buildings had been constructed with more attention to order and design. The shops changed from the work of the harbor to the business of a young city. This street had solicitors, accountants, restaurants, a cigar and tobacco shop, and a tailor advertising custom-made suits for gentlemen. On this pleasant day, city folk milled about on the boardwalks—families of men, women, and children.

As we rounded another corner, Kuno came to an abrupt halt.

"We got a problem," he said. A long line of men snaked along the boardwalk outside the government office. "Gonna take hours to get in there."

"Now what?" Jake whispered.

"I don't know," I mouthed back.

Kuno sized up the line. "C'mon, boys. Play along with me."

He marched us up to the front door and spoke so loudly to Jake that half the line could hear him.

"Now you tell that weasel of a beancounter in there, that Mr. Blatsford, that the Gov'nor can't wait. You get what he needs and get back out here on the double."

Jake was stunned. I nudged him.

"Go, lad! You're wasting the Gov'nor's time!" I held the door open while Kuno towered over the front of the line. Mr. Jones curled his lips back over his teeth and growled for added effect. One man opened his mouth, and closed it right away, like he thought better of arguing with a man two heads taller and arms the size of stovepipes.

"I hope Jake is quick," Kuno said to me as we turned away. "I'm a little surprised none o' them sods took exception to him barging in."

"You were very persuasive," I said, and Kuno stuck his chest out with pride.

We crossed the dirt street to a stall where some local women were selling fish and vegetables. As Kuno picked out a salmon for supper, the women pointed at Mr. Jones and exchanged smiles and comments.

I was browsing through their herb collection when familiar voices made my spine crawl. I peeked around Kuno's large frame, certain my ears were playing tricks on me. Boss and Clem, the two sorry miners who'd hounded me in San Francisco, were coming down the boardwalk right for us!

21

i

"Those men! Cover me!" I said to Kuno and dove behind the women and their baskets of fish. Kuno didn't miss a beat. He took a position to block their view until they'd passed. I got to my knees, apologizing to the two women who I swear had made themselves look bigger to hide me. The door of the government building opened and Jake came out.

I waved to get his attention. Boss and Clem would easily recognize him as the schoolboy from the burning boat. He was about to cross the street to join us when I signaled "hold up," like we used to do on the ranch, and pointed at Boss and Clem. Jake saw them, but it was too late. They'd already spotted him and were headed his way. I signaled to Jake again and he avoided looking in our direction, so the men wouldn't follow his eyes.

Kuno started for Jake and I held him back.

"No. Wait. Those miners were after me in San Francisco. They can't see me. They think I'm dead."

"That's the boss's son over there, and if a hair on that blond head o' his falls out, it's on me."

"Jake can handle them. Just back him up."

Kuno stuffed me back behind the fish baskets. "You stay out o' sight. And don't go anywhere!"

As Kuno hurried across the street, Jake was headed away from us, with Boss and Clem on each side of him, probably pestering him about what he was doing all the way up here in Victoria. They wouldn't hurt Jake, I was sure of that. He could talk his way out of pretty much anything. The bigger problem was Kuno didn't know the whole story. He could blow it all to smithereens by saying the wrong thing. I followed Kuno, keeping a few buggy lengths behind him so as not to be noticed.

Boss and Clem steered Jake into a nearby lane. Kuno was hot on their heels, and I was trailing all of them, concealed by strangers and storefronts. I could see Jake talking to the men. His expression was serious, but he was in control this time. They wisely kept their hands off of him, to make the conversation appear ordinary to passers-by.

Kuno stopped at the lane and said something to Jake and the men.

"Don't blow the story, Kuno," I said.

They exchanged a few words. The two miners, both looking up at Kuno with stupid grins, didn't object to whatever had been said. One of them shook Jake's hand! Then they continued on their way, looking satisfied with whatever they'd been told.

I waited for Kuno and Jake to retrace their steps, watching their backs in case the miners doubled back and followed them. They didn't.

Back at the stall where I'd hidden, I popped out and met them, Kuno no wiser to me having disobeyed his order to stay put until he returned.

"Mind telling me what just happened there?" Kuno asked, once the three of us were reunited. Kuno snagged me by the elbow and steered me off in the direction of the harbor. "We're getting both of you back on the ship right away. Tour's over."

"Thanks for the signals," Jake said to me. "Pretty sure they would have spotted who I was with if you hadn't done that. Gave me a chance to guide them away."

"What did you say to them?"

"Oh, we had a fine conversation. I told them I was here on summer research. I bored them to death with the details of it until they got restless and got down to what it was they wanted."

"Which was?"

"They wanted to know what happened after the beach incident. They were worried I might have implicated them. I said I didn't want to be dragged into any trouble myself. I told them the authorities ruled your death accidental by fire. A homeless person of unknown origin living in an abandoned boat."

"Smart thinking, Mr. Fitzquiddick," I said. Jake pinched his cheeks into a smile.

"Pick it up a little, you two," Kuno said. "I don't know what kind of story you got going here with those fellas, but I don't like it."

"You were outstanding in the role of concerned bystander, Kuno. You'd have been a fine actor," Jake said.

"Yeah, Kuno. First at the government office and then with those two losers," I added.

Kuno stopped to check our surroundings for threats. Our compliments didn't appease him. He studied the street behind us, then led us off again, making unexpected turns down different alleys. He knew his way around the town, and soon we emerged from a lane close to the pier where our two ships were tied up.

Back on the *Salish Wind*, I pulled Jake aside to go over every last detail of his conversation with Boss and Clem. Satisfied he'd gotten rid of them, I acknowledged that he'd been very helpful after all, and I was no longer annoyed with him for taking matters into his own hands. He reminded me we'd always trusted each other and worked as a team. I didn't think that arrangement could last unless I got my life sorted out, so I let the comment slide and asked him what he'd found out at the land office instead. I could tell from his downcast expression that it was more bad news.

"The gold mining company doesn't exist."

"What? That can't be!"

"The clerk knew right away. He said the document wasn't even legal here. It isn't locally registered. I should have realized that myself, come to think of it."

I couldn't hide my disappointment. "But Uncle was positive it was worth a fortune. And those men chased him and then me all over San Francisco for it. There must be some mistake."

He gave me back the certificate and I stared at it in disbelief. I'd prepared myself to hear it was too deep in the canyon to get to, and for more discouragement because of the lateness of the season and such. I wasn't ready to hear there was no gold mine at all.

"You're absolutely certain, Jake?"

"Sorry, Charlee. No mistake. The clerk showed me licenses and claim certificates. This is nothing like them. If what you've got really is valuable, it isn't valuable here."

Kuno had to report the shore incident to the Captain. Although he reassured him we hadn't been followed, he ordered a watch placed on the pier just in case. Jake and I were instructed to remain below deck.

Although our shore visit had come to a sudden end, Jake got to stay on the *Salish Wind* until the Captain cleared him to leave. As promised, Kuno took over the galley and prepared a delicious Polynesian dish of fish and rice. Drak grumbled that the fish was bland and buried his under a layer of salt. I pretended to add salt to mine, just so he wouldn't feel bad. As a reward for my loyalty, Drak took off without a word, leaving Jake and me to do the cleanup.

Jake chatted through the entire meal, about Boss and Clem and how we'd played them for fools again. He took great satisfaction in getting them back for the grief they'd caused in San Francisco. His lighthearted sense of victory even made Kuno relax about the whole encounter. I let go of being mad about him coming north after me. He had helped me with the mining certificate, but I stopped short of celebrating our afternoon adventure. My heart was much too heavy. The news that my shares in a gold mine didn't exist still stunned me. I'd come all the way to Fort Victoria for nothing.

"So what's your plan now?" Jake asked, interrupting a long period of gloomy silence that had come over me since we'd finished eating and everyone had left.

"I don't have one. This was nothing but a wild goose chase. The thing is worthless."

"I'm not so sure about that. I think we were looking for answers in the wrong places."

"What do you mean?" For the first time in hours, a flicker of hope passed through me again.

"Remember when I first saw it, I said I thought it looked like a promissory note?"

"Yeah. Those are things one person gives another when they owe something or agree to something."

"Right. Well, the clerk in the land office said the same thing. Which means we shouldn't be looking for the company at all. We should be looking for who signed it, and it's probably a lawyer or a notary right in San Francisco on behalf of the unknown third party."

"And they would know who the unknown third party is."

"Exactly."

"So you think it still might be worth something?"

"I don't know. But I think we have a few more rocks to look under before we give up, and none of them are way over in Yale."

"What about your father? He knows a lot of people in San Francisco."

"Are you suggesting we show it to him?"

"I mean, maybe he'll recognize the signatures. It might save us some time."

"Sure. You know he'll help you... if you let him."

I'd been dead set against getting Jake's father involved, but by trying to handle it all by myself, I'd gotten nowhere. I'd even set myself back, coming on this wicked journey north, thinking I'd be able to ride into the gold fields and claim ownership. For the first time ever, I wished I'd paid more attention to Jake's law books.

"I've got the sail back home to think it through."

I made coffee and we spent the rest of the evening at the galley table talking about what would happen when Jake got home. He really wasn't too worried about it. He knew his father would be angry, but Mr. Miller wasn't the sort to scream and yell, or take a switch to his children. He'd sit down with Jake and they'd have a serious discussion. As for school, he said he had only one examination left to write. He was certain the headmaster would be persuaded to let him complete it on his return.

"Must be nice," I said.

"What?" Jake asked.

"To always have everything go your way and work out. If it was me who'd stowed away, I'd probably be arrested and thrown in an institution. And without an important father, or even one that's still alive, I'd be failed for the whole school year."

Jake didn't comment. He knew what I said was true.

Drak stumbled in just before midnight, reeking of rum and tobacco, and ordered Jake back to his ship. We'd all be up well before dawn the next morning, preparing for an early departure, and we needed at least a few hours of sleep.

22

i

Dawn arrived with a soft, pink glow. With breakfast over early, the crew mingled, sipped a last bit of coffee, and waited for our ship's turn to be pushed away from the dock. Then all of us would spring into action hoisting the sails.

I paused to look east to the sunrise. Kuno said a pink morning sky was a warning of a change in the weather. As the sun rose, the pink darkened until the sky looked like it was bleeding crimson. We intended to get out ahead of whatever foul weather might be coming in.

I'd dressed ready to sail. I learned on the rough trip up that as soon as we were in the wind, the day would feel more like winter than summer. I had my hat and gloves ready in the pocket of my coat. Still, I shivered in the windless calm of the morning harbor. The thought of another sailing trip back made my stomach turn. Cook said, you're either a sailor or you aren't. I was pretty sure I wasn't. I'd had no idea what I was getting myself into when I decided to sail north. And now that they had taken me on, Cook expected me to stay with the crew for the last run of the season. I didn't know if I could stand another trip like the one we'd had to Victoria. If the trip back was even half as bad, I might never set foot on another sailing ship for the rest of my life.

I hung over the gunwale of the *Salish Wind* as our sister ship prepared to leave first. Jake was already at work on deck, minding coils of rope as a pilot boat set up to accompany them out of the inner harbor. The pilot boat would come back for us and we'd head out right behind them. Our two captains had gone ashore to gain clearance for our departures. Victoria had a lot of regulations for American vessels, Jake had said, because of all the money to be made in a gold-rush town.

As I finished my coffee, the captain of the *Sonoma Wind* came back alone. He spoke to Kuno, who seemed very annoyed by what he was told. Kuno immediately dispatched Paddy and Lu Chan to town, presumably to accompany our captain back.

I waved to Jake as the pilot boat pushed the *Sonoma Wind* away.

"See you in San Fran! Hope you get better weather," Jake taunted.

I made a face, but stuck a thumb in the air in reply.

There was still no sign of our captain when the *Sonoma Wind* raised her sails and started around the point of the harbor entrance. Drak and I loitered port side, where an impatient pilot boat driver waited to accompany us out of the harbor. Kuno paced the deck and finally joined us to look for signs of the Captain's return.

"What's going on?" I asked him.

"I don't know," he replied. "But I wish they'd hurry it up. We only have a small window to get out of here this morning."

Three figures approached the pier. It was the Captain. He'd come back with two new men.

"Where's our boys?" I asked.

"Don't know," Kuno mumbled. "Captain's brung replacements so he must have given them shore leave."

He handed me Mr. Jones, who stiffened like a corpse in my grip. I tucked him under my arm the way Kuno liked to do.

Two of the new sailors looked mighty familiar. We'd had a

lot of workers come and go in the past few days, unloading and loading our cargo. I'd probably seen them then. It made me uneasy to face new sailors. I had to smarten up my boy disguise all over again.

Kuno pulled Drak aside. I couldn't catch what he said to him, but Drak seemed to have no trouble understanding, in spite of his poor English. Kuno looked tense and Drak's expression was stormier than usual. Mr. Jones growled at the newcomers as they came aboard.

"Do we usually change crew like this?" I asked Kuno in a whisper. He frowned, hushed me up and didn't answer. Something nagged at me about his dismissal of the question.

The Captain gave orders to prepare for departure and Kuno took charge of the new crew. The new men seemed like capable sailors, seaworthy and earnest, but Kuno had lost his usual sunny outlook. I caught a concerned glance between Kuno and Drak. They were troubled. Something wasn't right about this sudden change.

Then I remembered where I'd seen those two sailors! It was in the backstreets of San Francisco, outside a tavern in Portsmouth. Dolly, the woman who'd given me directions when I was lost, had called them no-good louts!

My mind raced. What if the Captain had picked up a couple of pirates? That sounded ridiculous. This wasn't the last century and it wasn't the Caribbean neither. Pirates were nothing more than old history and storybook characters.

It seemed like a mighty big coincidence they'd come to work on the *Salish Wind* when we had a fortune of gold aboard. But nobody knew that. I put myself in the Captain's shoes and tried to figure out why he'd made a last-minute change.

Maybe someone on the old crew had found out about the gold. Or maybe Mr. Miller told the Captain to take extra precautions. For security reasons, he'd surprised the regular crew with shore leave for a few weeks. There were many logical explanations. I put my silly thoughts of pirates aside.

By the time we got underway, the *Sonoma Wind* had a two-hour head start on us and we were cutting it close for favorable conditions. I didn't pester Kuno with any more questions as he was studying the weather. I handed Mr. Jones back to him and he gave me a reassuring smack on the shoulder.

Fort Victoria looked small from a distance. Apart from almost running into the bad men, I didn't think it was such a scary place. I knew from experience that the beauty of a city from a distance disguised the dangers of its dark lanes, rowdy taverns, and shady tenements full of desperate men. San Francisco had schooled me in all of that. I wasn't afraid of city life. But I wasn't naive about it neither.

I paused at the steps leading down to the galley as the crew trimmed the sails, creating a billow of white cloud against the morning sky. I took off my cap, let the cool breeze blow through my hair for a moment, and then hurried below.

"You make coffee good," Drak said when I entered the galley.

For a second, I'd forgotten about the kitchen problem that Cook had left me with. "He's loyal," Cook had said about the broken sailor turned cook. He was at that. He'd been nothing but kind to me in his old billy goat kind of fashion. So there was that.

"You want me to make the coffee?" I asked.

He grunted approval, and tried to make it look like he was too busy and it wasn't really about the complaints he'd already had about his own watery batch. It was a step in the right direction.

When the coffee was ready and Drak had peeled half a pot of potatoes, I decided to tell him about the two men I'd recognized.

"Drak…"

"Da?"

"The new crew. I've seen them before."

He laid down his kitchen knife.

"Da?"

In the simplest words I could find, I explained how I'd run into them in San Francisco last summer and told him what Dolly had said about them being from Boston and no good louts and how I figured they might be pirates. Drak nodded as he listened, letting me know he understood what I was telling him. He stared at the boards of the ceiling as if someone might have an ear to the floor, eavesdropping on our conversation.

"No pirates here," he said when I was done. He picked up his kitchen knife and peeled a potato with so much conviction, I thought he'd lose what was left of a gnarly thumb.

"Yeah, the pirate thing is a joke." But he didn't laugh it off all the same. He was thinking.

"You say to Kuno?"

"No. I mean, he's got other things on his mind."

"Kuno and I never see. We crew five year, never see."

That wasn't good. Sailors in these parts recognized each other the way horses recognized neighboring herds.

"What about Paddy and Lu Chan? Did you and Kuno know about their leave?"

"No. Trouble ashore. Papers. No come so Captain bring."

So that was it. Our crew had been delayed with their papers and we couldn't wait for it to be sorted out. The Captain had hired a couple of quick replacements.

I was glad I'd talked to Drak before I'd made a fool of myself talking to Kuno or the Captain about pirates. They were just sailors looking for work and probably keen to do a run back to San Francisco. I wondered what kind of trouble our crew had with their papers. In any case, it could take days for some government office to set the matter straight. We had to go without them.

Drak didn't say another word for the rest of the morning except for "good coffee" when he tasted my brew and "more salt" when we made the supper stew.

Kuno and Mr. Jones came by for coffee once we were under full sail out in Fuca Strait. He seemed more like his old self now that we were underway. He and Drak didn't bring up anything about what had gone on back in the harbor.

I didn't mention the two men to Kuno. It was nothing more than a coincidence that I'd bumped into them before. It wasn't my business to question the ship's command.

I remembered my job. Get Drak to let me make the coffee. Check. Help Drak with his awful cooking so the crew wouldn't mutiny. I was already working on that and convinced him to reduce the onions and garlic in the dinner stew by half. And last but not least, my other secret job, to make sure Mr. Miller's gold made it to San Francisco.

23

i

A few hours later, in the early afternoon, the watch called, "Sails, ho!" and all hands scrambled to starboard to see what ship had appeared.

Kuno handed a spyglass to the Captain, who had joined him at the wheel.

"She's a sloop, Capan. No colors."

Cook had explained to me how ships flew their country's flag, and sometimes a second flag from a town or territory, to tell others who they were. The *Salish Wind* proudly flew the Stars and Stripes and the flag of the Bear Republic at the top of her two masts.

"Don't recognize her," the Captain said. "A merchant out of Port Angeles?"

"Should be overtaking us easy. Why's she hanging back?" Kuno asked.

They studied the situation further in silence. After a while, the Captain ordered the watch to look bright, which I'd learned meant to pay close attention. He instructed Kuno to stay the course and keep him informed. When he turned away, he caught me looking at him. He covered his troubled expression with a tight smile.

The afternoon wind picked up as we beat our way along Fuca Strait toward the Pacific. Thanks to our late start, everything was turning against us—the tide, the wind, the current, and even the weather. The morning sunshine had given way to overcast skies and gusty winds on our nose. It was hard, slow going with our ship fully loaded. And yet the smaller, more nimble ship continued to follow at the same distance.

I worried when the two coasts on either side of us faded into barely distinguishable lines behind thickening fog. In front of us, the open ocean disappeared in a descending, grey gloom.

Drak and I stood at the ship's stern and watched the follower tack after us yet again. It was clear even to me that the ship intended to stay with us all the way out to sea. Suddenly, the Captain ordered a change of course to the north.

"Capan, the rocks and shallows," Kuno protested.

"Plenty of room. I know these waters. Let them dare make a game of it," he snapped.

Kuno protested, but when the Captain wouldn't hear it, he obeyed his orders. The ship fell into irons, swung about and headed for the rugged northern side of Fuca Strait. Soon after, the wind shifted behind us and pushed us fast into the dangerous waters.

Every sailor was called on deck to man the ship. Kuno poured over a map and constantly checked our position. A thick band of grey lay ahead of us, thick fog that was a constant threat in the strait and we were headed right for it.

"He's taking us into it on purpose," I said to Drak.

"No good," he replied. Drak was superstitious. The day before, when I walked across the galley with only one shoe on, he'd said, "Bad luck, bad luck!"

The fog closed around us like curtains. Landmarks disappeared. The water churned and frothed and the wind came in uneven, changing gusts from the side and behind. After staring into the fog, looking for a horizon or landmark, I was lightheaded.

I lost all sense of direction. Then the worst thing happened. Kuno and the Captain disagreed on the ship's position. Nobody else said a word in the muffled air. Again, Kuno followed orders and commanded the crew to stay on a broad reach. We streaked through the damp cloak of low cloud.

An ear-splitting crash broke the silence. The impact was so hard, I flew headlong into the bulkhead and landed in a dazed heap. The sailors hollered and ran to stations. We'd struck something big! The ship seemed oddly lifted and tilted, unmoving in the water. Kuno pointed. The black sloop lurked in the fog some distance away.

Drak tugged at my sleeve, insisting I follow him to the galley.

"What are we doing?"

He started filling a small bag with clothing.

"Pack," he ordered and tossed a small canvas sack at me.

"For what?"

He shook his head as he rolled his rain slicker. "To leave."

I gasped. "Are we sinking?"

"Sloop come rescue? Nyet."

"You think they're pirates!"

Swashbuckling treasure hunters would have been exciting to me not very long ago. But this was no storybook. This was real and it was terrifying.

"Is no good."

"Maybe they just wanted sailing company, y'know, like us and the *Sonoma Wind*? Till we made the open sea?" My theory was logical, but I didn't believe it myself.

"Why follow here?" He shook his palms at me, alarmed. "Stay. I check. Pack!"

I still didn't know what to pack for, so I wiped my clammy palms on my trousers and put everything into my duffel. Drak wasn't gone long. When he returned, he was pale and breathless.

"They coming."

"To rescue us?"

He shook his head slowly and I clapped a hand over my mouth.

Drak crouched and popped a wooden panel off the wall beneath the galley counter, revealing a long, narrow cupboard.

"In," he whispered.

"You want me to get in there?"

"In! No come out. I come you," Drak said, stuffing my bag into the compartment. He poked me, and then shoved, urging me to get in.

"I'm not…" There was a loud crash above us, followed by yelling and the thundering steps of men running.

"In! You hide. I come get!"

"But Drak…"

"In!"

Loud bangs and muffled yells made us both freeze with dread. I immediately scrambled into the compartment.

"Stay." He gripped my leg so hard with his thick fingers, I thought they would leave a bruise.

"Don't forget me in here," I replied, trembling like a newborn colt.

"Da, da!"

The cupboard had been empty but for a roll of canvas used for sail patching. It was long enough to fit me with my legs bent, and wide enough for my bag to fit in tight around me. Since it was built into the wall underneath the counter, it wasn't visible to anyone who wasn't looking for it. I had been working that kitchen for two weeks and hadn't noticed it. Cook hadn't shown it to me. Why wouldn't they have stashed Mr. Miller's gold in here?

"You safe," said Drak. He smiled reassuringly, but his face twitched with worry. Once I had fit myself into the space, he jammed his emergency bag in with me. As an afterthought, he handed me a large kitchen knife. My eyes bulged with images of butchery about to happen.

"Shshsh. No sound."

"Da," I said, and he winked. Then he replaced the cupboard panel and I was plunged into darkness.

It took my eyes a couple of minutes to adjust to the blackness. Soon, a crack of light was visible between the wooden slats. Putting my eye up to it, I could see the floor by the counter to about knee height directly in front of me.

A rumbling crash pounded the deck right above my head. It sounded as if deck lumber had shifted or part of a mast had come down. I cringed, half expecting the deck to break and come down on my head. The ship lurched violently as if we'd hit rough seas or had hit a rogue wave broadside. I hit my head on the cupboard roof. Kitchen things banged and crashed to the floor.

The noises overhead grew loud and violent. A battle raged. Yelling, thumping, thundering feet and wretched howls filled my ears. Drak's feet shuffled back and forth in the kitchen a few times but I couldn't tell what he was doing.

Then, footsteps on the galley stairs near my head. Drak had company.

"Drop yer weapon, mate." A gruff order from an unknown man. A kitchen cleaver clunked to the wooden floor by Drak's feet. "Hands over yer head."

"You got gold down here and you're gonna show us where," said a second man in a raspy whisper.

Drak snapped back with an angry stream of Russian words.

"Ya don't understand English? That tells me yer Captain weren't lying," the first man said. "Where is it?"

Drak didn't answer. My pulse raced. If they tore the place apart searching, they'd find me hiding.

"Look in the stores, Hample," the first man said. "I'll take the cross this one's got around his neck."

Give him your cross, Drak. Please give it to him.

"Nyet!" Drak protested. There was a scuffle and then the rasp of a blade drawing from a sheath. Moments later, a body landed heavily on the floor beside me. I recognized the vest and shirt. I bit my sleeve to keep from screaming.

A pair of legs crouched beside Drak, who hadn't moved since hitting the floor. If this evil man looked to his right, he might spot the unusual panel and I'd be doomed. I couldn't see his face. I braced myself to be torn out of my hiding place.

"They got whiskey, smoked fish, salted meat and… a whole lotta gold," said the second man called Hample.

"You don't say." The first man stood up and kicked Drak's limp body.

A series of thumps behind my head meant another person had come down the stairs to the galley.

"We're done, Skulder. Her keel's failing. She don't have long."

"Get another man. Hample needs a hand with those barrels. On the double," he said.

"Aye."

The *Salish Wind* was going to sink! I could already feel it listing. My body pressed against the side of the cupboard with the opening. I braced my knees around the frame so that my weight wouldn't pop the panel off.

Thumping of feet meant other men had come to help. They were laughing, talking about a fellow who had gold in a bag around his neck, and how they might have missed it if one of their mates hadn't skewered him in the chest with a blade.

"Struck gold!" one said.

"That's mining on the forty-nine for ya," said another and they all laughed.

Water dripped on my head from somewhere. If they don't kill me, I'll drown in here, I thought, willing myself not to panic and burst from the cupboard.

"Let's move it, men."

Their voices faded as they left. "She'll be under by nightfall," I heard one say before the galley was silent.

24

i

Minutes ticked by as I listened to the muffled voices and thumps of the invaders overhead. Heavy feet stomped in every direction. I imagined the ship being looted from stem to stern, and goods of the greatest value dragged, stacked, and loaded into a waiting boat. They meant to take whatever they could use from the sinking *Salish Wind*.

I didn't move an inch in the cupboard. I had to stay hidden until I was absolutely certain they would not come below deck again. It was sheer luck for me that the ship's hull gave way just when they'd come to raid the galley. They didn't have time to search all the nooks and crannies. It wasn't worth the risk of staying below deck and maybe getting trapped themselves. They raided the pantry and got what they'd come for, along with a good amount of whiskey to celebrate their fine haul.

My legs stiffened from being folded and jammed against the cupboard frame. I was afraid to change position and risk knocking the panel off. I hoped rising water wouldn't drive me out of hiding before the men abandoned ship. They'd left the galley lantern behind so I still had light. Drak lay where he'd fallen, but a large pool of blood had spread out and covered the surrounding floor. They murdered him and didn't give it another thought.

There was nothing I could do to help him. Drak told me to stay in the cupboard until he came to get me. That wasn't going to happen. I was going to have to figure out when to get out on my own, without knowing what had gone on above.

After what seemed like an eternity, the sounds on deck changed. The scuffling, dragging, and thumping stopped. I hadn't heard a voice for a very long time. The only sounds remaining were creaks and painful groans, the rubbing of the hull as it crushed and tore upon the rocks, and water running somewhere on the other side of the wall behind my head. I stretched and all parts of my legs and arms butted up against the hard wood of the compartment.

There was a bulkhead mid-ship. I could hear water behind it by my head. That meant water had breached the main hold and was flooding the lower compartments. The galley was below deck. I had to get out before the bulkhead gave way. Drak had saved me from murder or capture. It was up to me to save myself from drowning.

I pushed a knee against the panel. It was jammed tight and needed more force. I wriggled my hands around and drew a foot up against it. With no way to kick, I pressed my back against the other side and pushed out as hard as I could. It still wouldn't budge. I couldn't let myself panic. No way I was going to survive gamblers and thieves and wicked men on the streets of San Francisco and then drown in a ship's cupboard at sea. If I was going to drown, it would be in the open water. Not in this tiny wooden coffin.

I took a deep breath and pushed with everything I had. The panel groaned, popped out, and skidded across the floor. I stuck my legs out and winced as they cramped and complained. I could barely wiggle out of the tight space. My body felt like it'd been poured into a mold and set like jelly. Every part of me hurt when I moved. Out of the cupboard, I leaned against the counter and rubbed my aching shoulders and knees. Nothing stirred any-where—not near the galley, not overhead on deck. Where was our crew? Had they abandoned ship, too, and left me behind?

Water trickled over the ledge by the galley door and ran across the floor. It made the room smell like salty metal and covered the floor with a smeary layer of blood and seawater. Drak was dead. I knew it when I saw him go down. But I owed it to him to be sure. I crawled over and peered over his side. I wasn't ready for the sight of his injury. His throat had been slashed so badly his head was barely attached to his body.

I scrambled back and away from him, holding my hand over my mouth. The bitter taste of vomit burned the back of my throat. I swallowed hard several times and tried to erase the hor-rific image in my mind. My head ached, but I had no time to sit there and feel sorry for myself or for Drak.

Drak said we'd row to the nearby island. He must have seen one. That was his plan when he told me to pack. I banged my forehead to make myself think. The rowboat was too big for me to handle alone, but there was a smaller skiff, almost right above the galley. It was only used for little trips into shallow coves and bays. I had to get to that skiff.

I snatched Drak's bag out of the cupboard. I wished I'd paid attention to what he'd packed. Now I had to trust he'd been thor-ough because I had no time for inventory. I pulled out my own bag. I flung out whatever I could—old ranch clothing and hat, a lot of Papa's stuff I'd never used—to make room for Drak's bag. I stuffed the rest of the empty space with any supplies I could lay my hands on. At the last second, I grabbed Cook's galley book, the one where he kept his foraging notes and recipes.

The trickle of water had turned into a gushing stream. It was all around me. It dripped through the boards over my head on the low side of the galley. It dripped onto the lantern by the door and made it sputter. If it plunged me into darkness, I might not find my way out. With the heavy canvas bag slung over my back, I stepped over Drak's body and made my way across the slippery floor.

Water was almost a foot deep outside the galley and almost waist deep to the starboard side. One of the new seamen the Captain had hired floated face down at the bottom of the stairs. I waded past him, water already up to my knees in that short distance.

The hatch was open above me. I set my sights on the patch of grey sky that filled the opening, the low light of an overcast afternoon. It was a steep climb up the cockeyed stairs to the deck. The bag was heavy on my back and my knees buckled under the weight of it. I got a good grip on the rail, mustered all the strength I could find and fought my way up, stair by stair, to the outside deck. It terrified me that someone might be lurking up top and a blade would come out of nowhere and take off my head, but I had no other choice.

I was halfway through the hatch when the ship lurched wildly. It knocked me sideways against the opening and I clutched a main sheet coiled nearby. It was attached to nothing and unraveled through the air with me. Before I could fall, the boat lurched again and flopped me back. I hung on to the edge of the hatch. The water below me gushed like a waterfall. A main bulkhead had given way.

I scanned the entire deck. It was a mess of ropes and sheets and sails. Bloody footprints and skid marks went in every direction upon the ordinarily pristine deck. Two sailors I didn't recognize had been dumped, or maybe had slid, into a heap near the starboard gunwale. I couldn't tell who they were, but both had gruesome injuries. Sliced by thick blades or heavy swords. That's what had killed Drak. Not a shot was fired. This raid had been sneaky and deadly.

Nobody had been left alive on the ship. The riggings banged

and the abandoned sails flapped unwittingly in the light breeze. The wind had blown off most of the fog when I was below, but it hung around in a few distant patches. The sun burned through a hazy cloud cover. The *Salish Wind* had smashed at full speed onto a submerged reef, the kind of reef these waters were known for, and had taken other ships to the bottom of the sea before her.

The ship's deck angled to starboard. Off to that side, a long band of rocks hidden beneath the water extended to a cove in the middle of a small island. Carefully climbing the deck to port side, I peeked over the gunwales to the east. More of the rocks that had caught the sailboat and were tearing her apart from below. Then nothing but water as far as the eye could see. I had to get to the island on the other side.

I tied my bag to the base of the mast so it wouldn't slide away or tumble into the water. The rowboat kept at the stern was gone. They must have taken it. I scrambled fore to where the smaller skiff was kept, tied down near the starboard bow. It was gone from its place, but its lines trailed over the gunwale. Already in the water, I told myself. I leaned over the bow. It had been crushed into matchsticks between the hull and the reef.

I had no way off the sinking ship.

25

i

I slumped against the main mast and clung to my bag. My aching stomach heaved. Fear bubbled up in choking sobs.

"You're done and so am I," I said to the helpless schooner. Every breaking board, creak and groan of the ship terrified me. I smothered my own unstoppable cries in the sleeves of my shirt.

I'd seen four bodies on the boat: Drak, one of the new sailors, and two other unknown men. Where were the others? Taken captive or drowned below? If anyone was alive or still on board, they'd be where I was or would have called out.

That small skiff was my only hope. Finding it smashed and useless felt like a death sentence. I rocked myself back and forth, wracked by sobs that took my breath away and shook my entire body.

Images of the dead flooded my mind, their twisted and mutilated bodies lying where they had been murdered. And for what? For gold. For stupid riches. I'd heard those men. They'd known about Mr. Miller's shipment. Who had told them? They'd stalked the *Salish Wind* and killed innocent people for money. Black-red blood streaked the deck beneath my feet. A familiar smell rose from the wood. It was the unforgettable odor of a slaughter-house. I wiped my blurry eyes on a wet sleeve.

The ship let out a terrible groan. It would not stay afloat for long. The starboard deck loomed closer to the waterline, the weight of the masts tipping perilously over the water. The ship would go under on that vulnerable side, unless it broke up sooner in the middle from the damage to the hull.

I could surrender to the pirates. But they'd gone. And would they really rescue me? I'd witnessed their crimes! I imagined my surrender and shuddered. They might kill me straight away, but if they found out I was a girl, it would be worse than death. I'd be captured and probably tortured. My sobs stopped. Anger burst wide open in my chest. If they were nearby, I'd drown before I'd let them get me.

I looked over the surrounding scene, taking in the devastation. Just this morning, I'd stood on this pristine deck. I'd spotted a magnificent pod of killer whales approaching in the black waters of the Salish Sea. I had stood with Kuno and Mr. Jones and we were in awe of the breaching whales, so close to our boat. It was a very rare sight, Kuno said. Whalers had hunted these beautiful creatures to near extinction.

Now all the crew were dead or missing, killed for valuable cargo that most of them didn't even know we'd been carrying. The regular crew, stuck in port over paperwork, had no idea how lucky they were. And Cook. Thankfully, he was safe on Admiral Island. But poor Drak, who'd been so proud to be chosen to fill in for Cook, he was anything but lucky.

Just then, I thought I heard a voice.

"Is someone here?" I didn't recognize the sound of my own voice. It was strained, rasping, ripped with fear.

Nobody answered, nothing moved. The boards of the ship creaked a mournful reply.

I scanned the water off the low starboard side. Bits of debris drifted in the frothing water. Not too far away, the small, rocky island peeked out of the surrounding fog. Although the island was close, I knew it was much farther away than it seemed. Even Jake, who was an excellent swimmer, wouldn't make it.

"Can't swim out of this one."

Saying the words out loud helped me calm my nerves and come to terms with my fate. Unlike the rivers and ponds back home, this water was too cold even in summer.

"Wouldn't last fifteen minutes," I said, repeating what Cook had said to me days earlier.

I pictured Jake sailing home on the sister ship, books spread out on a table below deck, studying some government papers. I had wanted him to return on the *Salish Wind* with me.

"If Jake was here, we'd figure out what to do."

Jake couldn't even imagine this disaster. As far as he knew, the *Salish Wind* was sailing a few hours behind the *Sonoma Wind*. As far as he knew, we'd be meeting up in San Francisco in a week to ten days.

You know what to do. I twisted around, startled. The voice came from somewhere aft, somewhere near the helm.

"Who's there?" I fumbled for my pocketknife.

My eyes groped the shadows. Nothing but lapping water and rustling sails. They were strange words, the same words I'd heard my papa speak before he died, when I had to get Thunder, the wild stallion, under control. I'd heard Papa's voice inside my head. He'd said, *You know what to do.*

"I heard you... Papa, are you there?"

Then I spotted two booted feet sticking out from behind the stacked lumber. I shifted to my hands and knees. Somebody was still alive! The man's voice had come from there, I was certain of it.

"What do you mean, I know what to do?" I said. The voice wouldn't answer now that it had my attention. "I don't know what to do. I'm going down on this ship with all the rest."

No answer.

A round piece of rigging tumbled past my fingertips.

"If I'm not killed first by something falling."

I crawled along the sloped deck toward the booted feet. I recognized the legs as they came into view. It was Kuno. And there beside him, tucked right by his side, guarding his body with fierce loyalty was Mr. Jones.

"Oh no! Kuno! Get up!" Mr. Jones stared at me, unmoving.

I reached out for him, but when my hand got close, he bared his teeth. He wasn't going to let anyone near his beloved friend.

I slowly raised my hands.

"It's Charlee, Mr. Jones. "You know me. I'm not going to hurt you."

A huge maroon stain had spread out from Kuno's right side. It had made a river across the deck, but had long since dried in the warmth of the sun. I edged over to him, not wanting to alarm Mr. Jones. He had to be alive. I'd heard a voice.

But he wasn't alive. His eyes were wide open. He stared straight up at the mizzenmast as if something horrible had been caught in his sight. His mouth hung open in a silent shout.

I stuck my fists in my eyes. Even though I'd known him for little more than a couple of weeks, we'd become friends. Kuno and his dog. The huge shepherd of a man, and the little wool dog he'd rescued, always tucked under his arm like a little lamb.

Mr. Jones was very much alive. Somehow, he'd escaped the attack.

"Kuno is dead, Mr. Jones. He's gone."

He stared at me with defiance, yet his posture was oddly rigid and uncertain. He knew it. I was telling him the obvious. He didn't want to accept it.

"I'm so sorry, Bubba. I know how you feel." And I did. I had an ache in my chest that took me back to the Miller ranch, to Papa's bedside. Like Mr. Jones, I'd curled up beside Papa willing him to come back to me, even when I knew he was gone.

The horror of it all filled me with rage. Kuno was a hardworking man, a good man, an innocent person. They'd killed him because he was in the way. A whole good life wasted with the plunge of a sword.

My stomach churned and I looked away. It was too much, the violence and death.

I remembered the voice. It wasn't Kuno who'd spoken.

"Is someone else here, Mr. Jones? I heard someone speak over here."

He shifted his weight from one paw to the other, but continued to stare at me, unblinking.

The ship lurched, causing me to slide down into the lower gunwale. Mr. Jones braced himself against Kuno's side. This sudden movement of the ship caused a log from the mid-deck pile beside us to shift. Ropes securing the timber had been severed. The whole stack was unstable.

Suddenly, a log from the timber pile dislodged and tumbled from the stack. It flew past my head, just missed Mr. Jones and crashed into the gunwale below us.

I gaped after it, paralyzed. Then I heard the voice again.

You know what to do, it said.

I turned in the direction of the sound. It came from Mr. Jones.

"You? You're the one talking?" There was no other explanation. No other living thing was anywhere near us. I shook my head and rubbed my ears.

"This is just what I need—to go mad as a hatter. If I survive this, I'll end up in an infirmary for people who have gone off their rockers. No, I won't be that lucky because I'm going to drown when this ship sinks. So why not die with a talking dog! Well, I'll tell you something. I don't know what to do, Mr. Smart Talking Bubba Jones."

I was distraught all over again but I refused to cry any more.

I surveyed the distance to the island and closed my eyes.

What did I know how to do? Swim for it? Too far in this cold water. I wouldn't be able to take anything with me to use on the island. I had to try. It was the only way out. Waiting for the sea to swallow me up with the boat was too horrible to imagine.

Build a raft.

This time the voice came from inside of me, from the heart of old memories. I closed my eyes again and felt peace come over me. The smiling face of Jake was in my mind.

26

i

I scrambled up the sloping deck to the pile of timber stacked mid-ship. Most of the wood was cut planks, long pieces of huge, fragrant cedar. All the pieces were too long and heavy to use. But in between the two stacks of planks were dozens of fence posts. It was one of these posts that had rolled free minutes ago and nearly struck me in the head.

It would be dangerous pulling them off the pile. Another tip of the boat could send the whole load tumbling down to the starboard side. The log stack reminded me of Jackstraws, a game I used to play with Jake when we were kids back on the ranch. The object was to remove one stick while causing none of the others to move. If you could do it, you scored a point. I was good at the game because I had real steady hands. Now I was about to play a giant game with pieces that could kill me. If I made a mistake, I'd lose a lot more than my turn.

I lifted one of the log posts from a side of the stack. It wasn't too heavy, maybe five inches thick and a foot taller than me. I needed a dozen of these to make a raft wide enough to hold me, with a couple of cross poles for a platform. I had plenty of wood and rope, that wasn't the problem. The problem was I didn't have enough time to build it and the lumber could dislodge and tumble, burying me where I worked.

I drew a log from the pile, dragged it down along the deck and laid one end on the starboard gunwale. Mr. Jones kept an eye on me from his post in the shadows beside Kuno.

"Too bad you don't have hands, Mr. Jones," I puffed, lugging a second log into position beside the first. "I might have a chance of getting this built if you could help."

I looked up at the tilted riggings. The wind had died right off. The sun burned behind the cloud cover leaving a hot stillness behind. I scrambled over to my duffle bag and dug out my canteen of water. I drank almost half of it before realizing I didn't know when I'd be able to fill it up again. I threw off my jacket and got back to work.

"You could at least cheer me on," I said to Mr. Jones, after I'd dragged six logs into place.

I carefully picked another log from the precarious pile.

Seven points. Nothing had slipped.

As I worked, I remembered all the rafts Jake and I had built during our summers growing up. The first one sunk on its maiden voyage. Our ties had slipped and loosened and it fell apart. The second one we built held together but sat about six inches below the waterline once we both got on it. Jake carried on for days about our weight and water displacement and such. He wrote out a lot of formulas and drew a lot of diagrams, but I knew instinctively we needed a bigger raft. The best design was the simple one based on science. There was no time for measurement and precision.

I had nine logs lined up beside each other on the gunwale. It had taken me almost half an hour to get them and gather rope to bind them together. As I pulled down a halyard from overhead sails, I noticed a bit of wind ripple in the loose sails. The wounded ship had been resting in the stillness of the afternoon. My heart fluttered with every quiver of the sails. When the ship woke up, it would be for the last time.

I sawed at lengths of rope with my papa's bone-handled pocketknife, the sturdy knife he'd given me on my fourteenth birthday. Although sharp, it was no match for the job. Within minutes, it exhausted me, my hands ached and I'd cut only one piece.

"Mr. Jones! I need a bigger knife!"

I dropped Papa's pocketknife back in my pants and scanned the deck for something bigger, like maybe a machete or sword dropped in battle. I spotted an axe wedged in the timber pile. It was big and heavy, but it had a mean blade on it. As I dragged it back to the ropes I'd collected, I noticed Mr. Jones, still in the same place, panting heavily in the heat.

"You need water!" Making a cup with my left palm, I poured a little water from my canteen into it and offered it to him. He got up slowly, took a few steps toward me and drank. I filled it three times before he backed up and resumed his post.

"You are a good, loyal dog," I said to him. Tears welled up in my eyes at the sight of him standing watch in the shadows. The ship lurched and let out another loud crack. I steadied myself and got back to work.

The axe cut rope and wood with a couple of well-placed chops. Soon, I was hitching the ropes around notches in the wood and tightening them snuggly into place. I kept my ears on the wind in the fluttering sails. It was definitely picking up, but not like it had blasted in on us earlier in the day. I hoped for nothing more than a light, evening breeze. Wind in unattended sails was bad. It made everything unpredictable.

The ship had been eerily quiet during the calm, but wind and waves with a breached hull would soon change that. The ship would continue to list, and eventually the cargo on deck would rip loose. A good chunk of the starboard gunwale would break off and the ship would go down on her side. My raft could be smashed to smithereens before I ever got on it.

By the time the evening breeze created ripples on the water, I'd hacked off a cabin door and made a platform on top of the cross poles. I used chunks of canvas from sails to wrap and stow my duffel bag, and attached a tether so the raft wouldn't be swept away if water gushed over the gunwale.

I had beaten the clock, thanks to the wind taking a long afternoon nap. Waiting was almost worse. The raft, one end on the gunwale and the rest on the submerging deck, was still a foot above the waterline and far too heavy for me to shove into the water. I'd placed it so it would launch itself as the deck sunk below the waterline.

A gust of wind caught a sail and heeled the boat. The log pile grumbled but didn't give way. The starboard gunwale was barely above water. Any minute now. I sat with my heart pounding out the seconds and my stomach in knots, waiting for the right moment to abandon ship. I had to be fast when the time came. I could get trapped by debris or sucked under with the boat.

Mr. Jones stood up, sensing something about to happen. If he remained where he was, the log pile would surely kill him as it rolled down the deck and into the water. I crawled to him, directly into avalanche territory. The ship yawned loudly, a sleeping monster about to wake up.

"You have to leave him now. You have to come with me, Bubba." He backed deeper into the shadows by Kuno's head as I crawled closer. An unexpected hand touching him might cause him to retreat even more. Or he might stand his ground and bite me, even though I was trying to help. Then I had an idea. Kuno had a yellow bandana tucked in his shirt pocket. I reached for it. Mr. Jones didn't stop me. The ship shuddered.

"C'mon, Mr. Jones. Come with me now." I held out my hand with the bandana.

A large sail filled and flapped wildly. The boat lurched again.

"We have to go! C'mon Bubba," I pleaded. I couldn't stay

there a minute longer.

I started back to the raft, the slope of the ship deck already more perilous. Halfway back, I felt a nudge on my leg. He'd followed me.

Relieved, I tied Kuno's bandana around his wooly neck and said, "Good boy, Bubba." He followed me to the raft. "It's just you and me now."

We waited for what felt like an eternity. My eyes were constantly on the move, from the timber pile to the sails to the rising waterline. The wind finally picked up and started whipping the loose sails around. I was ready with Mr. Jones at my side when a big gust filled the mainsail and sent the ship tipping severely to starboard. The logs gave way and thundered down the deck, crashing over the body of Kuno and breaking through the gunwale a few feet away from us. Water gushed wildly over the broken side.

"Let's go!" I scrambled on the raft as water boiled around my legs. Mr. Jones didn't move! I started chopping at the rope tether.

"Mr. Jones, get on!" The water was rising fast. I lifted the axe, ready for a final strike.

The gunwale broke and the raft tore loose. I grabbed for Mr. Jones, knocking the axe into the sea, but he was out of my reach. He sat frozen, water coming up around his shoulders as the raft slipped away from the ship.

"Bubba!" I cried. Icy water gushed over me. I gasped as a wave soaked my clothes. The raft was afloat but Mr. Jones had vanished.

"No!" My heart felt so much pain I thought it would explode.

The water churned with wood, sails, and lines. I could get tangled up and pulled down. Survival snapped me back to my senses. The tide was in my favor. The raft floated away from the ship on its own. Wood whined, snapped and exploded. The boat tipped and swayed, a terrifying sight still close enough to roll over on me. I took up an oar I'd salvaged and paddled.

Something between the boat and the raft bobbed on the surface and caught my eye. It was a bit of white and yellow.

"Mr. Jones!" His head turned and he swam for the raft. As soon as he came alongside, I caught the bandana and hauled him up beside me. He shook the icy water off and pressed up against me, both of us dripping and shivering and terrified.

I back-paddled until we were safe from a crashing mast and debris. We were silent as the ship cried out in pain and went under. As the hull disappeared, a terrible vision came into view. Anchored some distance away was the pirate sloop.

27

i

I flatten myself onto the raft deck, petrified. I drew the canvas cover over Mr. Jones and me, hoping it was enough to disguise us. Mr. Jones made himself small beside me as if he knew.

Had the pirates seen the ship sinking? Of course they had! They'd come back to watch their secrets disappear into the sea. Had they seen the raft? I didn't dare move a limb even though I trembled uncontrollably from fear and the chill of clinging, wet clothing against my skin. Mr. Jones shivered beside me, his sopping fur soaking the only dry part of my shirt.

"It's all right, Mr. Jones." I put my hand on his shoulders. The shock of cold water and the fright of the boat sinking out from under him had broken his usual streak of independence.

There was no sign of a boat launching from the black sloop. They hadn't spotted us. At least not yet. They weren't looking for a raft.

"It's all right, Bubba. We're safe for now," I said, attempting to comfort both of us. There were still far too many unknowns. The island. The sea. The wind and current. But saying "it's all right" made me feel a whole lot better, and more convinced we could make it.

We were afloat. The raft was doing its job, but it was far

from seaworthy. The occasional wave lapped over the edges of the raised platform. Cold water trickled underneath us, making for a soggy bed to lie on. At least we were not submerged in the chilly water.

The piece of canvas sail covering us kept the breeze off but didn't allow air in at all. It quickly became stifling underneath it. I adjusted the cover so we could breathe. Fresh salty air replaced the muggy, sweet smell of mildew.

"We have to look like a chunk of the boat. If the watch sees anything move, they'll come after us."

I hoped the tide that pulled us away from the shipwreck would also carry us to the island. Through my vent in the sail, I could only see the small patch of water directly behind us, full of wood and debris from the *Salish Wind*. The pirate ship appeared to be getting smaller. There was no sign of a rowboat coming after us.

I needed to see where we were going but it was too risky to sit up and look. I couldn't paddle to correct our course if we were drifting. I had to trust the raft until the daylight was gone. With nothing to do but wait, I put my head down to rest. Mr. Jones shuddered and sighed, and did the same. The waves lapped the edge of the raft in a soothing rhythm. I closed my eyes, rocked in our dangerous cradle.

Sometime later, I awoke with a start. Laughter and song drifted across the water. It was pitch black under the canvas. I peeked out into the last light of dusk. Far out in the bay, lanterns on the pirate ship glowed yellow against the still, black water. Mr. Jones stirred, I pushed the sail cover aside, and we both sat up.

The tide had carried us close to the island, but a current was taking the raft sideways. If we stayed on this course, we'd be caught on the rocky southern reef, or even worse, past the island's tip and headed for the open sea. I snatched up the oar and paddled fast and hard. The pirates in the sloop wouldn't see us against the black outline of the island.

The raft was difficult to steer. The current was so strong, I felt we were standing still. Within minutes, I was out of breath and losing strength.

"Stop flailing, Charlee," I heard Jake say to me. I was back on the Miller pond and he was teaching me to paddle correctly. "You won't get anywhere like that."

I remembered Jake laughed as I dipped the very end of my paddle in the water.

"Lily-dipper!" he'd taunted me. "That's how girls paddle." He laughed and I was furious.

"They do not!" I shot back. "Girls need a chance to learn." I smacked my paddle on the water, sending a rooster tail of water in his direction.

"Fair point," he'd said. "If you don't want to be a lily-dipper, then slow that paddle. Move your right hand down for a better grip. Dig it all into the water. Like this."

He took the role of teacher seriously, explaining in great detail how to produce an efficient stroke. I admired the way he could make something complicated seem easy. He could explain almost anything. I had noticed the muscles of his arms flex as he gracefully pulled the paddle through the water and the boat leaped ahead.

"Reach, dig, swing," he said, coaching my new style.

"I'm not as strong as you."

"Doesn't matter. It's about proper form."

Sideways drift snapped me out of my recollection.

"Form, Mr. Jones. I need form." I corrected my position by the edge of the raft. "Reach, dig, and swing," I said, pulling on each stroke with every bit of strength I could find. I had to get the raft turned around and headed back to the island.

A loud chorus of song rang out across the rippling water. The partying pirates were celebrating their stolen fortune. Their cruel indifference for the lost ship and her innocent souls fueled me like oil on a kitchen fire.

"Murderers, thieves," I said, in answer to their happy refrain. Fury burned inside and I dug the oar hard into the waves.

"Dirty pirates," I said.

Pledges punctuated each hard draw on the paddle.

"You."

"Will."

"Pay."

"One day." The raft swung around.

"I swear." It lurched against the current.

"You'll pay!" It inched closer to the dark cove on the island.

I paddled until my hands ached and my arms felt like they would drop out of their sockets. I fought with all I had against a powerful current. I couldn't let up for a moment or I'd lose momentum and distance gained.

Four pirate songs later, the raft started moving with ease. I'd broken free of the current. Once I'd passed inside a rocky outcrop near the southern end of the island, I let the raft glide. My arms and shoulders burned with fatigue. I dangled my torn hands into the cold water, wincing as the salt stung every broken blister.

"If this tide turns, we'll be taken back out to sea." I did some quick math on what I knew about the tides of the day. "Shouldn't turn for a few more hours, if I learned anything at all from Kuno and Cook."

Mr. Jones, now oddly fluffy from his earlier dunking, stuck his nose in the air and sniffed with acknowledgement.

"I know. I can't stop paddling."

I changed my grip to spare my wounds and set back to work. I had little strength left, but I didn't need it anymore. I made good headway in the island's direction with little effort.

Behind the black outline of the island, the setting sun had streaked the sky with blue and gold. I focused on the shadows and kept going. Sometime later, stars appeared above me, causing the water rolling past my paddle to twinkle.

I pulled the paddle in and fell back on the wet logs to rest. The raft had held together. Jake would have been very impressed that I'd built one so fast and all alone, but I had the advantage of everything I needed right at hand. I wondered what he was doing at that moment. I pictured him looking off the stern of the *Sonoma Wind*, hoping to catch a glimpse of the sister ship sailing along behind.

I'd met Jake when I was eight and he was ten, when Papa went to work for Mr. Miller. We hit it off right from the start and became inseparable. At least until Mr. Miller married The Missus and she came to the ranch with Bernadette. After that, we had to sneak around. He taught me all he'd learned at school, and once I caught up to him, I helped him with math because I had a knack for it. We swam, rode horses, fished, and built things.

But Jake had stopped going on adventures with me not long before Papa died. The happy, outgoing boy had vanished and in his place was a brooding, serious boy whose voice had cracked. I told Papa I thought Jake was avoiding me—he was always too busy studying to go on an adventure—and Papa had just smiled and said, "He is a young man now. And you are a young woman, even though you don't dress like one. He can't play with you anymore."

"That's ridiculous," I'd said. "We are best friends."

"It's complicated. You aren't like other girls, but you're still a girl."

"That's not it. I don't think he likes me anymore."

"I think he probably likes you too much and he is very confused because he's still the same boy you've known. He's becoming a man. Just give it time."

"I hate being a girl. It ruins everything."

"You think that now, Charlee. Wait and see."

The raft entered the protected waters of a cove. I hauled on the paddle a few more times to get us closer to shore. Overhead, stars sparkled in an indigo sky. I thought about Papa and how he'd taught me about the constellations.

"That's the big bear, right there," I said to Mr. Jones, who had taken up the job of night watch. He didn't look up to where I pointed. He kept his eye on the distant ship out in deep water.

My arms screamed for rest and my palms burned. I let the raft drift with the incoming tide.

"Papa, if you're listening. Give us a shove, will you?"

I collapsed onto the raft and fell into an exhausted, tormented sleep. I dreamed I was back in my hiding place in the ship's galley. The water was seeping in all around me. Suddenly, the cupboard opened and an ugly pirate threw a headless corpse in on top of me. I awoke with a scream, with my heart pounding, gasping for air.

The raft was bumping hard against something in the dark.

28

i

I wiped crusty salt and sweat from my eyes and strained to see in the darkness. The island loomed large in front of me, all black shadows and towering silhouettes of trees. The raft crunched as a breaking wave ground it into the shoreline. Then, as if satisfied they had my attention, the waves lapped the beach around me in a gentle rhythm.

"We made it, Mr. Jones," I said, feeling for his furry body in the dark mounds on the raft. He was gone!

"Mr. Jones!" I dangled a bare foot over the edge of the raft to feel for ground. My toes touched rock and sand. The water was only shin-deep, but icy cold. The shock sent a cramping chill up my leg. I dipped my other foot into the water, found the bottom and stood on wobbly legs.

"Mr. Jones!" That old familiar rat started gnawing in my belly as my eyes groped around in the dark outline of the island.

He couldn't have fallen overboard. He wouldn't have jumped off. He must already be on shore. How long had the raft been bumping the beach? I looked to the sky for the constellation of the hunter, Orion. He had moved a quarter turn. It was well past midnight. I fished what was left of the tether rope out of the icy water and used all my might to haul the raft higher up the beach.

Something rustled and cracked in the bush in front of me. My heart jumped into my throat. Mr. Jones bounded out of the underbrush and ran to greet me.

"You scared me!" I reached out to ruffle the fur on his head but he side-stepped my touch. "Miserable old boy. Well, I'm mighty happy to see you anyway."

I scanned the shoreline. The bay was the shape of a half moon, but jagged like the teeth of a timber saw. Rocky points jutted out on both ends. I'd landed near the north end of the cove, where the rocks of a long, submerged reef had sunk the *Salish Wind*. At the other end, where the current had almost taken us, huge rocks stood in the water like giant soldiers in black uniforms guarding passage beyond. In the cove itself, little rock monsters, half submerged, showed their ugly heads. I eyed them for several minutes to be sure none of them moved.

A new fear took hold of me as I peered into the darkness of the night forest away from the beach. Cook had said nobody lived on these rocky islands in Fuca Strait. That's what I thought he'd said anyway. Even animals, he'd said. Still, I didn't want to go into that bush. Definitely not in the dark, maybe not even in the light. And what if Cook was wrong and big animals did live here? Mr. Jones bounded back and forth along the shore in front of the raft. He wasn't nervous and that was a very good sign.

"I'm glad to be on land, too. Did you scout it out for us?" I said to him, as I untied my bag from the raft. The wet, loaded bag took a lot of grunting to lift. I dropped it on dry ground as Mr. Jones scrambled up a sloped path that led to a stand of tall trees. Ancient trees, like scarecrows, arms stretched out stiffly, pointing at everything and nothing.

Mr. Jones waited for me at the top.

"I get it. I remind you who did all the paddling. Just a minute then."

I donned my rubber deck boots and scanned the blackness of

the bay. Although no lights from the pirate ship were visible, I knew it was out there, hidden under the cloak of night. I couldn't see them, but they also couldn't see me. For now.

I took a few careful steps. Away from the water's edge, the sloped beach of round stones shifted beneath my feet. I lost my footing and fell on my knees. No sharp rocks here, I noted, pushing myself back to my feet, my hands clutching loose but smooth pebbles. A few more steps and I had the feel of it, like walking on a slipping sand dune. Loose bits of wood were strewn everywhere, trimming the high tide line. Lots to burn, even though I couldn't build a fire with the pirates watching.

Mr. Jones had stopped by a grove of old evergreens. Their tops towered into the starry blackness; their sweeping branches created a canopy that blocked most of the night sky from view. At eye level, I could only make out the shapes of the first trees, most of them at least two times my size around. From this spot, I was out of the ocean breeze and had a complete view of the bay. I fought the temptation to sit down.

"We've got work to do, Bubba." He started back down the slope and I smiled. Funny little dog always seemed to know what I was talking about.

With the tide high helping me, I timed the bigger waves and gave the raft a few more drags up the pebbled beach. I used an extra bit of rope to tie it up to a nearby rock. Satisfied, I shouldered the duffle bag and hauled it up to the trees.

Starlight, like a million tiny candles in the night sky, gave me just enough light to navigate the edge of the grove. The drooping boughs of the fragrant trees swept low around my head and almost touched the ground. Their scent was familiar, earthy, and inviting.

A fallen branch had caught between two trees. I draped canvas over it, making a crude tent that would shield me from the chilly night dew and ocean dampness. It was a perfect spot to shelter for the night.

I pulled off my deck boots and rubbed my cold feet. My clothes stuck and pulled against my skin—wet in patches, but mostly damp and sticky. Seawater had seeped into my bag, but damp wool was better than nothing. I peeled off my wet pants and shirt, wrapped myself in my wool blanket and crawled under the canvas.

"Mr. Jones. Come."

He didn't obey. He glanced over, then turned his head back to the water. His furry warmth would have been a great comfort, but he had chosen to continue the duty of night watch.

"Good ol' sea dog. Wake me up for middle watch then." I wasn't sure exactly when that was. Sometime during the night, I knew that much.

I leaned back under the canvas tent, cushioning my back with my duffle bag propped against the tree. Two survivors of the *Salish Wind*—a cabin boy who wasn't a boy at all, and a cranky old dog who thought he was a sailor. Tears streamed down my cheeks again as I thought of him sitting by Kuno, our lost friend.

Mr. Jones lay down, not making a sound, instinctively on the lookout for predators. He was not concerned with the forest behind him. He sensed no threat there and that gave me great comfort. As I let my tired body relax, he rested his head on his paws and stared into the darkness of the bay.

A chirping songbird woke me well before dawn. The sun hadn't yet come up, but dim light was seeping into the bay. Confused for a moment, like waking from a strange, deep dream, I shook the cobwebs from my brain. Shipwrecked. I remembered. The pirate ship was anchored, fat and gloating, on the far edge of the bay. Mr. Jones was sitting up, watching it.

"It's still there, I see," I said to him, nodding at the pirate ship. "They don't know we're alive. I'd like to keep it that way."

Mr. Jones looked down at the raft and back at me.

"I was thinking the same thing," I said, flinging back the sail and pulling on some damp but drier clothes than I'd been wearing. "One look at the beach through a spyglass, and they'll discover our raft. I have to conceal it before daylight."

It was impossible to move the raft into the trees. Even moving it another foot up the beach was out of the question. Back on the Miller ranch, Jake and I hid our rafts in the underbrush by the river. We'd tie them up at the bank and then cover them with leaves and fallen debris to make them blend in with the background. One time, our job of camouflage was so good we had trouble finding it. While we argued about its location, it was hidden less than half a dozen steps away from where we stood.

The tide had gone way out, leaving the raft stranded close to piles of driftwood. We were lucky to have landed during the night at high tide. Had we arrived on a lower tide, the raft would be part way down the beach and impossible to hide amidst grey sand and black mounds of rock. For a moment, I felt a bit of hope. Many, many things were going my way. Mother Nature had taken my side and I wanted to keep it that way. She is a fierce opponent when you get on the wrong side of her.

I hurried down the path and covered the raft with surrounding driftwood, seaweed, and kelp. It didn't take long for the roped-together logs to blend into the natural beach. I'd just finished when a flickering light from the east lit up the beach beside me. The sun was coming up. I crouched down and scrambled back up the slope, hoping the morning watch on that horrid ship hadn't been looking in my direction.

29

i

I quickly took down the makeshift tent and packed up my things. The pirates were still asleep out in the bay and I had to be ready when they finally woke up. I needed to find proper shelter where I could keep an eye on them, and be safely hidden if they came ashore.

I examined my surroundings in the dim light. The beach in front of me was open and unprotected; the forest behind me too sparse and too far away from the water. That left the rock face running from the north point of the cove, underneath the sloped clearing and angling down like a wedge to the beach on the other side. To my left, the rock face was too steep and vertical. To my right, it was maybe eight feet high but broken into layers and ledges. A tangle of scrub and low bushes grew between the rocks.

A shadowy crack caught my attention. I remembered the crevices and caves of the Sonoma Mountains on the southern border of the Miller ranch. I was riding with Papa, hunting for a mountain cat that had been killing the Miller sheep.

Look for the shadows, Charlee. Papa spoke inside my head. *Shadows are cracks, openings.* I crawled along the top edge, looking for a way down. A grassy patch marked the start of a potential route.

"Stay here, Mr. Jones. Watch the boat." He crouched down, eyes fixed on the bay. That is one smart dog, I thought, as I slid down over the boulders, concealed by the long grasses covering them. About half way down, I discovered a rocky ledge. It was part of the shadow I'd seen—a fine horizontal line. Where was the dark spot I saw perpendicular to it? The ledge narrowed and disappeared not far to my right. Left then, back toward the sloped path and forest. As I crawled along, the ledge widened, cutting deeper into the cliff. The rock above formed an overhang. Beneath it, the rock separated into a gap and a natural cave angled into the crevice formed by it. The morning light shone into the narrow opening. It was maybe six feet deep and widened to four by four inside. With a little work, it would be an excellent shelter. The beach was only a few steps farther down, near the sloped path where I'd first stood, practically right in front of it. It was easy to get to from below, now that I knew where it was.

I carried my gear to the cave in three trips. On the last one, Mr. Jones abandoned his watch and followed me to our new accommodations. Mr. Jones sniffed out the dark corners of the cave while I decided on how to set up my new camp. He carried some treasure he'd found over to the place I'd chosen for a sleeping spot and made himself comfortable. It looked like part of a dead fish. It was stinky and dirty, but he licked it like it was pudding.

"Yecch. Get that off my blanket." Only slightly offended, he moved to a more private spot to enjoy his find. A pang rippled through my stomach. I hadn't eaten for a whole day either. I rummaged in my duffel and pulled out my canteen and an oilcloth bundle, hoping seawater had not ruined everything.

I unwrapped a piece of smoked salmon. The oilcloth had kept it dry. I tore off a sizable chunk and shoved it in my mouth. Mr. Jones got wind of my fish and abandoned his own sad breakfast. He took the bits offered to him as gently as if Kuno had told him he must.

"Good boy, Bubba," I said, thinking of how he'd stood watch during the night on the raft and then again after we'd landed on the beach. "I'm sorry I called you a miserable boy." I straightened out his yellow bandana. "You are a splendid first mate, that's what you are. Kuno would be so proud of you."

His name lodged in my throat, a fishbone of pain. Sadness and despair gushed up from my chest and tears streamed from my eyes. I never used to cry at all. Now I felt like I could cry forever and never stop.

You're all right. You know what to do.

That voice in my head. It saved me again, as a whirlpool of grief threatened to drag me under. It yanked me back to safety, onto solid ground. Mr. Jones licked my hand.

"Sleep, Bubba. It's my watch now." He looked at me, head drooping, eyes bloodshot and ringed red with fatigue. "I'll let you know if something happens."

He circled around three times, scratched at the canvas sail I'd laid down as a ground cover, and curled up in a ball. His eyes were closed in seconds.

"I swear you understand everything I say," I said, petting his head.

The morning dragged by as we waited for the pirates' next move. I itched for something to do. I opened my saddlebags of books and papers, relieved to find only the outside leather a little damp and the contents completely dry. *Uncle Tom's Cabin* or *The Swiss Family Robinson*, I asked myself, not in the mood to read either. I could have tackled that book of Whitman's poems again, if I hadn't given it back to the Captain.

Where was the Captain? Did he die in his cabin and go down with the ship? Did they take him captive? He'd told them where Mr. Miller's gold was hidden, the coward. He'd arrogantly sailed us into dangerous waters, against Kuno's protests and better judgment. Now the ship was gone and people were dead. Why did he do it? I'd probably never know.

As the morning sun rose and lit up the shore, I observed the island cove. It looked like a harmless patch of beach under a clear blue sky, with no fog or hard wind. But on each end, rugged, rocky points stood like fortress walls. Half-submerged rocks stretched far out into the water.

The sound of voices and metal clanking broke the quiet lapping of waves on the sand. Mr. Jones awoke and joined me at the cave opening, where I was looking out at the water. Suddenly, his muscles tensed and he braced himself on the ledge, growling and baring his teeth. A boat had launched from the ship. The pirates were coming ashore!

"Bubba, shshsh! Get back." His tail fell and he was immediately quiet.

The boat departed the ship and the men rowed in random circles around the bay.

"What in Sam Hill are they doing?" I said to Mr. Jones, who was as interested and anxious about the activity as me. A sailor leaned over the water and hauled an object into the boat.

"They're scavenging! Picking up whatever didn't sink with the *Salish Wind*."

They disgusted me. As if they hadn't taken enough already.

But they'd also confirmed something.

"It's proof. They don't know we're here!" I said to Mr. Jones. "If they'd seen us, they'd be heading to shore and not fishing for flotsam. Stay close to me. Absolutely no barking. Sound carries over water."

He sat on his haunches, making himself small, as if he understood the detailed orders. It occurred to me that in the few weeks I'd known him, I'd never heard him bark. Growl, yes, but not bark. I had to believe he wouldn't start now because my life depended on it.

"Now we watch and wait."

The boat zigged and zagged around the bay. I couldn't make out what the men were saying, but they were loud and relaxed, like nobody was listening. Laughter erupted from time to time. After about an hour, the boat returned to the ship with its treasures.

Since I couldn't leave the cave and risk being seen, I did an inventory of my supplies. I emptied the damp contents from my own bag first. Drak had told me to pack, but I didn't understand he meant for survival. At the last minute, I brought my entire duffel bag, leaving behind old ranch things to make room for whatever was handy.

I sorted my things into two piles. In the useful pile, I stacked clothing, two blankets, toothpowder, some candles, soap, a water canteen, my papa's folding knife from my pocket, and the leather tool set I got for my fourteenth birthday. The other pile, for sentimental things, had a box of beads and shells, a nightshirt, a dress Mizzy had made me for school, and Papa's old spurs. I paused to consider where to put the saddlebags that held two storybooks, a notebook Jake had given me, and all my writing supplies. I placed them in the useful pile.

When I realized I'd have to leave the galley fast, I'd only thought to grab Cook's galley notebook and a bit of food. I had an oilcloth of salmon, a bundle of jerky, half a sack of rice and some potatoes. I stared at my sad pile in disbelief. There were so many things I could have brought. Like matches.

Drak's emergency bag was made of old oily canvas and stained white in places from drying seawater. It reeked of fish. Mr. Jones immediately came over to investigate. I pushed his nose out of the open bag and reached in. The contents were completely dry. Drak had waterproofed the bag, probably with whale oil. Stinky but smart.

He'd bundled everything in his bag to use the least amount of space. I pulled out a woven blanket, rolled up and tied with hemp rope. Tightly compressed inside were wool pants, a shirt, and a wool sweater. Another tied bundle had his black rain slicker and hat. I hadn't even thought to pack mine. A canvas bundle was next and it contained a cup, a plate, a pot, and some utensils. Stuffed into the pot were several cloth bags containing dried beans, grains, flour, tea, and spices. Drak had chosen foods to last. My smoked salmon was half gone after one small meal.

A heavy bundle with tools contained a small hatchet, a knife in a sleeve, and a sharpening steel. Another bundle revealed cotton strips, disinfecting powder, a sewing kit, a flask of rum, a bottle of strong-smelling fish oil, and two metal boxes. I used Papa's pocketknife to pry open the first one. Flint and tinder. I hoped I could remember how to use it. The other box contained a handful of fishing hooks and a roll of fishing line.

"Drak thought of everything, Mr. Jones. We'd be in rough shape without him. I wouldn't even be alive."

My eyes flooded again. My tears were unstoppable.

"No, I will not cry again. They're gone and crying won't bring them back."

Mr. Jones looked at me with sad, brown eyes.

"You haven't told me how you escaped those pirates," I said, changing the subject.

My comment troubled him. He didn't want to talk about it and he looked away.

30

i

The next morning, I woke up before dawn with one troubling thought. If the pirates came ashore and found the path, they might find the flattened spot where I'd slept the first night. Or they might discover the raft, if they got close to it. I had to return to the grove and cover our tracks.

Since I had no plans to take that raft on the water again, I used Drak's serrated knife to remove the ropes. The logs relaxed into a less obvious pile. Then, using a tree bough to erase my steps, I reversed up the path, through the grove and along the bluff to the rock steps. Along the way, I used handfuls of loose scrub to cover bent grass and disturbed ground. Mr. Jones and I returned to the cave. I'd made us disappear. Until the ship was gone, that's how I meant for us to stay.

Morning sun flooded the cove with bright light. The tip of one of the masts on the *Salish Wind* had reappeared at low tide along with the ugly, submerged rocks the ship had struck. With the tide so far out, it seemed almost close enough to walk to the shipwreck. Farther out in deep water, away from the scene of treachery, was the gloating pirate ship.

Warm air seeped into the shadowy cave. Outside, the sun burned through a thick blanket of haze. The chill and dampness of night was almost gone. I stretched out on the cool rocks of my hideout and considered my circumstances. I had found a good shelter, concealed in the rock wall. But since I couldn't build a fire to cook, I had very little food. The biggest problem could be water. By staying in the cool shade of the cave, Mr. Jones and I could get by for another day on what was left in my canteen. Once the pirates were gone, I could forage for food and water, and get my bearings. Until then, I had to ration. If they stuck around, I'd have to venture out at night.

The winding of a winch echoed across the water. A rowboat lowered from the pirate ship and four men clamored aboard. They rowed for the south end of the cove, the end farthest away from me. Mr. Jones stirred, as if he could feel the air change around him.

"They're coming ashore, Bubba." I tapped his shoulder and he stood in alarm. "Not a sound now." I pressed my finger to my lips. He blinked in reply.

The men in the rowboat were in no hurry, rowing at a snail's pace, which I took to mean they were still no wiser to the *Salish Wind* castaways watching them. Their boat ran aground far down the beach. The men stepped out onto the mucky sand, and lazily unloaded some barrels and jugs.

Two of the men shoved the boat back out and returned to the ship. The other two carried goods up the sand to the rocky foreshore. They ambled about like outlaws, bored now that their latest raid was over.

Soon, a wisp of smoke rose from a fire. They chopped wood, threw it on a pile, and scavenged around on the beach. I was almost bored with them.

"I think they're just having a bonfire. But why did they bring so much for a picnic? I hope they aren't planning to stay."

Mr. Jones looked at me, his brown eyes squinting. I pictured the barrels in the galley.

"What about the barrels?" I said.

He dug at the rock floor with a paw.

"Mr. Miller's gold. They've brought it ashore. They're going to bury it on the island."

The rowboat returned with three more men. That made seven ashore. The fire blazed and the sailors' voices got louder.

"Another drunken party, I suppose. I hope they all pass out and drown at high tide," I said.

A few hours passed and nothing changed. I yawned, fighting the urge to have a nap.

Just then, two pirates started up the beach toward us. They passed a jug back and forth between them, and staggered along without purpose. How far would they come? I didn't want them poking around the path, or discovering the logs from the raft that remained in a suspicious-looking pile.

The approaching danger made me alert. I felt my breathing get fast. Mr. Jones, sensing my alarm, stood up, his fur standing on end down his back. I touched his shoulder again and put my fingers to my lips. He reluctantly sat down, remembering my instructions. I carefully pulled a large bundle of loose scrub and branches into the entrance of the cave. I flattened myself out on my belly and found the best position to watch the approaching men.

One of them motioned to a big log on the beach in front of me. They sat down, side by side, only a stone's throw from the path I'd taken into the cedar grove and from what was left of the hidden raft. They passed their jug back and forth in silence for some time.

The man farthest was away, taller and thinner than the other, spoke first.

"Storm brewing." He turned his gaze from the eastern sky to the other man. My skin prickled as I recognized his voice. He was the man called Skulder from the galley! If he looked over his friend's shoulder, he'd be staring right at me through the under-brush. He squinted and ran a ringed hand through his greasy brown hair.

The other man had a bald, square head and a red beard. He had his back to me and I strained to catch his reply.

"… want us outta here… southeasterly… gale blows in…"

I recognized his voice, too. He was the other man in the galley named Hample. He belched loudly.

The other pirate clapped his friend on the back. "You don't have to worry, mate." He pointed at the ship with a left hand that appeared to be a few fingers short of a full set. "They're calling us back."

"… done our work… forlorn place… bloody haunted island…"

They rose and started back the way they came. Mr. Jones let out a low growl. I clapped my hand over his muzzle and froze. The pirate with the brown hair stopped and turned around. He looked right at the crevice in the rock face.

"You hear something?"

"That was me. I let one rip," Hample confessed with pride.

The pirate with the brown hair cracked a smile, but scanned the bluff where we were hidden. A sudden gust of wind rustled the canopy of trees near the rock shelf and drew his eyes away.

"Wife says I hear like a dog."

He shrugged his shoulders. The other sailor made some amusing retort that was carried away in the wind. They hooted over that as they marched back along the beach.

By the time they reached the others, the party had broken up and the fire had been extinguished. The boat was already making a trip back to the ship with the first group of sailors. By the time the second group left, thick grey clouds had gathered in the east. The wind caused the tree branches to swirl.

"I thought we were done for," I said to Mr. Jones. "You almost gave us away."

He could tell I had a bone to pick with him. He skulked behind my duffle bag, tail down, and glanced at me sideways as I spoke.

"I appreciate you acknowledging your error in judgment." He wouldn't make eye contact. "Don't be silly now. I'm not mad. You just did what comes natural."

Mr. Jones's left ear moved back and forth.

"Your growling tells me something's wrong. I appreciate it. But growling when we're trying to hide from pirates is not helpful. Luckily, one of those losers is half deaf. It would have been quite a different story if both of them had heard you. We'd probably have been slaughtered right where we sit." I shuddered at the thought. My nerves were shot, but I didn't want Mr. Jones to feel bad.

"They are dangerous men. That brown-haired one is real spooky. I won't forget his mean face anytime soon. Did you see? He even had the devil tattooed on his forearm. His mate was a bit of a pudgy sod, but I bet he'd cut a person in half for a jug of rum."

Chains clanged on the black ship as they winched up their anchor. Whitecaps had formed on the open water by the time the pirate ship sailed east, its mainsail flat and tight in the strong wind. Within minutes, it disappeared around the point of land where the *Salish Wind* had been ambushed.

"Nobody knows the *Salish Wind* is gone. Those pirates aren't going to tell anyone what they did."

Mr. Jones, his sins forgiven, moved to a spot on top of my blanket. He sighed and closed his eyes.

"Even worse, nobody knows we're here." A chilly wind gusted into the cave. The warmth from earlier in the day had vanished with the pirates. For the first time, my clothes felt thin and inadequate. We were definitely in for a storm.

"No time for sleep, Mr. Jones. We have work to do."

31

i

"I've got to get to that bonfire before high tide wipes it out. There should be hot coals in the ashes."

Since my sweater was still damp, I dug out the one Drak had packed. It was too big for me, and had a fishy smell, but it was clean and dry. I pulled it over my head. The bottom of it hung down to my knees.

Mr. Jones trailed me up the beach, sniffing the sand where the men had walked earlier. I picked my way just above the water's edge, which was much rockier than the sand at low tide. Most of the footprints of the pirates had already washed away, like they had never existed, never set foot on the island at all.

At their abandoned bonfire, I found the remnants of the afternoon party. A couple of empty rum jugs were lying on the sand. Piles of shells from the oysters and clams they'd been cooking on the fire were strewn about. I filled Drak's satchel with dozens of unopened shellfish they'd gathered and not eaten. Mr. Jones busied himself devouring morsels discarded with the opened shells.

"At least we'll have a grand dinner," I said to him. "These can be eaten cooked or raw. I prefer them cooked though." Mr. Jones didn't mind them either way.

Above the tide line, tracks led to several feet of disturbed ground in the brush. The pirates had tossed bits of scrub and beach debris about to make the spot look natural. They'd done a lousy job concealing where they'd hidden Mr. Miller's gold. I figured they were either very dumb or very new at buried treasure.

A blast of wind whistled through the trees. A tree limb snapped and fell onto the beach close to where I stood. No time to do anything about the gold. It wasn't going anywhere, but the incoming tide and breaking waves were about to ruin what was left of the fire.

The pirates had thrown a lot of seawater on the blaze, but it still smoldered. Taking out Drak's metal firebox, I probed the ashes with my hand shovel and uncovered red-hot coals. I filled the box with as many glowing coals as would fit and snapped the lid shut. I popped the box into my satchel, grabbed the two empty rum jugs and sped back to the cave with Mr. Jones on my heels.

The entrance to the cave, below the rock overhang, was a perfect spot for a small fire. The gap between the rocks formed a natural chimney, but it was still too exposed to wind and might be visible from the water. I hauled large rocks up to the ledge, stacked them up about a foot high and built a sheltered fire pit. I gathered dry bits of tinder, witches' hair and driftwood. With everything ready, I reached for the metal box from my satchel.

"Yeeow!" The hot metal box hit the rocks, the lid flew off and the coals broke and scattered. I sucked my burned fingers. "Oh no! That wasn't smart!" Mr. Jones agreed and moved away from the catastrophe.

The shattered bits of coal quickly fizzled to grey. I couldn't lose my chance at starting a fire. I rescued the tiny glowing remains with my shovel and carefully laid them on a nest of tinder. I blew on the coals until a thin plume of smoke rose from the bundle. Stoked with slivers of dry cedar, the tiny pile burst into flame.

As my little fire grew, the eastern sky turned heavy and black. The late afternoon felt dark and ominous. Wind whipped into the cave entrance. Raindrops hit my face and caused the fire to spit.

"I don't suppose you could tend the fire," I said to Mr. Jones, as I swapped out Drak's baggy sweater for his rain gear. Mr. Jones ignored my sarcasm and immediately took up residence on the warm sweater.

I hurried to the remnants of the raft. The only piece I could salvage was the cabin door. In the grove of trees, I hunted for a couple of straight, fallen branches.

As I worked, the sleeves of the slicker got in my way. Annoyed, I took my knife out to hack them off, but thought better of it and rolled them up. I'd alter Drak's clothing properly while hunkered down during the storm.

I jammed a thick branch across the cave entrance like a drapery pole and attached a piece of canvas sail to it. The wind blew the canvas around, making it difficult to secure. By the time I had it tied down tight, rain pelted my hat and shoulders.

I hauled driftwood and dry branches into the cave until a huge gust of wind nearly blew me off the ledge. The makeshift canvas door kept the wind from funneling inside the cave, and the fire burned well behind its rock mound.

Once inside, I fought my way out of the oversized, dripping rain cloak. My hands were a cold mess of dirt and torn flesh. They reminded me of my first day of work at the Livery last summer.

"Those coals were a stroke of luck. We'd probably still be sitting here in the cold. I've never had to use a flint, even though I saw Papa use one on our homestead. It might have taken me a while to make it work."

Mr. Jones looked pensive.

"I can thank those pirates for two things—being so lazy that they left the tide to put out their fire. What's the other thing, you ask? Leaving the gold buried here in plain sight." I smiled and added more wood to the fire.

It didn't take a big fire to make our cave cozy. The wind blew some smoke inside, but that was a small price to pay for the light and warmth. I stuck my cooking pot outside to collect rainwater streaming off the canvas. My pot filled up fast. I topped up my canteen and used what was left to wash up and clean my torn hands.

When my pot was full of water again, I heated it over the fire. I mixed up biscuit dough and wrapped it around a stick to bake over the coals. On a bed of rocks in the fire, I roasted oysters and clams in their shells. Mr. Jones and I ate every one of them, along with the last of my smoked salmon and the stick biscuits.

Over a cup of tea, I thumbed through Cook's notebook. Along with many good recipes using local ingredients, there were fascinating notes on foraging in the forests and on the shores around Vancouver Island. Cook loved the places and things he wrote about. He saw the beauty in nature's designs.

"He's practically a botanist. Look at all these detailed drawings and descriptions of plants."

Mr. Jones acknowledged my comment but didn't find my discovery important enough to interrupt his nap.

"I was so mad when he told me he was getting off the boat. Now all I can think of is how incredibly lucky that was. If he'd been with us…"

Grisly scenes of death on the *Salish Wind* flooded my head. They made my throat close and my stomach clench. I quickly pushed them away, turned to a new page and concentrated on a section Cook had written about native crops.

While I knew oats from home, I had never really paid attention to things like red clover, dandelion, and thistle. In California, we'd fed those things to our horses, or cattle grazed upon them in the fields. Cook's entries dated back almost two years, which

I figured must have been when Mr. Miller bought the merchant schooners and started doing business in the British colonies.

Cook's notes had the honest, personal touch of a diary. I may have been biased, but the way he described the tender, green spirals of the fiddlehead fern was as good as the poetry that Mr. Whitman wrote. I almost felt guilty reading his notes. I told myself it was all right because the information was so interesting, even though it was often his beautiful words that drew me in.

I turned another page and a folded slip of paper dropped out from between the pages. I recognized the large printing on it immediately. It was Mizzy's writing. I fingered the piece of paper for a moment, knowing it was private and not my business to read it. But then I figured I might end up dead, or never found on this island, and what would it matter then?

Dated September 1858, Mizzy had written a brief note to Cook and pleaded with him to look for me before he left for the east. It was just as she'd told me. She had sensed something had gone terribly wrong. The last line of her letter sent a deep pain through my chest. She had written, *Please look for her. Find my girl. MJ.*

The wind howled and the rain poured for hours. I read Cook's notebook from cover to cover and kept the fire burning low, eyeing the cave floor for leaks and flooding. I made the cabin door into a flat bunk to keep me off the hard, cold, and jagged rock floor, and away from any crawling critters, if there were any living in the rock crevices.

The warmth from the fire made me drowsy. Every time my head fell forward, I rubbed my face and pinched my ears to wake myself up. I was losing the battle.

"I can't fall asleep, Bubba. We need to keep our fire going."

Somewhere in the wee hours, the wind fell off and the driving rain changed to a steady, soothing patter on the canvas. I couldn't stay awake any longer. I stoked the fire, leaned back against my lumpy duffle bag and pulled a blanket around me. Mr. Jones tucked himself in by my side.

A few hours later, still in the rain and darkness, I woke up to the wet nose of Mr. Jones, nudging me awake so I could put more wood on the glowing embers.

32

i

The rain took a break the next morning, giving us a chance to leave the cave and walk along the beach again. My limbs loosened with the chance to stretch and move. Mr. Jones tagged along, investigating shallow puddles left between the rocks. The wind had made the sea choppy and wild. Waves rolled and broke on the beach, foaming around my rubber boots. The icy water pierced through the rubber, reminding me why swimming to the island would have been completely hopeless.

We walked to the south end of the cove, where the sand ended at the rocky outcrop. The shallow water at the base of it offered up several crabs and handfuls of green kelp. Rugged oysters clung to the rocks, but I'd eaten so many the night before that I didn't pick any.

Debris from the *Salish Wind* had washed up in the storm during the night—milled wood, a chunk of an oak barrel tangled with a torn piece of sail, what was left of a broken hatch. The sight of the remains made my heart heavy.

Past the northern rock reef, the tips of the masts had vanished. The storm had erased the shipwreck. Nobody knew the *Salish Wind* had gone down. Nobody would know until the *Salish Wind* failed to arrive in San Francisco. It would be a week before anyone even knew we were missing. Then they wouldn't even know where to look. Only the pirate sloop had seen us, and I was sure they weren't going to tell.

I fished the floating piece of hatch from the water and hurled it under a shoreline tree. I wanted to yell into the sky, rage against the unfairness of it all. But there was no one to blame for my predicament. I chose to come north in search of my own riches. This is where chasing that foolish dream had landed me.

The rough mound of dirt and sand left by the pirates beckoned. I would get even with them. They would not have the gold they'd stolen and killed for. I stomped back to the cave to get my hand shovel and canvas. Mr. Jones steered clear of me, sensing I was not in a mood for adventure or light conversation.

My shovel was small, but the ground was soft and the pirates had been lazy. Only a few inches of dirt covered the barrels. I shoveled fast, knowing I was racing against a short break in the storm. Without too much work, I unearthed three small barrels.

When I popped the lid off the first barrel, I was surprised to find wood chips. I dug through the thick layer and sat back on my haunches in awe. I'd never seen gold like this. It didn't sparkle the way my storybooks had said. It was heavy and cold. Muted yellow nuggets, hundreds of them, were nestled in the wood chips.

Each barrel was the same. I emptied all three, sifting the nuggets from the wood chips and collecting them on pieces of canvas. Then I refilled the barrels with rocks and wood chips, so they felt the same as they had with the gold inside. I buried the barrels exactly as I'd found them.

As I worked, the air became thick and hard to breathe. Sweat poured off my head, the result of exertion and nerves. A warning drop of rain splatted the back of my neck and thunder rumbled in the distance. Fat clouds hung low and heavy, ready to burst. I hurried along the beach and dug a new hole for the canvas bundles high above the tide line. Working against time had taken the edge off my anger. Mr. Jones came over to supervise as I made the buried treasure disappear into the ordinary features of the landscape.

"Those men may be pirates, but they don't know the first thing about being an outlaw. They've got themselves a nice collection of worthless stones for all their trouble."

I finished my job as the skies opened and rain poured down in sheets. I set up the broken hatch from the *Salish Wind* as a pointer. Only Mr. Jones and I knew where the gold was buried now.

I filled my arms with driftwood and hurried back to our shelter.

"I don't have any of the stuff they had on their island," I said to Mr. Jones, tossing my very worn book back into the duffle bag. I'd been reading *The Swiss Family Robinson* aloud to him as the rain continued into the next afternoon. "If you ask me, that whole family is a bunch of know-it-alls. They would get on my nerves if I were shipwrecked with the lot of them. They never stop."

I knew my survival was going to be a different story than theirs. I was alone, well, except for Mr. Jones. If I'd been shipwrecked in the colder months of the year, I'd probably already be dead, swept away on my raft by impossible wind and currents. I still had what was left of summer on my side. It would give me time to explore the island and figure out the best place to be for rescue.

When summer ended, the cave would become an unfriendly place. And when the pirates eventually returned for the gold, I needed to be as far away from them as possible. When would they return? I had no way of knowing, but I figured I had some time. They wouldn't have gone to all the trouble to bury the loot if they wanted it right away.

Drak said this was an island. But what island and where? It was somewhere west of Fort Victoria, on the northern side of

Fuca Strait. We had been only a few hours into our journey, heading for the Pacific, when our luck ran out. The black sloop had appeared, the weather had turned against us, and the Captain had made the fatal decision to outrun both.

"When this stormy weather passes, we'll take a day pack and explore the island. Seems like the path into the cedar grove keeps going, like it's there because people used it at some point. We'll follow it and see where it takes us. Maybe somebody lives here, although I doubt it."

Something bothered him about my plan. He shook his head and scratched nervously at an ear.

"We don't have to worry about animals. This cave hasn't been used. Cook said there aren't any animals on these small islands. No bears, no wolves, no big cats and such."

I hoped I'd remembered that correctly. I didn't pay full attention to the geography lesson that Cook was so willing to share when we'd sailed in from the Pacific. If I was wrong and this wasn't an island, the trail that led into the forest could get us lost or put us face-to-face with a predator.

"Besides," I reassured myself, "animals mostly mind their own business." The face of the murdering pirate with the devil tattoo came to mind and I clenched my teeth. "It's people you can't trust."

Mr. Jones agreed.

The rain and wind carried on for three days. Mr. Jones and I spent most of our time in or near the rock cave. In the daytime, between rain showers, I gathered dry wood from the cedar grove and foraged along the seashore. Mr. Jones ambled along behind me wherever I went, digging up things in the ground and waiting for me when I stopped to fill my canvas bag. The rain had filled my cooking pot repeatedly. By the second day, the two pirate jugs were full of drinking water.

On the one hand, it was a relief to be alone and not have to worry about pirates and murderers. On the other hand, I looked out to sea, wondering who was out there, and if anyone would ever find me. The thought of never being found terrified me, particularly at night when I tried to sleep. I couldn't let myself dwell on it.

"No point watching for a boat," I said to Mr. Jones as he looked out into the cove. "They'll have taken shelter when this storm came in."

When it rained, I huddled inside the cave and wrote in my notebook. On board the *Salish Wind*, the evenings were always the best time of day. That was when Cook and I would sneak a few minutes to relax over a cup of coffee. He'd tell tales of the sea and play his guitar. I'd get out my pencil and paper.

"What are you writing?" he'd asked me one evening.

"Stuff," I replied. "Sometimes stories, sometimes things I learn about. Right now, I'm writing out your recipe for crab cakes."

"You want recipes, I'll show you some real good ones I learned from the coast people." That's when he'd first showed me his special book. I was glad I'd saved it for him.

At night, when it was dark and the wind seemed to blow harder, I set to work on Drak's oversized clothing. I cut off the bottom of his wool sweater, hemmed it to a better length and used the rest of the wool to make two pairs of mittens and a scarf. The arms produced a good pair of socks. I altered the rain slicker and used the bits to sew a small waterproof bag. I was never much for regular sewing. I couldn't crochet or embroider and detested the thought of fussy work that didn't seem to have a purpose but to decorate. Papa had taught me how to repair harnesses and riding tack. We used to mend gear after supper on the ranch. I pushed the memories away because they made me feel too sad.

"I like spending time like this," I said to Mr. Jones. "Even though you don't talk, you're like Cook and Mizzy and Papa and me. You like to work on little projects when you relax." Mr. Jones was cleaning the fur on his paws.

"You'll meet them one day. Well, not Papa because he's gone. I lost him, like you lost Kuno…"

I'd said too much. He stared at me for several moments, as if reliving what had happened on the deck of the ship, then stood up and moved away. He settled at the entrance to the cave with his back to me.

33

i

On the morning of my fifth day on the island, I woke up in a sweat. The morning sun had come up in a clear blue sky. It beat on the canvas, making the damp air in the cave humid and warm. Mr. Jones and I were baked out of our sleeping quarters by the time breakfast was over.

"Time to go exploring," I said to Mr. Jones as I donned socks and ranch boots for the first time. "I have a plan. Today, we'll see where the northern shoreline goes. It shouldn't take us long to get to the end. Then, we'll come back the same way."

I packed food, water, and supplies into Drak's canvas bag. I'd collect plants and berries in the one I'd sewn out of extra bits of his rain slicker.

"I know. It seems like a lot to take. We aren't going to get lost, but Papa always taught me to be prepared. This island didn't look very big from the water. I figure we're pretty close to the southern end. Already know the beach is a dead end that way. We'll go north, maybe try inland another day."

Mr. Jones stretched as I took in the pretty morning. The sea was a deep blue. Waves sparkled in the morning sun, and the incoming tide lapped the stones of the beach with a soothing hush. I left fire embers buried and burning, hid our cave entrance and we set out along the beach with the sun still low in the cloudless sky.

Ten minutes into the exploration, I had to turn back. The beach was impassable at the north end of the cove. We returned to the path by our camp. I looked up at it with a little dread. The only way out of the cove by land was into the trees and away from the water.

I didn't say it to Mr. Jones but I was reluctant to leave the safety of the cove. I wanted to follow the shoreline. It gave me the advantage of knowing where I was while keeping an eye out for the pirates returning. I wouldn't get lost or run into trouble staying by the shore.

The woods was a different matter. I didn't know how far the forest would go. And what if I was wrong and this wasn't an island? What if it was a peninsula attached to a mainland on the other side? If it was, there would be animals. Big animals. Maybe even people. And leaving the beach meant the pirates might show up and I couldn't get back to my cave. I didn't have a choice. I had to find out where we had the best chance of rescue. Mr. Jones, bold as always, started off ahead of me.

After about fifteen minutes of hiking beneath towering cedars and pines, we left the forest shade and walked out across a flat, grassy bluff. The temperature jumped from cool to hot. We were unprotected from the blazing sun. I peeled off my vest and let the light breeze blow against my loose shirt.

"I recognize those plants from Cook's notebook. Those with the purple flowers. They're camas. Kind of like potatoes, I think. And these are oats," I said, swishing the golden grasses with a hand. "Funny. It almost looks like it's somebody's garden gone wild."

My eyes skirted the perimeter of the field. I had murderous pirates with machetes to worry about. I didn't need a crazed gardener with a sharpened hoe coming after me as well. But the field was untouched. No sign of trampled grass or turned soil.

"We'll dig a few camas on the way back. Looks like berry

bushes over there in the shade."

I headed for a group of peculiar trees, their branches red and twisted, like gnarly fingers pointing into the air and over the bluff to the sea. Sitting down in the shadow of one, I pulled out my water canteen and Cook's notebook. I flipped to a page I'd read the night before.

"Here it is," I said to Mr. Jones, who was drinking water from what I'd left in my cup. "This is an arbutus. It's sort of like the madrone tree back home. Here, it gets red berries in the fall that can be steamed or roasted." I looked at the many branches. Still too early for the berries.

"These berries can be added to bannock as well, Cook says, or crushed and made into jam. A piece of warm bannock bread with some of that on it would sure be nice." I had flour and soda but hoped I would be long gone, rescued from this place before these berries ripened.

"There was something else about this tree." Mr. Jones had wandered off to poke around in the rockery on the bank. He was almost out of earshot. I flipped through the pages and found the place where Cook had written, *If you peel the bark from the tree and do not use it, you will peel your luck away.*

I ran my hand along the beautiful wood of the trunk. It was hard and smooth, a bright lime green. Red paper scrolls rolled up its trunk.

"I have no use for your bark, and I definitely need to keep my luck," I said to it, patting its trunk.

"Let's go, Mr. Jones."

We picked our way down a rocky slope leading to the water.

At the bottom of the bluff was a tiny cove surrounded by steep rock faces. The land dropped straight off into the ocean. I thought it might be a great hiding spot for a pirate ship until I noticed all the submerged rocks. Only a fool would take a boat into that treacherous cove.

Heading north, thick bushes made walking impossible. We had no choice but to stick close to the water's edge. After a short trek over jagged, slippery rocks, Mr. Jones stopped. The northern point of the island couldn't be much farther, but the incoming tide would cut off our return. Mr. Jones turned around and I followed him back to the field above the bluff.

I found the blackberry bushes I'd seen earlier. I ate handfuls of plump berries and picked many more to take with me. I dug up a few camas, carefully replacing the soil where my shovel hurt the ground. Papa had taught me to leave the land as good as I found it, to treat it kind. I didn't take more than I could use.

I retraced my steps across the field and back into the trees. We'd been walking for several minutes in the forest when I realized we were on an old trail. It was going in the right direction, so I stayed with it.

Mr. Jones ran ahead and disappeared. The trail wound through the trees, in harmony with the shape of the land. It had natural steps of fallen logs, branches that seemed to sweep away from the passage. Sunlight burst through the treetops in openings like beams from heaven. For quite a while, I lost myself in the peaceful beauty of the woods.

Mr. Jones reappeared, racing toward me with excitement, urging me to hurry along. The path ended at a T. Left would take us back to the cave, right veered off and climbed a hill. Mr. Jones took off up the hill and I followed him. The path ended in a small clearing of thick, purple-flowered clover. A small, wood building with a flat roof stood at the far end, weathered but quite intact.

As I crossed the clearing, I noticed the ground had not been walked on. Still, I felt a little nervous, like I'd just wandered into someone's yard. Mr. Jones sniffed the air and trotted around the outside of the little building. I stuck my head in the doorway and peered into the dark until my eyes adjusted.

"Hello?" I called. Nobody was there. It was empty. "What is

this place, Mr. Jones? Who do you figure built this little shed?"

I didn't think it was my place to go inside. Whoever this belonged to might come back, and it would be rude to march into someone's house uninvited. Or worse, they could be lying in wait, hiding in the nearby forest, ready to ambush me. I didn't really believe any of those things. There would have been noticeable human signs. I hadn't forgotten what Papa had taught me. It was definitely abandoned, but I decided not to trespass.

Just then, an eagle cried out above me. It circled over the clearing and landed on the top of a tall, dead tree at the opposite side of the clearing. It folded its wings and looked down, tilting its head as if looking at something on the ground below. I followed its gaze down the trunk. A person sat at the base of the tree! I could see part of a man's jacket. His dark boots.

He appeared to be leaning against the trunk, sleeping. I didn't want to startle him, coming up on him from behind.

"Hello, sir!"

He didn't answer. My muscles tensed as I rounded the trunk to face him. I gasped and clapped a hand over my mouth.

The man was dead. He'd been there for quite some time, all blackened remnants of flesh and white bones in tattered clothing. His skull was in his lap.

How had his skull ended up in his lap? Had it fallen off his crumbling spine or had it been hacked off? Had the pirates murdered him, too, left him up here for dead?

I took a step back. His clothes weren't those of a sailor. The coat and cap were tweed. His cap was on the ground beside him, like it had dropped from his hand when he took his last breath.

A foul smell wafted up from the decomposing body. In an instant, I was back on the deck of the *Salish Wind*, standing by the gruesome body of a dead sailor. Mr. Jones barked and took off, calling for me to run. I backed out of the clearing and bolted after him.

34

i

I tore down the path as if that corpse had jumped up and was running behind me. Fear gushed through my veins and the pulse in my throat almost choked me. I'd stumbled upon the scene of another gruesome death. Everywhere I turned, death seemed to find me. I saw Papa, lying in the dust with his head smashed into a post. Drak, twisted in a bloody heap in the galley. Kuno, mortally wounded on the deck of the *Salish Wind*, eyes screaming at the sky.

I raced away from the horrible scene as fast as my legs could carry me. My shoulder bag swung wildly as I changed directions, zipping down through the trees, gasping to breathe. On a crooked section of the trail, I made a sharp turn and the strap of the bag caught a branch. It yanked me sideways and threw me off balance. As my left foot came back down on the path, my weight caused it to twist violently. I hit the ground like a sack of potatoes. My body whipped and my head cracked against something, sending a searing pain through my skull. And then there was nothing.

It must have knocked me out for a while. When I opened my eyes, the sun had moved to the west, leaving the forest in a flat, gloomy light. I pushed myself up to a sitting position, wincing at tenderness in my right elbow. I moved my foot and a wicked pain shot up the side of my left leg from my ankle. I cried out from the shock of it and then sat still until I could determine what else I'd injured.

I ran my fingers over the back of my head and found a huge goose egg. No blood, but I already had a skull-splitting headache from it. My right shoulder and elbow ached, but I was still able to move and bend them. The heel of my left hand was dirty and scraped. Right leg, definitely bruised but nothing torn or broken. Left ankle excruciating to move even an inch.

The camas and blackberries I'd picked were scattered on the path around me. Cook's notebook lay open in the dirt. I looked at them, puzzled about what I'd been doing with them when I fell. I'd gone foraging in a field, I remembered, with Mr. Jones. Where was Mr. Jones? I called out for him as I started to gather my things.

"Excuse me. May I help you?"

A soft, female voice came from the shadows near the path. Startled, I tried to slide away on the seat of my pants. Images of headless ghosts and murdering pirates and dead people danced in my head.

"Agh!!" My foot screamed at me to be still.

A young woman emerged from the trees.

"Don't be afraid. You've had a bad fall. I'll help you," she said, crouching down. She picked up Cook's notebook, brushed the dirt off, and handed it to me. Her long black hair fell around her shoulders. She wore a plain brown dress, woven with a fringe, and shoes made of hide. A pendant made of shells dangled around her neck.

"Where'd you come from? Do you live here?"

"No, but this is my family's land." She carefully gathered the spilled contents of my bag.

I thought of the eagle that had circled the clearing just before

I discovered the body. The image of the man came flooding back. I pushed it away.

"I'm Charlee. I'm stranded here alone. Wherever this is. With my dog."

"Your dog?"

I looked around for Mr. Jones but he'd disappeared. "He took off."

"When you found the man."

"Yeah. We both ran. Scared me half…" I stopped. How did she know about the man? Had she seen him in the clearing? Had she been watching me?

"He won't harm you. He's waiting."

"For what? An undertaker?"

She looked puzzled. My head throbbed. What had I been doing in that clearing? I couldn't remember.

"I'm not far from my camp. I mean, I don't think it's far. Where…?" I looked in both directions along the path, not sure which way would take me back to my cave. I tried to get my good leg underneath me to stand.

"Wait. Don't get up. I'll find you something to lean on."

She searched the ground under the nearby trees. She was definitely older than me, but not by too many years. She broke a long branch and returned with a sturdy piece that had a fork on the end.

"This will work," she said, showing me how to lean on the stick to keep weight off my foot. "Let's go." She helped me to my feet. The forest spun and my stomach twirled with it.

"Mr. Jones!" I called. "That's my dog's name. Well, he's my dog now but I haven't had him long and now he's run off although that isn't like him. Not like him at all. Mr. Jones!"

My head wasn't working right. Everything I said sounded like I was speaking into a pillow. My head was a cracked egg with words spilling out of it, landing in muffled thuds around me.

"He is white with yellow cloth around his neck?"

"Yes! You saw him!"

"He's at your camp," she replied.

"How do you…?"

"Put your arm around my neck now. We'll go slow."

She threw my bags over her shoulder and we set off. Our first few steps were awkward, as I hopped and lurched out of time with her even steps. Each jarring movement made my head pound and my foot throb.

"Don't jump. Step right, lean left to me," she instructed. "Slower… there it is."

Soon, our motions synchronized and we made headway. We walked for what seemed like an hour in silence. I didn't know where I was going. For a while, I thought I was on the Miller ranch.

"How do you know where my camp is, Jake?" I asked at one point, when it occurred to me that I wasn't leading the way to my rock cave, a hideout known only to me and Mr. Jones.

"I'm not Jake. But I know where everything is on this island," she whispered. "I come here often."

"Well, good thing you aren't a stinky pirate," I said, swooning like I'd been drinking all day with a bunch of them.

"I'm glad to see you awake," she said as I opened my eyes to flickering firelight. I was propped up against the cave wall. She was kneeling beside me, cooking something over my fire.

"You've been out for half the night. That bump on your head is very bad." She handed me a cup with a small amount of liquid in it. "You need to drink this now."

I sat up and a soggy compress came loose from my hair.

"It's medicine. It will take the swelling away," she volunteered before I had time to form a question about it. "How do you feel now?"

"Awful," I said. "Like I ran down a path at full speed and dove headlong into a tree."

"You did. Drink the medicine. It will make you better and relieve the pain."

I swallowed the dark liquid. It was bitter, smelly, and horrible.

"Blech... that tasted like manure."

She laughed. "You are familiar with a manure drink? What is the medicinal purpose of such a drink?"

I leaned back, wondering if she was joking or serious.

My foot rested on my duffle bag. It was wrapped in a compress of muck and herbs, and tied up with thin strips of cedar bark.

"How did you get my boot off?"

"I'm sorry. I had to cut it."

My riding boots were tossed beside my things. The left boot had a crude slice from the ankle to the top.

"I don't remember..."

"They are beautiful boots. It was the only way, but you will fix them, yes?"

"Yes. I used to work with horses..." My thoughts were on the Miller ranch, with Jake, with Miss Molly and Papa. Where had they gone?

She took my cup and filled it with tea that was heating over the fire. When she gave it back, I couldn't hold it steady with one trembling hand. I curled both hands tightly around the cup.

"I can repair my boot," I said, after drinking half of the cup's contents and suddenly remembering what we had been talking about. The tea was unfamiliar and earthy, but also warm and soothing. "I've got leather tools," I said, taking another sip. "What kind of tea is this? I haven't had it before."

"Dried nettle with several other plants and roots. It will help the swelling and make the sickness go away."

I struggled to think of something I knew was important. What was it? My mind took me back to the *Salish Wind*. The raft was pushing off and I was desperately reaching for something.

"Bubba! Where is Mr. Jones?" I tried to make myself upright, but my limbs wouldn't obey.

As I slipped back into the deep, I thought I heard her say, "The little dog is right here beside you."

35

i

"How long have I been sleeping?"

I blinked my eyes to focus. The young woman was still sitting by the fire, but daylight crept into the cave from where the canvas had been drawn back.

"Two days," she replied. "Can you sit?"

I got as far as leaning on my elbows, but I was too weak to go any farther. She offered me her hands so I could pull myself up. As I did, the sleeve on my left arm drew back, revealing the nasty scar I had on my wrist. She leaned forward to examine it, but I pulled my arm away.

"This was another very bad injury," she said, propping me up with a blanket.

"Yes, it was."

I remembered my encounter with two street punks outside of Chinatown last winter. They'd thrown a bottle at my friend Taitai and her daughter Jing Yi. I'd knocked it out of the air before it struck them, but the glass had shattered and left a shard buried deep in my forearm. Taitai's good doctor friend sealed the wound, but it left me with a scar that looked like the brand of the Miller ranch.

"It's a very unusual shape," she said.

"It's a horseshoe."

"Horses wear shoes now?"

I laughed and immediately clutched my head. "Ouch. Yes, well, in this case, it might be considered a symbol of good luck."

"It is working, I think."

I thought about that as she prepared a warm piece of bannock and smeared it with purple jam. The aroma of fresh baking. My mouth watered.

"I guess I'm lucky. I didn't get killed by pirates, didn't drown when the ship sank. This fall wasn't very lucky though."

"Wasn't it?"

"You're talking in riddles."

She handed me the bread and I took a huge bite.

"Not too fast…"

"This is so good…" I said between hungry bites, savoring the sweetness of the bread and the tartness of the berry jam.

"It's good your appetite is returning. You must not eat too much though. You have been very sick."

"You speak English well."

"I don't speak it at all," she replied and her lips didn't move.

I sunk back onto my bags to think, to sort out things in my head. It was possible I was in a dream, but I'd never had a dream go on for so long and have so many scenes and details. No, I was definitely shipwrecked. And I was injured. I pinched my cheek. It hurt.

She filled a cup with tea. It was the same kind as before, but didn't seem as strong. Had the young woman stayed with me this whole time? Did she say it had been two days since my accident? I couldn't remember her name. Had she told me her name?

"Shenoa," she said softly, picking up some cedar strips, and a woven square. I studied her as she threaded strands of cedar in and out of others, carefully tightening them in an intricate pattern.

"Your family will be missing you, Shenoa."

"No, they will not. I am often away, caring for people, or collecting plants for my medicines."

I remembered having a nasty fall on the path from the clearing. I remembered her appearing out of nowhere in the trees. I didn't mean to take advantage of her kindness. What had I said to her? Everything in my head was mixed up. It was like a notebook with pages missing, and illegible scribbles all over the pages that remained.

"Why are you helping me?"

She put the weaving down. "Because you are family."

"That makes no sense."

"You do not remember talking to me about your birth mother?" she asked. "You said you could not remember her."

"I remember her well enough," I snapped back.

"Tell me what you know of her then."

She picked up her weaving again and quietly examined her last section of work.

My eyes stung. This conversation was going to a place that always upset me.

"Her eyes were like mine. When she rode her horse, she didn't like to use a saddle and her hair floated out behind her like a long, beautiful mane. And she had a way with animals."

I stopped. My chin was quivering. A single tear came out of nowhere and ran down my cheek. I quickly brushed it away. I knew so little about my mother. I had one piece of beaded leather that belonged to her and nothing more.

"I can't remember her because I was too young. She died of a fever when I was little."

"That's what you were told. That is not what happened."

"How do you know? You don't even know me!"

Raising my voice hurt my head. I wouldn't do that again. My chest also hurt, but from a different pain, one from a very long time ago.

"You said it yourself. It's time you accepted the truth."

"What do I know? Tell me then. Tell me what I said I should accept."

"Ask your mama."

"Another riddle. You mean ask the one you say didn't die from the fever? Ask that one?"

"I mean the mama who raised you. She knows."

My mouth opened but I was unable to form any more words. I drifted off, watching light and shadows play on the side of her face.

I awoke in the dark to the wonderful smell of roasting fish. Shenoa was working over the fire.

"You're still here."

"Yes, and it is very good that you remember me now."

"What day is it?" I had lost track.

"It is a good day to be well," she said.

I sat up and touched the back of my head. The bump was almost gone. The place where it had been was still tender to touch when I pressed my finger on it. My ankle didn't hurt at all. Both of my feet were in the wool socks I had made.

"Did you put these on me?" I pulled the left sock down. My ankle was streaked with purple and black, but no longer swollen.

"You have many questions. You put those on yesterday. You were telling me about your friend Cook and his writing book. I taught you some recipes. Do you not remember these things?"

I did not. But in the back of my mind, I had a sense of cooking over the fire. And I recalled her recipe for bannock.

"This bump on the head was horrible," I said. "It scrambled my head like breakfast eggs."

She laughed. "Do you remember doing this with bird eggs yesterday to make Cook's… what did you call them… clam fritters?"

My blank expression answered her question.

"No matter. It will all come back to you in time. Now. Let's have some of this salmon that Eagle brought us."

Eagle. A faint memory floated like a feather drifting to earth. She had gone to the beach. She had returned with a good-sized fish, claiming that Eagle had provided for us. Flying low over the water, he had snatched a salmon from the ocean and dropped it in front of her.

"Where's Mr. Jones?" I asked as we enjoyed our salmon and bannock.

"Outside. I gave him a piece with the skin."

"Oh, he'll enjoy that. Fishy things are his favorite."

Her thoughts were on something else. She hesitated, as if almost changing her mind.

"Tomorrow, I will go. You do not need me anymore."

"You can't go yet! My head is still too muddled. I won't know what to do."

"You must listen carefully now, so you will remember. You can remember if you try." She stopped and waited for me to agree. "When you are well, you will pack a bag and climb the trail again. You must help the man in the clearing so his spirit may rest."

"Oh no. No way. I'm not going near him."

"He will not harm you. Mr. Jones will be at your side."

"You want me to…"

"Give him a place to rest."

This was asking way too much.

"But I'm not well enough…"

"You will be soon. You are the only one who can help him."

"Why me? Why can't you? I'm getting another headache."

She didn't acknowledge my protests and complaints. I pouted for at least a minute.

"Promise you will do this for the man. You will understand why soon enough."

"All right! I promise!"

"Good. When you have done this, you will go to the end of the clearing. You will find the trail begins again behind the little house. Stay in the direction of the setting sun. It will only take a few hours, but you will need to be well for the journey as the trail is very difficult. On the other side of the island, you will find a lighthouse."

"A lighthouse? I'm on Deception Island!" I sat up much too fast for my woozy head. "It's the lighthouse island and there's a keeper."

"Yes. The keeper of the light will see you get home. She is a friend. But you must wait to do all of this until your foot is strong and your head is clear. You will know when it's time. I will leave medicine."

"Can't you stay until it's time? Can't you go with me?"

"I cannot. You do not need me. *You know what to do.*"

That phrase. From Papa at the corral. From Mr. Jones on the *Salish Wind* before it sank.

"How can you be so sure?"

"It is what they tell me."

"Who?"

"The ancestors. Who sent me."

36

i

I woke up with the sun streaming in through the open flap of the cave.

"Shenoa?"

Mr. Jones sat up beside me.

"Where have you been, Bubba? I've been looking for you."

A lot had happened. Memories swirled around in my head like puzzle pieces thrown into the air. But when I closed my eyes, I could see pieces fall and click into place, one by one.

Mr. Jones nudged my hand and pushed the cooking pot with his nose. I laughed and reached for a bundled of sticks and dry wood. The fire had dwindled to embers. I sat up and fanned it back to life.

"Still the keeper of the fire, good boy."

The keeper. Shenoa had told me about the lighthouse on the other side of the island. I remembered the dead man in the clearing, on the path across Deception Island.

I stuck my legs out on the ledge by the fire and steadied myself against the rock wall. I couldn't remember how long it had been since I had stood. Days? Weeks? My left foot wobbled. It wasn't ready to handle too much weight on it. I took a careful step. It didn't hurt. I leaned against the rock face and took in the beauty of the peaceful cove.

"Shenoa!" I called out. She was gone—I knew she was—and she was not coming back. I probably would never see her again. She had returned to her family, wherever they were.

I remembered pleading with her not to go.

"I am such a child sometimes. I nearly kill myself out of silly fear, and then expect her to stay and wait on me head and foot?" I remembered the scrambled eggs and how we'd laughed.

The air was fresh and slightly cool. Puffy clouds dabbled the blue sky. A hint of fall rode the breeze, the smell of fallen leaves and withered grasses. The season was changing. Time was running out for my cave at the beach.

I had to think for myself now. The first thing to do was to get the strength back in my foot. I would start with little walks and build it up gradually. Once it was healed, and I could walk to the north point and back without pain or swelling, I'd be ready to tackle the hike over the hill to the lighthouse.

Mr. Jones was having a nap on my warm spot when I crawled back into the cave. Everything in the cave was exactly how I'd left it. Shenoa had been there, but no trace of her remained. No cedar strips left behind. No tiny shavings dropped on the rock floor. The basket she was weaving was gone. It was as if she had never been there caring for me at all.

An herbal compress was drying by the fire. I didn't make that. My left riding boot had a slice in the leather. I couldn't have removed my own boot. Bannock from last night's meal was piled on a plank of cedar. I didn't know the recipe. Or at least, I hadn't known the recipe until we made it together.

"It feels like a dream, Mr. Jones. But it wasn't. I would be dead on that trail if she hadn't come along."

Mr. Jones dismissed my bewilderment with a sigh and resumed his nap.

I spent the rest of the day planning. I took fifty steps on my left foot before I noticed swelling. Shenoa had told me to put it in the ocean, so at high tide, I sat on a rock and dangled my foot into the chilly water. After, I applied the compress, which would aid the healing.

That night, I pulled out Cook's notebook. I found his Clam Fritter recipe, the one I'd made for us, using birds' eggs and fresh clams dug on the beach. Shenoa must have got the clams. I couldn't have.

I took out Cook's pencil and turned to a blank page. Bannock. I wrote the title in the neatest letters possible. It took me a long time to form the words. Recording the recipe made my eyes ache.

Over the coming days while my foot was healing, I was going to add all I had learned from Shenoa about plants and recipes to Cook's collection. I knew Cook would approve. No, it would delight him that his love of food and the abundance of the land had rubbed off on me.

By now, Cook would believe I'd been lost at sea aboard the *Salish Wind*. He'd feel responsible for letting me sail with him. Mizzy. It would break her heart to have had me back, only to lose me all over again. And Jake. I'd already faked my death once. This time wasn't my fault, but I remember how crushed he'd been when he thought I'd died.

I had to get to the lighthouse. I had to get well, get home and set things right.

Each day after meals, I worked on improving my ankle. It tested my patience. I had twisted it so badly I thought I'd broken it. Shenoa told me the bones were strong, but it would take weeks to get the purple, blue, and yellow to drain from the flesh.

"C'mon, Mr. Jones. It is time to walk," I'd say. Mr. Jones, always enthusiastic about going on any exploration beyond the cave, would run ahead, behind and around me, taking one hundred steps to my every ten. When I walked, I remembered what Papa taught me to do for a lame horse: Walk them in the corral, just a few laps to start and with no rider. Each day, add a little more to keep them working and improving. If handled properly, a horse would be back to galloping on an uneven field within weeks. A pain shot up the outside of my leg. Push the horse too hard or too fast, and you'll end up having to start over.

My foot was actually less of a worry than my head. After my daily exercises, I worked on organizing my thoughts. Although the bump was entirely gone, and there was no visible mark to see or feel, the thoughts in my head had been dropped like a box of colorful beads. Everything was out of order and mixed up. I'd misplaced so many memories. When I tried to string together all the things that had happened since I set sail from San Francisco, I found it difficult to remember the order of things. I lost time. Or at least badly muddled it. Mr. Jones had to listen to me try to untangle it all. I wrote my recollections into my notebook and reviewed them every day.

"The *Salish Wind* set sail on July 29, 1859. Good. I have that to start. Now then, when did the pirates sink the ship?" I looked to Mr. Jones for help. "August, you say? But what day?"

He sat up and scratched his neck thoughtfully.

"How long have we been cast away on this island?" Something in the logical part of my brain tried to come to my assistance. "The weaker sun and the cooling temperatures mean summer is almost over. So we can be sure that a few weeks have passed."

And then there was the accident. How many days did Shenoa stay, tending to my injuries? Was it three days? No, five? I couldn't say and had no way of even asking.

The questions swirled around and around in my head until I thought they would make me crazy. I had no answers. The harder I tried to remember, the more tangled the memories became. I couldn't force them to return. But when I put my mind on other things, I found memories would mysteriously reappear. Just one day earlier, I'd sat on the beach repairing my leather boot. As I stitched the leather back together, I saw Shenoa applying an herbal pack to my bare foot. I knew how to make it.

But while something like that would suddenly make sense, I still had so many fragments of broken memories in pieces around me. I tried to sort them and glue them back together, but chunks were missing. It was like a giant puzzle I was trying to put together without knowing what the full picture was supposed to look like.

I thought of living with Papa on the Miller ranch, working with the horses, growing up with Jake. What was it about my mother? I couldn't find that piece. Miss Molly was my mama. *Don't call her that*, a voice said. Mama? *No, Miss Molly. She's Mizzy.*

I thought of going to live in San Francisco with Uncle Jack after Papa died. Then Uncle took off and left me with crooks on my tail. Did I really come all this way to find the gold claim Uncle had won in a poker game? I did. Jake found out there was no such mine. It wasn't registered. Jake had come north on the *Sonoma Wind*, and sailed home ahead of us. We sailed for home on August 13. It was Saturday, August 13.

Then there was Cook. I had his notebook. And Kuno, whose dog was now with me, and Drak, who had lost his life saving mine when the ship was attacked. And Mr. Miller's two schooners. And the San Francisco underground.

The pirates and the gold! I'd made a promise to Cook. My first assignment was to see Mr. Miller's gold made it safely to San Francisco. I'd forgotten about the pirates. They might return any day.

"We're getting off this island, Mr. Jones. And I swear I will get that gold back to its rightful owner."

37

i

The day I picked to make my trek was sunny and clear. I stood on the beach with Mr. Jones and checked the sky in all directions for signs of cloud. Not a trace of white in the blue. It was a good day to go. The thought of the expedition made me nervous, but I wouldn't let myself put it off one more day. I knew I was ready.

I chose my smaller canvas bag for the trip and fashioned shoulder straps out of rope in order to carry it on my back. Since I couldn't take everything on this first trip, I laid all of my belongings out, and made two piles—what was necessary for a day trip and what wasn't. Then I challenged myself to pick only ten items from the necessary pile. Since my accident had left me somewhat unsteady on my feet and quick to tire, I had to mind the weight of my pack.

I dressed in layers to be prepared for weather. Into my bag went a blanket, a piece of canvas, my rain gear, extra clothes, some rope, the hatchet, the flint kit, a full canteen of water, and food. At the last minute, I packed Cook's galley book and my own notebook, telling myself they were necessary to divide up the weight of all my belongings. Out of habit, I put my Papa's knife in my trouser pocket. It might be a tool or a weapon, but I hoped it would be nothing more than a lucky charm.

I returned all the things I was leaving behind to my duffle bag and stowed it as far back in the cave as possible. I stacked kindling, wood and the rest of my cave supplies with it, in case things didn't work out and I needed to move back in. If I could stay at the lighthouse, I'd come back for the rest of my things when I was able.

Once I was ready to go, I covered the fire pit. I couldn't imagine letting the fire go out altogether. My fire had burned every day since I'd rescued coals from the pirates' bonfire on the beach. It had become a strange friend.

I set out early, taking my time and picking my way through the trees until I came to the cross-island trail that led west to the clearing. Mr. Jones, who had been frolicking along in his usual way, now fell into an even stride behind me. This route marked something serious and he sensed it. He kept his nose to the ground, sniffing the trail as if someone or something had recently walked ahead of us.

The first leg of the trail felt vaguely familiar. Within twenty minutes, we arrived at the T in the path, where it intersected the woodland trail that led to the field of oats and camas. Mindful of my footing, I carried on and climbed the hill.

I hesitated in the bush before stepping into the clearing at the top, partly to catch my breath, partly to brace myself for the scene. The fright I'd had and my panicked flight from the place churned in my memory. It would take all my courage to walk all the way through the clearing to the cedar hut. I straightened up and pushed on before I could lose my nerve.

Half way across the clearing, I had an eerie feeling that someone was watching me from behind. I spun around. Nobody was there. My mind was playing games with me. I took a deep breath and exhaled it slowly, trying to calm my fluttering heart.

Don't be afraid, I heard Shenoa say. The memory of her calmed me, like an unexpected warm breeze. I willed myself forward again. Mr. Jones stayed so close to my right leg that he bumped his head every time I took a step.

I did not look over to the tall tree where I'd seen the body. I steeled myself and walked past, knowing the dead man was only a few dozen steps away. Finally, we reached the other end of the clearing. I found where the path continued behind the building and we disappeared into the trees.

I exhaled loudly, shaking off the prickling sensation crawling through my hair and over my skin.

"That wasn't so bad."

But saying it didn't make it true. As we set out again, a big knot formed in my stomach. To make matters worse, Mr. Jones was bothered. He ran back and forth behind me on the path. After about ten minutes, I couldn't take it anymore. I stopped to clear my mind and think. Mr. Jones turned and headed back toward the clearing until he was almost out of sight.

"No! Don't leave me!" I didn't expect him to decide he wouldn't go with me to the lighthouse. "Stay!" I said. I couldn't bear to be alone.

He stopped in the path. I took out a bit of bannock and fish for us to share as a snack. The sight of food seemed to change his mind for a few minutes. He came back and sat patiently as I divided a bundle of food for the two of us.

Just as I had talked myself into thinking everything was fine, an eagle cried out high above the forest. It circled above the clearing. I shot to my feet in horror.

"I forgot to help the dead man! I told Shenoa I'd take care of him. Why did I say I'd do that? This is a disaster!"

I paced the trail for several minutes, questioning why I'd told her I'd bury the man, and debating whether I had the nerve to do it. Mr. Jones waited for me to sort myself out.

"I don't know what happens now, but I made a promise." He cricked his head to one side and it came to me. "You tried to tell me."

I looked up at the sky peeking through the trees. I held my head in my hands, and ran fingers through my dirty hair.

"My head doesn't work the way it used to. I can't keep anything straight anymore. It is so frustrating!" I looked at Mr. Jones, who was sitting quietly, waiting for me to calm down. I paced back and forth a few more times. When I stopped, he was sitting on the path heading back to the clearing.

"Well, of course, we're going back." Mr. Jones got up and started walking. "Go ahead and say it—I told you so."

I stuffed the rest of our snack into my pocket and we retraced our steps.

As soon as I entered the clearing, my eyes locked onto the tree.

"I've seen dead people before. This is no different." Mr. Jones said he'd seen enough to last a lifetime himself.

I knew nothing about digging graves, but I'd been to my share of funerals where people respectfully laid flowers and said very nice things about people they didn't even really know. If I was this man, I'd appreciate someone laying me to rest and saying some nice things about me. I didn't want to look at him, but at the same time, my eyes were drawn to the horror.

He'd been there a while. Mostly just a skeleton now. Tufts of grey hair. Tattered clothing, badly weathered.

I plunged my shovel into the earth beside his body.

"I don't know who you are, mister, or what happened to you, but I'm real sorry it ended this way for you, all alone."

Although the soil was soft and easy to dig, my shovel was small. I had to settle for a hole about a foot deep. The worst part was moving the body into the grave. When I pushed a leg bone with my shovel, it separated from the rest. I felt like running again.

A voice in my head stopped me. *What if he was your papa or your friend?* It wasn't Mr. Jones speaking to me this time. He sat solemnly in front of the new grave, like a pastor waiting to deliver the sermon.

I summoned my courage. The man had been wearing a tweed coat. I picked it up and transferred most of his bones into the hole. I used my shovel to add the remaining pieces where they belonged.

As I covered the body with dirt, a small notebook fell out of the inside pocket of the man's coat. The paper had disintegrated, pages ruined by weather, but the cloth cover still had its gilded gold trim. It gave me no clue who he was or what he was doing on the top of this island. I placed it back where I'd found it.

When I was finished, I said a few words I remembered from other funerals, and added a special comment about him being a man who loved books. I figured he'd appreciate the personal touch. I would have, if it were me. Then I recited a prayer Mizzy would say when she tucked me into bed when I was little. I was surprised I remembered the exact words without trying.

I brushed off my knees and hands and backed away, pack in hand. I imagined the man's spirit scattering like the seeds of a dandelion, dozens of white, fluffy umbrellas floating up and away in the summer air. I wasn't afraid anymore.

Mr. Jones waited for me by the cedar hut. He fell in behind me with no more fuss and we walked together quietly for quite a long time. I ruffled the fur on his head.

"You are one smart dog. You knew I'd forgotten my promise. What I can't figure out is how you knew."

Mr. Jones pretended he didn't understand. He wasn't going to tell.

The trail continued its gradual climb, ending on an exposed bluff on the highest point of the island. Vancouver Island wasn't far off to the northwest. In front of me, the sea stretched as far as the eye could see. Down on the far southwestern tip of the island, alone on a bleak, rocky point, stood a tall, white lighthouse.

I surveyed the distance left to go. If I was an eagle, I could coast down there in fifteen minutes. But I had to wend my way down through the dense forest and scrabble over steep, rock faces. It would be slow and challenging.

The first part of the hike hadn't been too hard. But grave digging on top of it had worn me out. Since hitting my head, I tired easily. I dropped my pack and sat in the shade to rest. Sometime later, Mr. Jones nudged me and I scrambled to my feet. I'd dangerously fallen asleep in the middle of nowhere.

The trail I'd followed appeared to end at the bluff. If I ever hoped to find my way back to the spot, I had to mark the way. Papa had taught me how to set up trail markers when riding in the bush. I'd learned to snap branches in certain ways or use natural objects to indicate direction. The skill was going to come in handy, since I couldn't trust myself to remember the way. I pulled a handful of clamshells out of my bag.

"To the lighthouse, then, Mr. Jones," I said. I picked a friendly opening in the bush and we started our descent.

38

i

Within an hour, we had reached the barren bluffs that sur-rounded the lighthouse. A woman was working in the yard, back turned to me, hanging wash out on a line that ran from a little white shed to a crooked arbutus tree. The blinking lighthouse towered beside a square wooden cottage.

"I don't want to sneak up on her. She won't be expecting a girl and a dog to come marching out of nowhere. We have to let her know we are coming. Perhaps some friendly barking from you would help on this occasion."

Mr. Jones looked indignant, as if such a request was beneath him. I patted his hindquarters and we continued on.

Seagulls rode the warm afternoon breeze as we crossed an uneven field of grass and rocks to the lighthouse. The wind behind me felt like a friendly hand on my back, helping me over the final stretch.

When I figured I was within hailing distance, I shouted. "Hellooooo!"

The woman stopped to listen. She wore a brown jacket with big, sagging pockets, and pants tucked into rubber boots. A white apron was tied around her pear-shaped frame. Her short, silver hair whipped around her face as she looked right and left. Not seeing us, she took a couple of clothespins from her mouth and clipped a towel to the line.

"The wind is stealing my voice, Mr. Jones."

I waited until we were almost all the way across the field and called out again.

"Hellooooo, lightkeeper!"

As she spun about, I waved my arms back and forth over my head. I hadn't noticed the rifle leaning against her wash basket. She pointed it at me, then at Mr. Jones, then back at me. I stopped flapping my arms and held them still, hands high in the air.

"Don't shoot!" I hollered.

"Where in tarnation did you come from?" she said. "What's your business here?"

"May I come forward, ma'am?" I asked. "It is just me and my dog."

Mr. Jones growled and I shushed him under my breath, hoping she hadn't heard. "We are friendly," I said, but wasn't really sure if this applied to Mr. Jones.

"Come on over then. Slowly now, so I can get a good look at you."

I took one step, then another, keeping an eye on her trigger finger.

"You can walk faster than that. I haven't got all day," she said, shifting from one leg to the other.

"Sorry. Do you think you could point that gun somewhere else? It makes me nervous."

She was squinting now, taking me in, sizing up her invader. As I got closer, her expression softened.

"Why, you're just a lad," she said, lowering the barrel of her rifle. "And that's a Salishan wool dog."

I set down my pack without making any sudden moves.

"I've been on the other side of this island, alone for... for weeks. I'm Charlee LeBeau."

"Mrs. Dalworth. Lighthouse keeper," she said, as I moved closer. "Good heavens, you're a lass! How the dickens did you get here, Carly?"

"It's Charlee, ma'am."

"Charlee. Right then. Come on to the house. I'll put the kettle on. Are you hungry? You can tell me everything while I fix you something."

My head spun. Uncle used to talk like this lady, a bit too loud and barely taking a breath. Most of the time, Uncle waxed poetic about what he'd do when he won the big jackpot. This Mrs. Dalworth wasn't like that, but she was obviously fond of conversation.

"Your dog is welcome inside. I had a dog myself when I was a lass. We were inseparable, we was. Oh, I still miss him. A border collie. Used to herd the sheep. But his favorite was rounding up the children at the church picnic." She laughed. "He was a wonderful dog, friendly as can be. What's this fella's name?"

"Mr. Jones."

"Well, Mr. Jones. There's a nice rug by the stove. I think your old bones might enjoy that spot. I'll fetch ya some water."

Mr. Jones lay down and closed his eyes. I hadn't really thought of him as being old. Did I know how old he was? Had Kuno told me? I was too tired to remember.

Mrs. Dalworth added split cedar to her fire, and it burst to life with snaps and crackles. Then she filled a kettle and plunked it on her stove. It clanged on the iron top, echoing inside my skull. I sat down in a chair by the door and cradled my head in my hands. The trip across the island, burying the dead man, all the sudden noise—it was too much. The room was blurry when I looked up. My stomach rolled.

"Lass, you're white as bloomers on a clothesline. You're not well, are ya? You need to lie down."

"If you don't mind, I think I will. I'm very tired."

She helped me over to a bunk behind the stove and pulled off my riding boots. She was as kind as Shenoa said she would be.

"Ya know horses then, do ya lass?"

"Yes." I leaned back slowly so as not to rattle my aching head.

"Not a lot o' horses in these parts."

"I have a horse called Magic. On a ranch in California."

"California! You're a long way from home. Hush now. You rest. Unless you have somewhere else you're supposed to be?"

"I... no. No place."

Mr. Jones abandoned his soft rug and curled up on the bare floor beneath me.

"Loyal dog you got there. How'd you come by him?"

"Long story." I slurred my words. She covered me with a brightly-colored patchwork quilt.

The bunk mattress was soft and comfortable. I closed my eyes and drifted in and out of sleep. I was on the raft again. Then the sounds of the homestead kitchen—spoon clinking on china, knife striking a cutting board, chair legs scraping a wood floor, dishes being placed on a wood table—kept pulling me back. They were so soothing and familiar. I tried to think about nothing and listened to Mrs. Dalworth go about her business in the kitchen. It was like she was playing beautiful music.

"Come now, lass," she said sometime later. "Can ya manage a seat at the table? You could stand some nourishment, you're such a waif."

"I feel much better," I said, as she helped me stand.

A pot of tea, baked scones, and jam were on the table. She poured tea into a lovely china cup and placed it in front of me.

"I put a little honey in the bottom, so give it a wee stir. It'll perk you up."

The tea reminded me of faraway countries. The Missus served special teas like this in her parlor. Papa liked tea, too, and we often had a cup in the evening just like this, but in plain mugs.

"It's very good, thank you."

"So let's start at the beginning since we were not formally introduced," she said. "I'll go first because my story is short. The government built this lighthouse because too many ships were running aground and sinking off that long string of hidden rocks."

Submerged rocks were everywhere around this island. It was a nightmare for mariners.

"This is Deception Island, right?"

"Right. Got its name, they say, because of how it tricks so many sailors. My husband, Edgar, was appointed by the governor himself, if you please. I lost him at sea a few months ago…"

I thought I would choke on a mouthful of scone. "He was…?"

"… lost at sea. Went out in the rowboat one afternoon and never came back. When I saw the capsized rowboat drift by, I knew he was gone."

She paused, her smile fading away with the quiver of her chin. She slurped a bit of tea and dabbed the corner of each eye with her apron. After a moment, she steeled herself and resumed her story.

"The very day he was lost, I took over tending the lighthouse. All the boats coming through this passage weren't going to stop because Edgar had disappeared. Nobody even knows he's gone but me. They only come out here quarterly, you see. Well anyhow, I knew how to do it. Edgar taught me how to mind the lantern. We'd always worked side by side, he and I."

She stopped to eat some scone. "Do you like my black-berry jam?"

"Very much. It's all delicious."

She put her teacup down and continued. "So when the government boat comes to bring supplies at the end of September, they'll find out Edgar is gone. They'll want to get a new light-keeper, but I'll say, 'Where am I going to go?' I got no place else to go. Anyway, since I've been doing the job for a couple of months, and doing it properly, they should let me stay on. I'm the first woman lightkeeper and mighty proud of it, I'm not ashamed to tell you. It's a bit lonely out here though, without Edgar. Now. What's your story, lass?"

The sudden quiet in the room was jarring. I cleared my throat.

"I don't know where to start. So much has happened."

"Well, how about I just ask some questions, get you warmed up, and we'll see where it goes?"

"All right."

"Where are you from?"

"Where was I born? Or do you mean where do I live?"

"Good Lord! It wasn't supposed to be a trick question. Let's try again. Where were you before this?"

"Victoria. I mean, San Francisco. Before that, Sonoma. Oregon when I was little..." My voice trailed off. Where was I born though? I couldn't remember.

"What in God's green earth are you doing all the way up here in the British colonies?"

"I was a cabin boy on a merchant schooner."

"A cabin boy," she repeated.

"Yes."

She paused to consider this.

"And where is that merchant schooner now?"

I didn't answer. I was picturing the shipwreck, all the horrific murders.

"Lass..."

"What day is it today?"

"It's September 15. I hope ya still know what year you're in." She raised a greying eyebrow.

September? The *Salish Wind* left Fort Victoria on August 13. Over a month had passed.

Mrs. Dalworth smoothed a linen napkin with her hands. Finally, she laid it on the table, neatly folded, and looked at me sternly.

"Since you have appeared out of nowhere, I think you better come clean. How did you get to this island?"

I owed her an explanation. As I told the story, my memories got tangled up. Keeping facts straight in my mind was exhausting. I told her how the *Salish Wind* left Fort Victoria, how we were followed and attacked by pirates, how Mr. Jones and I escaped the sinking schooner on a raft I'd built.

Mrs. Dalworth's eyes narrowed. "That is quite a tale. Storybook, almost."

I knew it sounded far-fetched.

"I had a terrible fall, here on the island. I get dizzy sometimes and a little confused."

"That explains a lot." I was pretty sure she assumed I'd made the whole story up. "You'll stay with me. We'll get you sorted."

When Mrs. Dalworth excused herself to tend the lighthouse, I returned to the cozy bunk behind the stove. I pulled my wool blanket out of my pack and made a spot for Mr. Jones to sleep.

I was almost asleep when she came back in the door. The wind snatched it out of her hands and caused it to slam. I saw the lumber load coming loose and rolling down on top of me. I screamed and flew off the bunk. Mrs. Dalworth grabbed me and held me tight.

"You're all right, lass. There, there. You're safe now. Mrs. Dalworth will take care of you."

39

i

It had been months since I'd slept in a real bed. When I woke up the next morning, Mrs. Dalworth was in the kitchen with breakfast ready. Mr. Jones was supervising underfoot.

"Good morning, lass. I've got coffee for ya on the table. I'm hoping a good sleep set you right."

I'd woken up feeling pretty good and was keen to get outside and do something. Mrs. Dalworth told me the supply boat was due in two weeks or so and I could get passage back to Fort Victoria. That gave me a little time to figure out what to do when I got there and how I was going to get back to San Francisco.

Over breakfast, we got talking about how I ended up on Deception Island.

"Whatever possessed you to take a job on a merchant schooner in the first place?"

"My uncle was a gambler and a bit of a loan shark. One night he hit it big. He won shares in what looked to be a gold mine. I had to get out of San Francisco because it wasn't safe there, so I decided I'd come north to find the company myself. But it didn't pan out."

"What you lack in judgment, you make up for with courage, I'll give ya that."

"The thing feels like it's cursed. I was heading back to San Francisco like every other broken bum on a get-rich-quick scheme, and I end up shipwrecked, of all things."

I told her how the pirates had followed us and attacked the ship when we ran aground in the fog, how we sank on the eastern shore, and how Mr. Jones and I were the only survivors.

"Pirates," she said. "Never heard o' pirates in these waters. I heard of a lost schooner, August sometime. Never found a trace of her. Lost somewhere at sea, they figured."

"The *Salish Wind*. That was her name," I said. "They killed some of the crew. I saw them. The rest are missing. Probably went down with the ship."

I felt tears well up in my eyes and I tried to will them away. This time, I couldn't stop them. Mrs. Dalworth sat back in disbelief. But Mr. Jones remembered the horror. He pressed himself against my leg and tucked himself between my feet.

I mentioned the young Indian woman who had helped me after my fall and Mrs. Dalworth said, "But there's nobody else here…" Then, after giving it some thought, she said, "Although this time of year, the Lekwungen come to fish and forage." She patted my arm thoughtfully.

I didn't want to talk anymore. The conversation made me sad and everything I said sounded so far-fetched even I wouldn't believe it if someone was telling me the story. I wiped my tears away and pulled myself together.

"There, there, dear. You've been through quite the ordeal, that's for certain." Mrs. Dalworth handed me a handkerchief. At least she believed the part about the shipwreck.

I thought it best not to talk about Shenoa and how she had stayed with me for days until I was well. If she didn't believe pirates had attacked the *Salish Wind*, she wasn't about to believe that an Indian woman who claimed her ancestors had sent her had saved my life. And I couldn't tell her about the dead man in the clearing either. It was all too much.

I thought it best to keep my mouth shut about pirates, corpses, and ancestors. I definitely wasn't going to mention Mr. Miller's gold. It could stay buried forever, as far as I was concerned.

After breakfast, I helped her with some easy chores in the yard. I did my best to give her the impression that I was fine. No staring off into the clouds, no glum face or slumped posture. As I worked, I caught her sneaking peeks at me, like she thought I might run screaming off the nearby cliff. She stayed close by me, obviously not ready to let me out of her sight. To be fair, I wouldn't have trusted me myself.

"She thinks I'm not right in the head. I hope she isn't right," I said to Mr. Jones. Insisting I mustn't overdo it, she'd given me the mindless job of weeding around the chicken coop. Mr. Jones was soon bored and set off to explore the yard, busying himself with digging at the ground and sniffing little dirt creatures out of their homes.

When I finished the weeding, she had me fill a box on her porch with kindling. As I made my first trip with an armful that weighed next to nothing, she leaned on her garden shovel and hollered, "Smaller loads!"

"I can manage. I'm fine," I called back.

She wagged her finger. I sighed and obeyed.

It relieved me that Mrs. Dalworth was in the habit of ending work at three in the afternoon for tea. Even though my jobs weren't hard and we'd stopped for a hearty bowl of vegetable soup at lunch, I'd had enough tottering around. An old familiar headache rolled in with the fog swirling around the base of the lighthouse.

"I've got one final job for ya," she said, taking the tea cozy off her pot. I lifted my heavy head, thinking my offer to work might have been a mistake. "After tea, you're going to have a good long soak in my big tub. I've got pails on the stove warming water for ya."

A wash in warm water wasn't a chore at all. It was a luxury. I hadn't been in a proper bath since Taitai's laundry in San Francisco. I couldn't wait.

"A lass has to mind her grooming, even one that dresses up as a lad to crew on a ship. That's mighty crafty, if I do say so myself. Not so sure you could get away with it much longer though." Her eyes dropped to my chest for a moment and she gave me a knowing look. I blushed.

"Do you prefer your hair long, or do you want it short like mine? Edgar didn't fancy long hair. What a blessing! Said long hair was a hazard and made him sneeze. I was lucky to have him, I tell you. Seems your hair can't decide if it wants to be long or short. You just let me know—I can trim it up for ya if you like."

"I don't know, but a bath sounds wonderful. I'll use the water to wash my clothes after. They smell like a campfire."

"You leave those to me. I'll wash them up and hang them in the breeze. In the meantime, I'll give you one of Edgar's shirts and a pair of trousers. Edgar wasn't a big man. About your size. May as well wear his things. No point leaving them in a drawer for the moths."

Later that evening, after a supper of smoked fish and vegetables, we retired to a pair of rocking chairs in front of the fireplace. Mrs. Dalworth picked up a very worn Bible and started to read. I watched silently, with Mr. Jones snoozing in my lap, as her eyes stumbled over the lines and she adjusted a pair of glasses that didn't seem to help her very much.

She put her finger on a spot and looked up. "Can you read then, lass?"

"Yes. I went to school on the ranch. I have two reading books, but they're with the rest of my things on the other side of the island."

I remembered I had to hike back to my cave to get the rest of my belongings before the supply boat came. The distance wasn't far, but the trek was tough. It would take all day to go there and back, and a round trip like that was still too much for me. I hoped I had enough time to get my strength back before the supply boat showed up.

"Edgar's got some books over there. You can help yourself. I've got no interest in them myself. The traders won't give me anything for them either, all science, numbers and the like. I've been trying to get my hands on something by one of the Brontë gals, but so far no luck."

I put Mr. Jones down by the fire and surveyed the titles. I didn't recognize any of them. No fiction books among them. All very advanced reference material.

"Who are the traders?" I asked, picking out an interesting book called *The Elements of Geometry and Trigonometry*.

"The traders stop in when the weather is good. They bring food and things they get up and down the coast. I can get whatever I need." Her voice trailed off. "And so I barter and swap."

"What do you trade?" I asked, and then noting her silence, thought it was a question that was probably none of my business.

"Well, you'll find out soon enough because I could use your help, if you're up to it."

She looked around, as if others might be in the room listening, and then said, "I make wine in that little barn where my root cellar is. It's in demand. Don't touch the stuff myself though. Well, the odd snort for medicinal purposes. Last thing I need is to get lost in drink out here alone on the rocks."

"You peddle moonshine?" I asked, astonished that this Bible-reading woman was making liquor on government land.

"Heavens! It's not moonshine. What do you take me for? I'm a vintner, if you please."

"Sorry. You peddle wine then?"

Mrs. Dalworth bristled. "A lightkeeper's wage would make a frugal person sweat trying to stretch a penny. Some thanks we get for keeping the light on and saving lives. With my business on the side, I can get things the supply boat never has. I trade for butter, sugar, yeast, seeds for my garden—all kinds of nice things."

"But liquor? I've seen how men carry on when they have too much of it. They fight and steal. Sometimes they manhandle women and sometimes they even kill."

"Aye, but ya have to ask if it is the liquor that makes the man, or the man that makes the liquor."

I puzzled over that. She continued.

"Some men have bad blood. Liquor brings out the worst in them. They're not likely to want my wine if they're fixing to go on a bender. Those aren't my customers. But if they were, it's not my place to judge."

"My uncle was one of them with bad blood. Drinking made him worse. I'll judge him to the end of the earth."

"That book make any sense to ya?" She thumped the open pages as she passed my chair.

"I can follow most of it."

"Huh. Clever lass, are ya? Put a log on that a fire while I tend the light. Tomorrow I'll show you my wine operation. With your help, I'll have my bottles laid away in no time."

40

i

Mrs. Dalworth and I worked over four days, sterilizing bottles in boiling water and then siphoning off the wine from the vats into the clean bottles. Each full bottle had to be carefully sealed with sterilized cloth and hot wax.

"We are ready for your traders," I said when we had all the bottles filled, sealed, labeled and shelved.

"Oh no. These aren't going anywhere. This is next year's batch. I'll be trading last year's vintage, the ones in the cellar."

Mr. Miller would appreciate this, I thought, since he'd started a wine operation himself. Uncle had said his wine was some of the best he'd ever tasted. Mr. Miller used the beautiful grapes that ripened on the Sonoma hillsides. Mrs. Dalworth had to settle for the hardy, wild berries that grew in spite of unfriendly soil and weather.

That evening, I announced I felt strong enough to hike back to the cave for the rest of my belongings. The sunset had been clear and stars sparkled in the cloudless sky. The next day promised to be a good one.

"Now lass, you've recovered nicely, which I figure is the result of good rest and fine cooking. You've color in your cheeks again and a little spring in your step. Still, I don't like you going off to the other side of the island on your own. If something happens, I can't come after you."

"Nothing will happen. Besides, Mr. Jones will come with me. It's only about five hours of hiking all in. I promise to take a rest before starting back. If I leave right after breakfast, I'll be back by tea."

Mrs. Dalworth wasn't quite ready to agree. "We'll review the situation in the morning. I have to be sure poor weather won't sneak in on ya."

"I promise I won't go if there is so much as a suspicious haze way off in the distance."

"All right then. I wouldn't know where to send the supply boat fellas to look for you if you didn't come back."

Worry pinched her forehead into deep lines. She was thinking of the day Edgar left. She'd been unable to look for him when he didn't return.

"If you have some paper, I'll draw you a map."

She rummaged in a drawer and pulled out stationery and a long, sharpened pencil. I rolled it around in my hand. All I'd ever used were leftover stubs.

I drew the shape of the island, starting with the rocky point where the lighthouse stood.

"They call it Anguish Point," she said, and I marked the name on the map. "Hidden Cove is just down from the lighthouse, and then Clamity Cove is around the corner on the eastern side, where you came ashore."

"How do you spell Clamity?" I asked, and she told me.

"I've never been to that cove myself, even though it's close by."

I'd placed it much farther away than it was. She took my pencil and moved the southern point closer to the lighthouse.

"Ten minutes by boat. Edgar rowed around to that cove all the time for shellfish. He's the one named it, not just for the clams, but also because a mighty current could pull you out to sea in a jiffy if you weren't minding currents and tides. The day he disappeared, that's where he'd gone."

"Just around the corner?"

"Close enough to spit and have it almost land there. He'd done that trip dozens of times. It was a perfect spring day. Tides were good. Edgar didn't make mistakes. But a sudden wind came outta nowhere and that was that."

It was a heart-breaking story. I wanted to ask what she thought happened to Edgar, if she thought he'd capsized and drowned or if he even knew how to swim. I didn't look up from the map and hoped the painful moment would pass.

I drew in the side I knew well and roughed in the middle of the island where the main trail led to the clearing. I sketched in the western side as I remembered it, looking out from the highest point on the bluff.

"What's to the north?" I asked, pencil poised over the unfinished section. "I couldn't get to the end."

"That's Lekwungen land. They don't live there, but sometimes they camp on the northwest end where it's closest to the big island. They keep to themselves, and to the north half." She drew a dotted line across the middle of the island.

Shenoa must have come from there. I'd seen the natural garden, the land that seemed oddly cultivated. I'd dug up camas and picked blackberries there. Maybe she'd been out gathering herbs in the area when I had my accident.

I drew a zigzag path from the lighthouse up to the bluff, and then east from the bluff to the clearing. I didn't mark the burial site of the unknown man. I called it a clearing with a cedar hut and nothing more. From there, the trail snaked down to Clamity Cove. I drew a sinking ship on the water where the *Salish Wind* had gone down, and put a big X on the spot where I had lived for almost a month in the rock cave.

"If I should disappear, I'll be somewhere along that route. That'll give you a good start at finding my body."

"That's not funny, lass," she said.

She was right. I knew the risks of the island all too well, and they were no laughing matter.

Mr. Jones and I set out for Clamity Cove the next morning just after eight o'clock. The air was salty and a little cool, but the sky was blue in all directions and the sea was calm.

Mrs. Dalworth and I had made a deal. I would go in the morning, weather permitting. After climbing to the top of the lighthouse to survey every horizon, she gave her reluctant approval.

"See you for tea," I said, when a worried look wrinkled her forehead.

"Don't be late," she replied with a brave face. I set out across the field to the trailhead with Mr. Jones trotting along behind me.

That first trek to Mrs. Dalworth's lighthouse seemed like a long time ago. Mr. Jones found the rock pile I'd made to mark the trailhead and we began our climb.

A few times on the way up to the bluff, I had to stop and search for the path. Fortunately, I'd thought to use the clamshell markers on trees. It didn't take too much hunting to find them. When I got temporarily off track, Mr. Jones knew it. He'd put his nose to the ground and hunt for our scent from our recent passage. With our two systems at work, we weren't stumped for long.

We reached the bluff within an hour. I paused for water. To the south, I could see the lighthouse blinking on the point. Trees blocked the northern view of the island coast. The Lekwungen camp was somewhere down there. I wondered if anyone was there, or if they'd left when Shenoa had gone.

The trail from the bluff to the clearing was easy. It was as if a magnet pulled me to it. When we came out of the bush, I glanced over at the fresh mound of dirt marking the shallow grave. I felt like I should stop and pay my respects, but was mindful of the time.

"I'll visit on the way back, mister."

Mr. Jones must have heard because he didn't stop. I followed him through the clearing.

"No skeletons today," I said, oddly relieved as we started down the cross-island path. "Mrs. Dalworth was right. I'm much stronger now than I was when I left here. If all goes well, we'll make it back with time to spare before tea."

At the cove, I set my bag down and took in the familiar view. I felt a powerful kind of comfort but also a dreadful, hollow sadness. It's like going back to a place that was once your home, and even though a lot of bad things happened there, you realized you miss it.

"So this is Clamity Cove. It's a perfect name. No shortage of clams or calamities here."

Hidden Cove and the lighthouse were just around the southern point. It was so close by water, yet Edgar didn't make it back. What had happened to him the day he set out for Clamity Cove? I remembered the wicked current not far off the point. I was almost dragged out to sea myself. If a wind had come up that night on the raft, I wouldn't have made it to shore either.

The fog that clouded my mind since the accident had lifted with each passing day at the lighthouse. Most of the details of the pirate attack, the shipwreck, and my time at the cove had fallen back into place. Standing on the beach where I'd survived, I knew I could start to trust my memory again.

Mr. Jones sniffed out the cave. No surprises inside. I took off my pack and climbed in. It was as exactly as I'd left it, except for a few dead leaves that had blown in. Something about the place felt calm and serene. I sat for a few minutes in the silence, and let the cool dampness refresh me. The ledge at the entrance showed the remains of my fire pit, where hot coals had burned and blackened the rock surface. I crawled over to the darkest end of the cave and retrieved my duffle bag.

"That's a good sign. Exactly where I remember leaving it."

My bag was much lighter than I remembered, but then I'd been very weak for most of the days I'd spent here. I opened it, to remind myself of what I'd left behind. A small woven basket fell out.

"How did this get in here?" It was the little cedar basket that Shenoa had made while I was recuperating. Mr. Jones didn't find it odd and pawed at my rucksack for lunch.

"This wasn't here when she left. I didn't put it in there." The basket felt oddly familiar, but it was as real as I was. I'd almost convinced myself I'd imagined Shenoa. She was real. Everything I remembered was real.

I unpacked lunch and leaned back against the cave wall.

As my memories untangled, I remembered other important things. I still had to get Mr. Miller's gold back to San Francisco. By now, he would believe it was lost with the ship. But I promised Cook I would get it to him. He'd called it my first mission for the railroad.

"I can never tell anyone it's here, Mr. Jones. It's our secret and it stays buried until I can figure out how to get it back to Mr. Miller."

I pulled off a section of sandwich and gave it to Mr. Jones, who sat listening and contemplating my dilemma. Suddenly, he went to the cave entrance and growled. My heart jumped into my throat.

"Who's out there, Bubba?"

I peeked over his shoulder at the cove. The black pirate ship had come into view.

"They're coming for the gold!" I said.

But the sloop didn't stop. It continued south and dropped sails just past the rocky outcrop.

A horrible thought struck me. They were headed for the lighthouse. Mrs. Dalworth was alone and in danger.

41

i

I grabbed my bags and charged up the path leading to the clearing. In less than five minutes, I was breathless. A sharp pain in my side forced me to stop and rest. Sweat burst out on my forehead. I couldn't keep such a frantic pace. On the other side of the island where the trail was difficult, I could miss a marker and lose time getting back on course. Even worse, I could misstep and have another terrible fall.

My duffle bag, which I'd slung over one shoulder, flopped around, thumping against my leg with every step. I quickly rigged shoulder straps so I could carry it on my back. With my belongings no longer a nuisance and a hazard, I set off again at a steady pace, a swift march sprinkled with occasional trots on the flat bits.

As I reached the clearing, I imagined the pirates anchoring in Hidden Cove. There was no quick way back to the lighthouse. Mrs. Dalworth would have to handle them on her own. Even though she thought my talk of pirates was nonsense, I should have insisted she listen to me.

I hurried over to the shallow grave and kneeled down. Mr. Jones crossed the clearing and waited for me at the other end by the little hut.

"Hello, mister. It's me again. I meant to visit for a spell, but the lighthouse keeper is in danger, and I have to get back right away."

A small gust of wind blew across the back of my neck and I shivered. I stood up and walked away, then turned and looked up at the top of the eagle tree. I felt like the bird was watching me, but I couldn't see it in the branches.

I resumed a quick pace on the other side of the clearing. Mr. Jones had to run to keep up. When we reached the bluff, I didn't stop. There was no time to rest. I could see the lighthouse in the distance and it was still much too far away. Part way down the bluff trail, a shot rang out. I recognized the report. Mrs. Dalworth had used her rifle!

Worry and dread pushed me on, but I kept my feet focused on each step as I tackled the difficult descent. My path markings were easy to follow going back. I reached the field in half the time it'd taken going the other way. I was about to leave the protection of the tree line when a voice called out behind me.

Stop, Charlee! Wait!

"Papa?" I spun around. Mr. Jones had stopped some distance back. I crouched down and he came to my side. We both looked out across the field to the lighthouse.

Just then, two men left the cottage with Mrs. Dalworth between them. If I ran at them, they'd probably kill me. That wouldn't help Mrs. Dalworth if they were taking her hostage. I sized up the situation, surprised it didn't seem at all hostile. In fact, they walked in an almost friendly manner down the path leading to Hidden Cove.

I moved south, skirting the sloping field, staying in the cover of scattered trees, until I reached the cliff overlooking the cove. By the time I got there, a rowboat was on its way back to the black ship. Mrs. Dalworth stood on the beach, waving. I stayed out of sight, heart pounding in my chest like a huge drum. Mr. Jones growled.

Mrs. Dalworth didn't wait to see them off. She trundled back up to the lighthouse, as if it was just another day in the yard. She limped a little, but that was her bad hip causing her grief. I waited until I heard the ship's anchor clank. Then I slipped back from the lookout and hurried across the field to the house.

Mrs. Dalworth was in her kitchen, completely unharmed, humming to herself and putting away supplies. I stopped in the door behind her, seething, waiting for her to finish. She heard Mr. Jones's nails on the wood floor and spun around.

"Good heavens, lass! You scared the wits out of me! I thought you were the traders comin' back!"

"Traders? Those horrible men are your traders!" My voice rose with anger. "Those are the men who sunk the *Salish Wind* and killed my friends!"

"No, dear," she said sharply. "You're mistaken. They are coastal merchants, polite as can be. You must have them mixed up with some others."

She examined me from head to toe. I must have looked a fright. I'd snatched my cap off my sweaty head and knew my hair was a plastered mess. I was dripping in sweat. She couldn't understand my alarm.

"No. I remember them. It's the same sloop that chased us and the same men. I can't believe you do business with them!"

I threw my duffle on the floor, narrowly missing Mr. Jones. Mrs. Dalworth was silent as I yanked my boots off. She turned away and went back to unpacking her goods.

"Now lass, don't get all worked up," she said, in a voice that was really saying I was having a spell again and making things up. She tried to soothe my mood. "They're traders. They come here regularly. They are good customers, and I get fine supplies from them in exchange for my wine. They have always been cordial, although a mite smelly from being at sea…"

"I'm telling you, they are murderers! I saw their boat on the other side of the island, coming 'round the bend and headed your way. I ran back almost the whole way, thinking I'd find you robbed and dead!"

Mrs. Dalworth gasped. My anger cracked into jagged heaves and sobs. Alarmed, she dragged a chair over and sat down next to me.

"There, there." She patted my hand and rubbed my arm. "I don't know what happened on that *Salish Wind*, but I do know that shipwreck has struck terror into your heart."

I looked at her lined face, her nose and cheeks rosy from the warmth of the kitchen. Her eyes pleaded with me to let go of the nightmare. It was the same look she had when I first told her how I came to be on the island.

She picked up my hand and held it in hers. She had tried, but she couldn't believe my tale of raiding, murdering pirates. There was no point trying to persuade her otherwise.

"I'm sorry I raised my voice. I was scared they'd hurt you," I said.

She sat back in surprise at my concern for her. "Oh, lass! I'm a tough old bird. I can handle myself. But I know them anyhow."

"But I heard your rifle!"

"Oh that. One of the fellas is a crack shot. He bagged a duck for our Sunday dinner."

I sighed. She'd made up her mind. They were her friendly traders. But I knew their dark secrets.

Mrs. Dalworth, relieved that my bad spell had passed, returned to her kitchen and set to work baking bread. As she prepared her dough, she told me news she'd heard from the traders. I wasn't at all interested until she got to a dispute that happened on an island not far from us.

"Some American shot an Englishman's pig," she said.

"Why?"

"Seems when they were drawing up the new border here

between British and American land, they forgot about a set of islands called the San Juans."

"I remember seeing them when we sailed in."

"Well, last summer, a bunch of American miners started settling there. They'd tried their luck with Fraser Canyon gold, and when that didn't work, they turned to farming. Hudson's Bay fellas weren't thrilled to see them move in, bag and baggage."

"Who gave them their land?"

"Nobody. Both sides think they have rights to it, but neither of them officially does."

"So now they're fighting over a pig?"

"There was a scrap over sheep a few years back. Trouble's been brewing for a while. Anyhow, apparently the Royal Navy sailed by, saw a big ol' American flag flying and took exception to it. Things are mighty tense."

"What about the locals? Weren't they there first?"

"Of course they were. But nobody ever asks them. Our folk come here and lay claims. Government gives them a paper that says here's your homestead. Or they get a piece of paper, hammer a stake in the ground and they got a gold claim. The locals don't have a say. They either go along or move along."

"Where do they go?"

"Where they can. But it's hard, you know. Sometimes they get pushed out of places where their ancestors have lived for hundreds of years."

We were both silent. I'd been one of those seeking a land claim in gold country. I hadn't thought about how the land already belonged to others.

"This lighthouse is on government land," she said. "How do you suppose the government got this island?"

"Nobody wanted it?"

"Well, there is that. But inhospitable nature aside, they just took it."

I shook my head.

"What'll happen to the Lekwungen land at the other end of the island?"

"I expect they'll leave it alone for the time being. Luckily, nobody cares about this mean piece of rock. Unless they find gold on it one day, Heaven forbid," she said.

"Pretty sure there's no gold on this little island." Mr. Jones and I exchanged glances.

"Indeed. If I had a dime for every rock I hit with my garden shovel, I'd be as rich as the King of England."

I yawned loudly. Mr. Jones, also tired from our trip, headed for the blanket under my bunk.

"You have black circles under your eyes, lass. Better have a rest so one of them headaches don't come on."

I stretched out on my bunk. I couldn't fall sleep, so I did an inventory of the things I'd brought back. My ability to picture and remember things was returning, and I had a strange feeling I'd accidentally left something behind, like one item was just outside the picture frame and out of view in my memory. But nothing was missing. I'd double-checked the cave before leaving.

Dinner was a steaming bowl of chowder and freshly baked bread topped with butter Mrs. Dalworth got from the traders. I was famished, but had to wait for her to work herself into the opposite chair and say grace. I threw in my own special "amen" when she kept her prayer down to one short sentence.

"Dig in!" She dipped a shiny silver spoon into her bowl.

"You have new silverware!"

"A little present to myself," she said with a coy smile. "The traders offered it for a steal. It's not a complete set, but I don't mind. Just because I live on a rock doesn't mean I can't have a few nice things."

I picked up the spoon next to my bowl. It was heavy, polished and elegant in my hand. It had ornate writing on the handle. I tipped it into the light. The initials S.W. were engraved on it. My hand shook and the spoon clattered to the table.

S.W. stood for the *Salish Wind*! I recognized the silverware from the Captain's serving tray.

"What's wrong, dear?"

I rubbed my hand like it had a sudden cramp, then picked up a slice of bread.

"Nothing. I'm clumsy when I'm tired. Your new silver is beautiful."

Mrs. Dalworth smiled, but her blue eyes were filled with worry.

42

i

"Fine start to trading I've got here," Mrs. Dalworth grumbled, a few days later. She'd expected customers to come in a regular stream in late September. But thick fog socked us in and hung around for days. Only one group of miserable looking creatures with bad teeth, matted hair, and runny noses came calling and that was the day after the pirates. We hadn't seen anyone since.

On the third day of fog, Mrs. Dalworth invited me to go with her to tend the lighthouse. The brick and stone tower was three times taller than the keeper's house. No chance of a big wind knocking it over. I figured even a cannon blast couldn't topple it.

A steep, circular iron staircase wound its way to the top on the inside.

"Hold the railing. Don't look between the stairs," Mrs. Dalworth said. "It's a bit of a fright the first time you climb it, but you get used to it."

At the top of the staircase was the biggest lantern I'd ever laid eyes on. I'd have to lie down twice to stretch across it. A narrow platform circled the round room, and a huge magnifying glass was positioned in front of it.

"How did they build this? The lens is gigantic."

"That smart invention allows the light to be seen for miles.

When I come out on my watches, I check the wick and oil to make sure the lantern is burning properly. If it isn't, it could go out or smoke up the glass, which would make the light invisible from the sea. And if the light can't be seen, particularly on a day like today, it could mean disaster. Mariners rely on it now."

Mrs. Dalworth spoke about her work with great pride. She made her trips to the lighthouse like it called her to it. Six times a day at exactly the same time, including the middle of the night, she would quietly get up, put on her jacket and boots, and head for the lighthouse. Once in a while, she'd come in and say the lantern needed attention and she'd be gone for maybe an hour. Every week, she'd top up the oil and do some kind of maintenance work on it. She never asked for help and she never complained, even though I knew her hip pained her climbing the steep staircase.

As Mrs. Dalworth did her inspection, she told me the government planned to add a foghorn in the coming year. The light wasn't strong enough to cut through the dense fog that rolled around the rocky point in winter. An important ship had run aground a few years ago. The captain couldn't see the light through the fog until he'd run right up on the shallows and it was too late.

"One accident. One, and they want to change it all," she said. "Can you imagine trying to sleep through a blasted foghorn all night?"

"I used to, in San Francisco, at my uncle's house near the wharf. We had a lot of bad fog in the bay around this time of year, too. It would linger for days and I would hear that horn every night, all night long. But it wasn't right up close, like not right in your ear like this one would be."

"I suppose a person gets used to it then," she replied. "Probably no worse than a husband who snores so loud the rafters shake."

"Mr. Dalworth?"

"Oh no! That man was quiet as a lamb, bless his soul."

Mrs. Dalworth slipped into a private memory. She took a moment to visit some faraway place before starting down the staircase.

"Do you think you'll stay here? I mean, if they put in a foghorn and such?"

"I've nowhere else to go. No family anywhere. I don't know if they'll even let me stay on once they find out Edgar's gone."

"You'll be alone again when I leave."

"I'm used to it. Even with Edgar here, he'd often be in his books or off somewhere studying something. The Lekwungen people look out for me. They'll bring their wares as soon as the weather lifts. I trade with them, too. We trust each other. Edgar helped them and they don't forget."

"What'd he do for them?"

"Told the government the lighthouse didn't need the entire island. Edgar was a mathematician, a scientist. He did all the calculations on the lantern lens and mechanisms, you know. Anyhow, he convinced them the rest of the island wasn't useful. So they let it be."

"I don't think it takes a scientist to figure out this island is worthless, no offense to Mr. Dalworth."

"Ah. But imagine if a place was sacred. And imagine if a certain scientist knew that, and used his influence to keep it so."

"Then that would be a good thing," I said.

"Indeed."

The next morning, the fog vanished and we were back into the warmth of late September. I was reading Mr. Dalworth's mathematics book in the sunshine out on the cliff when two large canoes rounded the point and entered Hidden Cove. The front ends were long and pointed, like the ones I'd seen in Fort Victoria. I ran back to the house for Mrs. Dalworth.

"That'll be the Lekwungen," she said. "Now mind your manners. They'll wonder what you're doing here, want to be sure you aren't up to no good."

"I'll be on my best behavior."

"Make sure Mr. Jones doesn't bite anyone's leg off." Her voice trailed off as she hung up her apron and headed for the cove. She turned to add, "And don't gawk!"

I marched obediently behind her. Mr. Jones darted around, excited we were having company.

The paddlers let the canoes drift onto the beach as Mrs. Dalworth welcomed them ashore. Once the boats were hauled onto the rocks, the men and women carried their goods up to the house.

A man wearing a distinctive top hat with a big feather spoke at length to Mrs. Dalworth. To my surprise, she replied in his language! When they both turned to look at me, I knew they'd been discussing my presence. He nodded as she explained something I couldn't understand. One woman asked a question and pointed at Mr. Jones. That discussion continued for a few minutes. I shuffled my feet and hoped their curiosity would soon shift back to trading.

The group laid their things out on the porch for Mrs. Dalworth to see. They had brought fish, dried herbs, baskets of root vegetables, fruit, and a selection of handmade items. They smiled as they spoke, and pointed at various people and things as if they were talking about the weather, fishing, gardening, and the latest family news. I followed as they strolled off to the liquor barn.

The woman from the leader's boat walked along beside me while the others waited at the house. She crouched down to pet Mr. Jones. I wanted to warn her he wasn't fond of strangers, but not knowing how to do that before she lost a hand, I said, "Be nice, Bubba." It wasn't necessary. His tail wagged. He seemed quite pleased to meet her.

As we stood outside the barn, the woman said something and handed me a bundle. I turned to Mrs. Dalworth for help.

"It's a gift. Go ahead and take it, lass. It's herbal tea. She's made it, she says, for your... oh dear, how to translate?" She exchanged some words with the woman. "Ah! It's for your vision, she says. You know, behind the eyes. Does that make sense?"

"I guess so."

The woman's eyes were deep and searching. It was like she knew what had happened to my head, sensed how my memories had been rattled out of place.

"I don't have anything to give back," I said.

"A gift is not measured that way," Mrs. Dalworth replied.

The woman spoke to me again. I listened politely but understood no part of what she said.

"She has named you Eagle Looking," Mrs. Dalworth said. "She says she has seen you."

I looked at the woman with surprise. Had she seen me in the field where the camas grew? Or in the clearing? I remembered feeling like I'd been watched. Or did she mean she'd seen me in a dream?

Mrs. Dalworth looked back and forth between us with curiosity. She must have sensed I was uncomfortable as she took the gentleman by the arm and started herding all of us back up the path to the porch.

She'd only given them four bottles of wine. It didn't seem like much for all the food they had brought. But then Mrs. Dalworth dug in her pocket and pulled out a thimble-size nugget of gold. I caught my breath. It was just like Mr. Miller's gold, just like the ones in my secret pouch.

My secret pouch! I'd forgotten a little pouch of Mr. Miller's gold in the cave!

43

i

"My, my! It is quite an honor to be given a name, lass," she said to me as they paddled away. "And from the Chief's wife, if you please. You made quite an impression."

I was madly sorting through memories. When I dug up Mr. Miller's gold after the pirates had left, I'd put three little nuggets in a cloth pouch for safe keeping. I thought I might need them to pay for my rescue.

"Did you hear what I said, dear?"

"Mrs. Dalworth, where did that gold nugget come from?"

A storm formed on her brow and her expression turned dark as a thundercloud.

"I'm a business woman. I make deals."

I kept my mouth shut and carried a basket of fish in from the porch. If given enough room, Mrs. Dalworth would usually go on talking. She was working up to it as she unpacked her goods.

"Since your next question is likely going to be 'what's it worth?', that little nugget will buy what they need for winter."

"One gold nugget!" I knew gold was worth a lot. "But why did you give it to them in exchange for fish and vegetables?"

"Because I can't use it. What would the government think if the old lady in the lighthouse was trading in gold? These people are my friends. They'll use it for their people. And all of us will benefit. We work together. You see?"

"I think I do. Is that how you learned to speak their language so well?"

"No. That's another story." She dropped into her chair at the table with a heavy sigh.

"Before Edgar became lightkeeper, they hired him to survey land for development. We had quite the society life when we first arrived. Lots of money. Important people as friends. We had everything you'd ever dreamed of having in life, but both of us were miserable."

"Why?"

"Edgar couldn't abide the damage being done. The ladies' circle was a dreadful bore, so I taught English to the local people. In exchange, they taught me their language. When the lighthouse was finished, Edgar asked to be assigned as keeper. Once here, he returned to his numbers and research. He was happy again. We both were."

"I wish I'd met him. I've been enjoying his math book. I particularly like the places where he corrects what was written or shows a better way. He was really smart."

Mrs. Dalworth's cheeks quivered. She turned away and busied herself folding linen napkins.

"Yes, he was. I know he'd be fond of you. You would've won his heart in an instant with that comment about his notations."

I caught my breath as the mantel clock chimed and the kettle whistled at once. That feeling of somebody watching crept over me again. Mrs. Dalworth took the kettle off the heat, unaware of my eyes darting around the room looking for something that wasn't there.

"So yes, I gave them the nugget, Charlee. It doesn't make up for what they've had taken from them, but I hope it's for the good. Now. Would you care for a little honey in your tea?"

I couldn't sleep at all that night. I tossed and turned, thinking about gold and my problems.

Getting off the island would be the easy part. When the supply boat came, I'd go with them to Fort Victoria. Mrs. Dalworth said she could fix it for them to take me and it wouldn't cost anything. But taking Mr. Miller's gold with me was impossible. There was no way I could dig it up and lug it along without having to tell a whole bunch of people I didn't trust. It had to stay buried and I'd have to bring Cook or Mr. Miller back to fetch it.

Then there was the matter of what I'd do when I got dumped off in Victoria, and how I'd get back to San Francisco. There was the cost of a ticket for passage, and where to stay until departure. One little gold nugget from the pouch in the cave would more than cover it. But the supply boat was due in a few days. I was running out of time. And if I tried to buy a ticket with gold, it'd be like San Francisco all over again. Immigrants and children couldn't deal in gold without being taken for thieves.

I heard rustling in the dark cottage. Mrs. Dalworth lit a small lantern and slipped out the door. Four o'clock. It was like watches on a ship all over again. But here, she did all the shifts by herself. I noticed she didn't sleep a lot. She'd doze in her rocking chair until the midnight check and then turn in. She'd be up at four for the early morning check and then she'd be in her chair reading her Bible until breakfast.

I rolled over on my back and stared into the dark. Mr. Jones grumbled and changed position beside my legs.

I dreaded the trip home. My head was finally starting to work the way it was supposed to, but a journey by sea would make me sick all over again. I needed my wits about me to travel back alone.

The latch on the door clicked and Mrs. Dalworth came back in. She quietly eased herself into her chair. The gold she had given the Lekwungen people had to have come from the pirates.

Like me, they'd probably kept a few nuggets aside before burying the rest. But what did she have that was so valuable that they would pay such a handsome price? Maybe she owned some jewelry from her society days. I couldn't think of anything she had that could be worth so much.

Mrs. Dalworth's breathing became heavy and regular. I looked over. Her head had fallen to her chest and she'd nodded off in her chair, one hand marking the page she'd been reading, the other hand holding her bad glasses. I remembered old Mr. Porter in Santa Rosa, the man I almost went to work for. I thought he needed glasses, but he was actually going blind.

When I left, she'd be alone. Her vision wasn't great and she had a bad hip. She didn't want to tell her bosses about Edgar's death for fear they'd replace her. If they wouldn't let her stay, what would happen to her then?

"Trouble sleeping last night, lass?" Mrs. Dalworth inquired over breakfast. I looked up, my tired eyes surely giving away the answer.

"A little." I was reluctant to confess the whole truth.

"I'll bet a bottle of my prize vintage wine that it's that gold nugget on your mind."

I didn't want to talk about it, even if it was the truth.

"I tell you, lass. Gold turns people. Once they get it in their minds, it possesses them."

"Mrs. Dalworth, it's not my place to ask. But what did you trade for that piece of gold?"

She put down her cup and folded her hands on the table.

"You're not going to care for my answer."

"I know you deal with those... privateers." A nice name for pirates, I thought. I didn't want the conversation to go off topic on names.

"And I suppose you figure I got that gold from them?"

"Yes, that's what I figure."

"You've known me now for almost two weeks."

"About that, yes."

"Do I seem trustworthy? Do you think I would steer you wrong?"

"I don't think you would steer me wrong, no." She didn't notice I ducked the first part of the question.

"Good. Because what I traded for the gold belonged to you."

I gripped the edge of the table.

"What! What do you mean?" I went through a mental list of the things I possessed. I had nothing of value. "My gold mining shares. You traded them away!"

"Yes, I did. And I'm not sorry."

"How could you?"

"You said yourself, it's no gold claim and it's worthless."

"It wasn't yours!" I said. "I could have sold it for passage home."

"Ya figure now?" she shot back. "And just who do you think would buy a worthless share certificate off a young lass? Or should I say a young lad? You'd be arrested and thrown in jail. Do you know why? Because it's fake. I heard stories of these forgeries a few years ago, but I'd never seen one with my own eyes till you come along. I thought you'd figured it out. Your uncle was swindled and the claim is worthless."

I was stunned. "You wouldn't have known it's a fake if I hadn't told you."

"Of course I would've. It doesn't have any of the usual marks and seals of Victoria or the governor."

"But it names the place. Yale."

"I can explain that," she said, holding up a hand to stop me from interrupting. "Some of those first miners from San Francisco figured out gold was scarce. One or two got lucky. But most didn't. When they staked their land and registered the claim, they were given a piece of paper. So when claims turned out to be no good for anything, a couple of them got wise. They started collecting useless registrations from the desperate and the dead, and selling them to the next round of fortune seekers down south. Those claims didn't have gold. Swindlers have been playing this game and turning a nice profit."

I sat down with nothing to say. Jake had gone into the land office to check on the certificate. The agent in Victoria told him the same thing. It wasn't a registered gold mining company.

"But you traded a fake certificate for gold. Those men will come back and kill you—or us—when they find out."

"Those men aren't going up the Fraser River, I can tell you that right now. They'll trade it and make even more off of it than I did. I told them straight up, it's a fake. But I convinced them it's a good fake in the hands of a clever trader. They'll fetch twice the payment they gave me because they'll sell it with a little sample of gold."

Uncle would have loved the cleverness of the grift. I thought it was the worst possible way to get rich.

"It was wrong of you to take it," I said.

"Even when it was for the good?" she asked. "Have you never taken anything without asking, even when it was for the good?"

I thought of vegetables I'd stolen from Jake's rooming house yard when I was hungry. It wasn't the same thing.

"I'm sorry, Charlee. I didn't think you'd be so upset over a worthless piece of paper. Besides, you weren't here to ask. Your uncle's fake certificate is going to bring many people comfort this winter."

Edgar's math book was open on the table. I stared at a page with geometric diagrams. The illustration reminded me of Deception Island.

"Where's the map?"

"Heaven's alive, lass! What map?"

"The map I drew of the island, with the paths and the location of the shipwreck and everything."

I searched the room for the piece of paper I'd left on the table for Mrs. Dalworth.

She looked concerned for the first time.

"Last time I saw it was when that trader laid the fancy silverware out on top of it."

44

i

I brooded for days after my fight with Mrs. Dalworth. She had
gone through my personal things and taken something from
me. While I understood why she traded the claim away, I was
still mad that she took it without asking. It was stealing, plain
and simple.

As a last attempt to solve the mystery of the mining company
shares, I'd hoped to get Mr. Miller to look into the signatures. I
used to know exactly what was on the certificate. Drawn a fake
copy of it. I'd memorized it. But since my accident, all I could
remember about it was the names "Yale" and "Fraser River."
That it had found its way back to hustlers and cheats was a rather
fitting ending, given all the trouble it had caused me. I hoped it
caused them nothing but grief.

Every time Mrs. Dalworth called those men traders, I felt
anger boil through my veins. She called them traders like they
were pleasant fellows conducting proper business. They were
murderers and criminals.

A far greater disaster was Mrs. Dalworth letting my island
map fall into the hands of her smarmy privateers. The theft of
the map made me extremely anxious.

What would the pirates want with the hand-drawn map? They

didn't know I'd moved the gold and I hadn't marked it on the map. Not even Mrs. Dalworth knew about that. So if it wasn't because it showed where the gold was buried, then what was it?

They probably wanted the map so nobody would ever find the *Salish Wind*. They sank her, and that map showed at least one other living person knew exactly where. If they poked around the cove, they might find my cave. Maybe they'd discover the secret pouch of nuggets I'd left behind.

I tried not to think about it because the images from the shipwreck rushed back into my head. I had an uneasy feeling in my stomach whenever I thought of those wicked men. They terrified me half to death.

If I thought about them too much, I'd end up with a dreadful headache or a nightmare. I still had bad dreams about the attack on the *Salish Wind*. An evil pirate would chase me with a bloody sword, or a dead man would grab me as I swam to safety and pull me under.

My map in the hands of the pirates was worse than any of those nightmares. In my dreams, I fought them. In real life, I was helpless and they were getting away with everything.

"Soup's on," Mrs. Dalworth called from the porch as I busied myself re-stacking the leaning woodpile. Since we'd had our fight, I'd made up all kinds of chores to do, just to be outside, away from her and on my own.

A black mood settled over me as I hung my jacket on the hook behind the door. I sat down at the little table across from her as we did at every meal. We ate in pained silence.

"Weather coming in from the west, seems," she said, clanking her spoon in the hot bowl of soup. I nodded but didn't look up. A long silence followed.

"I was thinking of doing a ham for supper tomorrow. You'll be on your way any day after that, I expect."

I glanced at the calendar hanging on the wall behind her. The last week of September had arrived and the supply boat was due at month's end. Last year at this time, I was working at the Livery in San Francisco, thinking everyone I'd ever known or loved had abandoned me. Now I was on some far-flung lighthouse island with this headstrong woman who probably had no business being here on her own.

I finished my soup, said thank you, and got up to wash my bowl and spoon in the basin on the counter.

Mrs. Dalworth put her hand on my arm. "Lass."

I didn't respond.

"Charlee. Sit down." I obeyed, but lifted my head and glared at her, eyes cold as two frozen puddles.

"I don't know what I can do to set things right with you. I can't bear it a minute longer. You're leaving in a week and you won't speak to me anymore."

"Should have thought of that before you stole from me."

"I am not one bit sorry for trading that fake claim of yours away. But I am sorry for breaking your trust because that's worth much, much more."

"You went through my things." I sounded childish, whinging.

"Day after you arrived, I did that, matter of fact. While you took your bath. I'm alone here. I had to know who I had under my roof."

Another confession. This time, I wasn't surprised.

"Did you ever snoop to find out about me?"

"No!" I said too quickly, but I had. I remembered how I'd flipped open her Bible when she was out of the house. I'd checked the cupboards for guns and to see where she kept the ammunition for her rifle. I'd even snooped a little in Edgar's desk when I was getting dressed after my bath. I did it for the same reasons as her.

"Well then, the difference between us is I'll survive and you won't."

She got up from the table and cleared away the dishes like the conversation was over. I followed her.

"That's not true! I survived a sinking ship and weeks as a castaway!"

"By the grace o' God, mostly. Or you got lucky. But life doesn't work like that most of the time. With life, you gotta think ahead."

"I think ahead," I said, crossing my arms.

"Is that so? Is that why you came north chasing after a fake gold claim?"

I didn't have a smart answer for that. She was right. I hadn't thought it through because I desperately wanted to be rich. If I was truthful with myself, I'd used the bad men after me as an excuse to get on the Salish Wind. I could have stayed in San Francisco, gone to work for Mrs. Plea or something, and hidden right under their noses as a girl.

"I thought the claim was real." It sounded so foolish.

Mrs. Dalworth shrugged. "You're not the first to get gold fever. All that business is water under the bridge now. You need to look ahead. What's your plan for traveling when you leave the island?"

"I'll pose as a boy, like I did on the *Salish Wind*. I'll wear Edgar's clothes and you said you could cut my hair."

"And?"

"And what?"

"And what's your story?"

"I need passage back to San Francisco."

"'Is that so, young man,' they'll say. 'And you're traveling all that distance alone?'"

Mrs. Dalworth clasped her hands behind her back and paced like a lawyer as she made up her questions.

"Yes," I said.

"That'll be 'yes, sir.' And how old are ya, lad?"

"I'm, uh, fifteen, no thirteen years old."

"Are you fifteen or thirteen?"

I cursed under my breath. I'd made that same mistake when Mrs. Plea had interrogated me.

"I think younger is best. What do you think?"

"Go with fourteen," she said, resuming her role. "And what's the purpose of your trip, lad?"

"I was crew on an American merchant schooner that sunk here. I have to report it."

"Heaven's no, lass! You'd have trouble convincing the supply agent on the boat to take you off the island with that answer. You can't be a boy traveling alone who says he came off a shipwreck!" She wrung her hands as she considered the problem. "We'll craft a story for you. You are Charlee... can't use your real last name."

"Fitzquiddick." I'd use the code name Jake and I had made up.

"What? Is that an actual name? Use whatever you like as long as you can remember it and spell it. So. I hired you off one of the trader's boats after Edgar disappeared, to give me a hand. You've earned your keep doing chores, helping at the lighthouse."

"That's a fancy string of lies."

"And you're an orphan."

"That part is true. And what if they ask why I'm going to San Francisco?"

"You will tell them you are going on behalf of me, since I can't leave, and I'm sending you to the sister of my recently passed husband, Edgar, to take her the sad news and a few of his worldly possessions."

I was so drawn into her story that I almost believed it as she was telling it.

"What about Mr. Jones? What do I say about him?"

"Nothing. He'll have to stay here with me."

"No! I can't leave him behind." Tears were not far behind my sudden protest.

Mrs. Dalworth frowned, then softened. "Very well. How about

I tell the supply boat captain we trained the dog to protect you? I'll give the captain money, ask him to purchase a round-trip ticket for you on the next steamer to San Francisco... and that you are to remain in his charge until he puts you on it."

"A round trip?"

"If the story is to be believed, yes," she said. "I doubt that you'll want to use the return ticket once you get to San Francisco. But if you did, you'd always be welcome here."

She turned her back to me and fussed with things in her kitchen. She wanted to pay for my trip home, but she was also saying I was welcome to come back and stay.

"Mrs. Dalworth," I said, getting up from the table. "I will repay you. I promise." I thought about Mr. Miller's gold. I knew he wouldn't mind if I gave her a piece for all she had done. She'd probably give it to the Lekwungen and they'd take care of her. The gold in the pouch would be useful for that, if I had it.

"Forgive me, dear. That is payment enough. I'm looking out for ya, best I know how."

"It's a great story you made up. If I can remember it past tonight, I might even use it."

"Good heavens, I hadn't thought o' that."

As we stood in the kitchen, doing the dishes and putting things away, I realized time was running out and I was going to miss her. Soon Mr. Jones and I would leave the island forever.

Where was Mr. Jones? He hadn't followed me in for lunch. I called his name from the porch. He didn't come running. Then I noticed him off in the distance. He was sitting in the middle of the field that led to the cross-island trail. He was waiting for me.

45

i

While Mr. Jones sat in the field, a fall storm had rolled in from the west. Black clouds gathered in bands on the horizon and the wind whipped the steely water into frothy whitecaps. The lighthouse blinked its warning in silence.

"Looks like I'll have to go get him," I said to Mrs. Dalworth, after going out to the porch for the third time. I couldn't persuade Mr. Jones to come in.

"I'll stoke the fire and make tea," she said, pulling on another sweater. "I've got a terrible chill this afternoon."

By the time I reached the field, the wind was blowing the rain sideways. Its icy droplets stung my face and made my eyes water.

"What's wrong, Mr. Jones?" I kneeled down to rub the fur on his cheeks. He stood on stiff legs and looked in the direction of the cross-island trail.

"You're telling me to go get Mr. Miller's pouch of gold, aren't you? I know I have to. But we can't go today. The weather is too foul."

He took a few uncertain steps, stopped and looked back at the trailhead, then up at me, the wind blowing his curly, white fur back from his face.

"I promise we'll go on the first good day. C'mon home now."

Reluctantly, he followed along behind me. Cold rain pelted my face. I held my collar closed at the neck as we pressed into the howling wind in the direction of the house.

Mr. Jones couldn't keep up. He was too cold. I picked him up, tucked him under my arm like Kuno always did, and hurried back to the house.

The fireplace was blazing when I came in the door, a welcome change from the dampness and chill.

"There you are. You two must be freezing," said Mrs. Dalworth, coming out of her bedroom. She was twice her size, bundled up in layers of sweaters and a wool shawl over the works.

"He didn't want to come. I had to carry him."

"Mr. Jones isn't himself these days," she said, holding his damp head in her hands. "Put his blanket in front of the fireplace. He's shivering."

"Me, too, and I was only out there for five minutes."

"Summer's barely over. This is nothing yet."

Mr. Jones curled up on his blanket by the hearth. Although the warmth of the fire did him good, he was restless. He'd stay by the fire for a while, get up and wander over to the door, nudge my leg in passing, and then return to his blanket. His tail drooped over his hind end.

"Something's bothering that boy," Mrs. Dalworth said, sniffling her nose with a handkerchief.

"I know. My papa always said animals have a way of knowing things that people don't. They sense danger before people do, like they know what's going to happen before it does."

Thinking about that made me nervous. Mr. Jones was on to something and it couldn't be good. He wanted me to return to the cove right away. It had to be the gold I'd forgotten. How would I explain to Mrs. Dalworth that I had to hike to the other side of the island one more time?

I was lost in these thoughts when Mrs. Dalworth sneezed.

"Oh dear," she said. "I feel terrible."

Her ordinarily rosy face had faded to grey. She'd taken her reading glasses off and set them next to her Bible on the side table by her chair. Her eyes were puffy and wet. She rubbed her forehead with a shaky hand.

"You'd better crawl into your bed," I said. "You don't look so good."

"No, I want to stay where it's warm."

I got up, put two more logs on the fire and cleared our teacups away. Mrs. Dalworth had vegetables washed and set out in the kitchen, ingredients for some kind of stew.

"I'll make supper for us tonight."

Mr. Jones did another restless lap from the hearth to the door and back.

"That would be lovely, lass, but I've no appetite," she said, putting her head back and closing her eyes.

"I'll be insulted if you don't eat my cooking. This is my first chance to take over your kitchen."

"Haha," she said, unable to muster her usual hearty laugh.

On this cool fall day, the storm had stolen the last of the daylight. Away from the fireplace, the house had turned dark and gloomy. I lit the lanterns early, to lift the heavy mood that fell over us like cold dirt on a grave.

Mrs. Dalworth threw her blankets off and staggered to the door. She looked ghostly. Beads of sweat dotted her forehead as she struggled to put an arm in the sleeve of her coat.

"Mrs. Dalworth!" I rushed to her side. "You're burning up!" I could feel the heat of her body raging through her clothing.

"The lantern. I must tend the lantern," she said, swaying back and forth. "Help me with my coat."

"I'll do it. I can do it for you. You're not well!"

She persisted in trying to dress herself, batting at my hands as I tried to stop her. Her strength didn't last.

"The wick needs a trim. It was smoking this morning," she said.

"Don't worry. I'll take care of it." Mrs. Dalworth squinted her eyes, trying to bring my face into focus.

"You aren't Edgar…"

I felt her full weight in my arms as she slumped to the floor, unconscious. I crumpled to the floor with her. At least I could keep her from falling hard, hitting her head or injuring herself on something on the way down.

"She's sick, Bubba. I don't know what to do for her!"

I kneeled by Mrs. Dalworth, hoping her fainting spell would pass and she'd open her eyes. She didn't come around.

Mr. Jones stood up from his blanket by the fire and moved to the side. He gave me an idea. I pulled the mattress off my bunk and laid it on the floor in front of the fire. I hooked Mrs. Dalworth under the arms, dragged her over by the hearth and arranged her on the mattress. Then I covered her with every blanket I could find.

I remembered having a fever a few years earlier. I was so cold, I couldn't stop shaking. But I never fainted. This was much worse and there was no doctor anywhere near the island.

Mrs. Dalworth groaned and came around. Her arms and legs twitched uncontrollably as if something had possessed her. She was burning up with fever. I got a basin of water and a cloth to cool her head.

"Edgar," she said, clutching my forearm so hard I thought it would snap.

"It's me, Charlee."

"Yes, Charlee. That's her name. You know it. Have you met her then, luv?"

Her jaw chattered as a huge shiver ran through her body. Her eyes rolled in her head.

"Oh, you'll get on well with her, Edgar. She understands your numbers. But she won't stay with us."

I stopped wringing out the cloth and looked at poor Mrs. Dalworth. She was talking about me leaving. Suddenly, her expression turned anxious and she stared at the ceiling, a look that reminded me of all the death I'd seen.

A string of words in the Lekwungen language followed. It sounded like some kind of prayer or chant. She repeated it over and over and over until she finally slipped into a fitful sleep.

I kept the fire going and stayed by her side for hours. I held her hand and told her I was with her and she'd be fine. I tried to believe it. It terrified me to think she was dying of an illness I knew nothing about and couldn't stop. For hours, she would open her eyes, rant about something that made little sense and then fall back to sleep.

I stoked the fire and put her blankets back on when she threw them off. I changed the water in the basin and wiped the sweat from her face and neck. It seemed to soothe her agitated state. Finally, she stopped twitching and lay still, breathing quietly. I decided she was either getting better or dying and I couldn't tell which.

I looked at the clock on the fireplace mantel. It was eight o'clock and pitch black outside. The lighthouse hadn't been checked. For the first time ever, Mrs. Dalworth had missed her early night watch. She had always said, "Come hell or high water, the lantern must not go out." I stretched awkwardly to get a glimpse out the kitchen window. The beam from the lantern cast a glow on the window as it swung around. It was doing its job for now. Mrs. Dalworth could not be left alone when she was half out of her mind with fever. The lighthouse lantern had to wait.

"You need to drink. Fever needs drink."

I remembered the medicine tea Shenoa had made for me. I still had some in my bag.

Mr. Jones took up my vigil as I rummaged through my things

for it. He curled up next to her side and watched me move around the kitchen.

"I don't know what's going on today, Mr. Jones. First you act strange out in the field, then Mrs. Dalworth takes sick and now I'm gonna make medicine tea like I've done it all my life."

When the tea had steeped, I let it cool and filled a mug.

"Mrs. Dalworth, wake up." She didn't respond. "Mrs. Dalworth." I prodded her arm. She opened her eyes.

"What time is it? I have to go to work." She spoke as if nothing at all had happened and she'd just woken up from a little nap.

"No, you don't. The lighthouse is fine. The lantern is lit and I'll take care of it. You need to drink this tea."

I propped her head up. Her eyes toured the room. Finding some focus, she looked at me and said, "How did I get here? What's happened?"

"You fainted. You took ill with a fever and you collapsed. Here, drink this down." I helped her with the mug of special tea.

"Oh, I have such a terrible headache." She took a sip. "This is good. It's Lekwungen medicine."

"You've had it before?"

"Many times. It will help. I'm quite thirsty."

"Drink it all. There's more." She finished the cup.

"How did I get here?" She tried to sit up, but I held her back.

"Stay where you are. I carried you over here when you fainted by the door. Do you still feel cold?"

"A little. Not like before."

"You need to stay by the fire, under these blankets. Promise me you'll do that. I'm going to go tend the lighthouse. I know what to do. You taught me, remember?"

She laid her head down. The tea was taking effect. "I had a dream I saw Edgar. He was sitting against a tree. In a clearing."

Her voice trailed off and she was fast asleep. The fire sparked and I jumped.

In a clearing, she said. A memory came back to me then. The book with the gold trim in the dead man's pocket. I'd seen others like them.

When I first came to the lighthouse, I'd taken my bath in Mrs. Dalworth's bedroom. Her washtub was on one side of the room. On the other side, was a large wooden desk with a roll-top cover. It had been open when I'd soaked in the tub that day.

I ran into her bedroom and drew back the cover on the desk. Gold-trimmed notebooks were neatly lined up in a row.

"Oh no! Edgar."

46

i

I paused at the door of her bedroom to consider what to do. Should I tell her I'd found him or let her go on believing he was lost at sea? If I told her, there would be so many questions, many of which I couldn't answer. I dreaded having to dig around and unearth the gruesome memories. But if it were me, I'd want the person who knew something to tell me the truth.

I pushed aside my dilemma. It wasn't the time. Other things needed attention. Mrs. Dalworth was sound asleep on the mattress. I hoped the tea would keep her that way long enough for me to check on the lighthouse.

"Stay here, Bubba. Watch her for me." His eyes tracked me to the door.

"Good boy. I'll be back as quick as I can."

I threw on my jacket and left the house for the tower. The wind had let up a little, but rain was turning the yard into muck. I climbed the lighthouse stairs carefully, mindful that my boots might be slippery from the mud.

It puzzled me to find the lantern wick neatly trimmed and not smoking at all. Mrs. Dalworth's fever must have made her confused. There was nothing for me to do. Just then, the door opened and banged closed at the bottom of the stairs.

"Mrs. Dalworth, is that you?"

No answer. It couldn't be her. She's sound asleep, I thought, and much too weak to leave the house. It must have been the wind. Maybe the wind pulled the door open. I descended the spiral staircase, my figure casting a huge, grotesque shadow on the stone walls. When I got to the door at the bottom, the door latch was still in place. Hooked on the inside. Just as I'd left it!

The hair on my neck stood on end. The wind moaned as I opened the door and closed it behind me.

Someone had been in there tending the lantern.

Back in the house, I secured the door behind me, and checked it twice. My hands shook as I fiddled with the latch. Mrs. Dalworth was resting exactly as I'd left her, as if I'd never left the room. Mr. Jones was lying down beside her, his eyes trained on the door as I came in.

I stoked the fire and put the kettle on again. She was no longer shivering and her color was better, which probably meant her fever had broken. Still, I planned to wake her up and make her drink more of the medicinal tea.

"Mrs. Dalworth," I said, nudging her as before to wake her. "Time for your medicine."

Her eyes blinked and she rubbed them with her fists.

"What time is it?" she asked, slurring her words.

"Just past nine o'clock."

Her brows drew together with worry. "Did you check the lantern?"

Another shiver ran up my spine as I thought of the eerie presence I had encountered in the lighthouse.

"I did, and everything is perfect," I said. "How are you feeling?"

"Much better, but very groggy... and a bit too warm now." She pushed a layer of blankets off of her body. This was a good sign.

"I've made another cup of the tea for you. I think you should drink it all. Then I won't bother you for the rest of the night."

"Will you remember to do the night checks?"

"Of course," I said, and shuddered to think of returning to the lighthouse in the dead of night. I wasn't sure I had it in me to set foot in there alone again, particularly in the pitch dark. Mrs. Dalworth propped herself up and sipped her tea. "Thank you, dear. You're a kind lass." Her face was relaxed and peaceful, her cheeks a little pink. "Dear, would you mind reading me something from my Bible?"

"Sure. What part?" I asked, picking up the worn leather book on the table beside her rocking chair.

"I like to flip it open anywhere and see what God has to say to me."

I opened the book to a random page and put my finger on a line. She smiled and closed her eyes as I began to read.

"Ruth, chapter one, verse sixteen," I began. "And Ruth said, Entreat me not to leave thee, or return from following after thee: for whither thou goest, I will go: and where thou lodgest, I will lodge."

Mr. Jones got up slowly and leaned his body against my legs. I lifted him onto my lap. He rested his chin on my wrist, the one with the horseshoe scar.

"Thy people shall be my people and thy God my God. Where thou diest, will I die, and there will I be buried."

The tea was taking effect. Her mouth relaxed and opened slightly. I put the Bible down, drew her extra blanket over me and sunk back into the chair.

She didn't want to leave. She wanted to stay on the island with Edgar. Mrs. Dalworth, the good Christian, the clever vintner, the shrewd coastal trader, the devoted keeper of the light. The loving wife of a good man gone too soon.

Sadness filled my heart and spilled over. I knew her pain. My tears fell onto her blanket. Her God had taken care of her this time.

"I haven't forgotten my promise, Bubba. We'll go as soon as the rain lets up." I fell asleep in the chair with him curled up in my lap.

I woke up some time later with a start. The fire had died down. The clock on the mantel showed just before midnight. An eerie pang gripped my stomach. I had to go check the lantern for Mrs. Dalworth and I didn't want to go. What if it was Edgar's ghost I'd heard in the lighthouse? He had no reason to hurt me. If anything, he had fixed the lantern. I couldn't explain how the wick was trimmed when I didn't do it and Mrs. Dalworth was sound asleep in front of the fireplace. My thoughts were foolishness, I decided, like I was the one with the raging fever. I shook off my silly fear along with my blanket. I was out the door before I could change my mind.

The wind had died down and the rain had stopped. I paused at the bottom of the lighthouse steps, my legs as heavy as blocks of stone. I couldn't make myself go up there. The light was shining. I could see that the lantern was lit. It really didn't need me to check up close, I told myself about half way up the stairs. I stopped and returned to the house, relieved but also heavy with guilt. Mrs. Dalworth wouldn't have been afraid to go all the way up.

I dozed through the night, somewhere on the edge of sleep. Crumpled into the rocking chair, I twisted and turned and changed positions all night long. Whenever I glanced at Mrs. Dalworth, she seemed to be sleeping comfortably. Finally, exhausted from being awake, I slept. It was well past dawn when I woke. Mr. Jones was scratching at the door.

I got up and let him out while heading to the lighthouse for the morning rounds. The sun was shining with only a few scattered clouds overhead. A light breeze was all that remained of the wind. The weather had cleared, but fat clouds to the west still warned of more rain to come. As I walked to the lighthouse, I wondered what had gotten into me last night. Everything looked different, and very ordinary, in the light of morning.

Mrs. Dalworth was sitting in her rocking chair by the time I got back.

"Why didn't you wait for me to help you?" I said, surprised to see her up and about.

"I wasn't sure where you were. My old legs and back had gotten so stiff, if I didn't move right away, I thought I might never get off that mattress."

"I was doing your rounds."

"Thank you. Did trimming the wick give you any trouble?"

I shook my head and looked away. "It was fine. Do you think you could eat something this morning?" I changed the subject with a little too much enthusiasm.

"Yes, I'm famished," she said. "I feel quite a bit better this morning, although dreadfully achy."

"I'll make breakfast then. And after, I think I can put my bed back where it belongs and get you settled in your own. You need to take it easy. You scared me half to death last night."

"It came on so sudden. I'm lucky you were here. I might have been in quite a situation all alone. I bet I picked up something from that outfit of filthy pirates."

It did not escape my notice that she called them pirates and not traders. I set to work making bannock while she slowly folded the blankets lying in a heap on the floor.

My stomach was growling as I laid our breakfast and tea on the table.

"This is lovely," said Mrs. Dalworth, biting into a piece of warm bannock covered in berry jam. "When did you learn to make this?"

I was about to reply that Shenoa had taught me, but then said, "It's one of Cook's recipes."

"He sounds like quite an interesting chap, that Cook."

"He is. I adore him."

"Do ya then," she said with a mischievous grin.

She took a sip of her tea and rattled the cup back into the saucer as if it weighed as much as a bag of flour.

"Where's our Mr. Jones gotten to now?" she said, scanning the room.

"He's outside. He helped me all night while you were sick, stayed by your side when the fever had you, watched over you while I went to the lighthouse."

I got up from the table and went out to the porch to check the field. He was out there again, waiting for me. I looked at the sky, with puffy clouds gathering above us.

"I'm going to have to go get him again," I said, pulling on my boots and jacket. "He's sitting out in the field again."

"He's trying to tell you something."

"I know," I replied, not willing to say what I already knew. I had to return to Clamity Cove one more time.

"He's an older dog, you know," she said quietly. "I bet he's right up there with me in dog years."

I didn't ask her what she meant. I didn't want to think about it.

Like before, I had to go get Mr. Jones because he wouldn't come.

"We can't go today, Bubba. We'll go soon though. I promise."

He looked over his shoulder at the trailhead, then got up and followed me back to the house.

47

i

Mrs. Dalworth made a quick recovery. That day, I did the lighthouse checks for her, including the night watches, pleading with her to let me handle it so she could rest. Although she was better, she was slow to get up and wobbly when she walked. I worried she would stumble and fall on the lighthouse staircase. She agreed to let me help her and gratefully slept most of the day away.

The night of her illness felt like one of my bad dreams. It had been a hard night, full of worry and empty of sleep. Whenever I closed my eyes, I had visions of ghosts and pirates sneaking around the lighthouse.

With Mrs. Dalworth back in her bedroom recovering, Mr. Jones took up the unusual spot by the door when I got into my bunk. During the night, I would hear him get up and pace around the room, his nails clicking on the wooden floor. I lay awake in the dark.

I had to return for the pouch of gold. The supply boat was due in a few days. Mrs. Dalworth was going to pay for my ticket home, but I was pretty sure she couldn't really afford it. One small nugget could do so much.

After lunch the next day, I cleared our dishes away and went outside to fill the woodbox and carry in water. Mr. Jones was sitting half way across the field, in the same spot as before. It had rained again overnight and the sky was a plain canvas of pale grey.

When my chores were finished, I started out to the field to bring him back. He wasn't there. I called out to him, looking around for his white fur and yellow bandana against the oranges and browns of autumn. When I reached the place he'd been sitting, his tracks led to the trailhead.

He had given up waiting and had gone alone.

I ran into the house and threw things into my rucksack.

"Slow down, lass. What's gotten into you then?" Mrs. Dalworth asked, pushing herself up from her chair.

"It's Mr. Jones. He's gone."

She let out a heavy sigh.

"I'm going after him."

"It's too late. It'll be dark in a few hours. Even if you do find him out there, you won't have time to get back."

That comment prompted me to add the flint and steel, a wool blanket and a roll of canvas into my pack.

"He's returning to the cave. I can make it there by dark."

"No. Leave him be. He'll come back on his own, if that's what he wants, if that's what God intends."

"I'm going. He wants me to go."

"I'll not let you risk your life chasing after him," she said, mustering her most stern, adult voice and putting herself between me and the door.

"Is that why you didn't look for Edgar? Because it was too risky. Because it was in God's hands?"

My comment stung.

"I didn't have a boat," she whispered.

"Edgar didn't drown, Mrs. Dalworth. He tried to get home through the island trail and… and he didn't make it."

She caught her breath. Her eyes well up with tears.

As soon as I blurted out the words, I deeply regretted them. Not because she didn't have a right to know what really happened—I was going to tell her before I left the island—but because I flung the words at her out of my own pain.

"How do you know this?" she asked. "Tell me."

"Because… I found him."

Our eyes met and pain flashed between us like lightning. "I have to go." I pushed past her out of the house, and ran across the field for the trailhead.

"Charlee! Come back!" she called behind me. I didn't listen.

I found his paw prints in the mud at the trailhead. He was following the path we'd traveled before. The ground was slippery and I fell twice while climbing the sloping trail. By the time I reached the bluff, I was damp from sweat and my trousers were muddy to the knees.

"Mr. Jones!" An anxious knot twisted my stomach into a tight ball. He'd had a considerable head start on me.

Slow down, I said to myself. You know where he's going. His tracks led from the bluff to the clearing. I looked up at the sky. Rain started to fall and a quiet hush filled the thick forest.

I reached the clearing as daylight faded. Mr. Jones's tracks vanished. There was no sign of the eagle that lived in the tall tree.

Guilt about my harsh words to Mrs. Dalworth had hounded me all the way up the bluff. Shenoa had told me the lightkeeper was a kind woman. She was so much more than that. Some thanks she'd got from me.

A branch had fallen on Edgar Dalworth's grave. I pushed it aside and brushed away needles and leaves that had fallen during the storm.

"She thinks you and I have a lot in common," I said. "But from what she's told me, you'd never do what I did. She didn't deserve that. I promise you, I'll set things right."

The trail past the clearing was only damp. The huge canopy of branches kept the light rain from landing on the forest floor. I made quick time down the path, past the terrible place of my bad accident without giving it a second thought.

I made it to Clamity Cove by dusk. Light still lingered out on the water, but the land on shore was all black shapes and dark shadows.

I scrambled down the slope, found the rock cave and peered in through the dwindling light. There he was, curled up like a perfect crescent moon, in the place he always slept when we'd spent our first days on the island in the cave. He looked very small.

"Mr. Jones."

I touched him and he lifted his head. I ran my hand over his head. His fur was wet and cold.

"Bubba, we didn't need to come today."

I groped for the little pouch of gold in a notch in the rock wall and found it in the place I remembered only days earlier.

Mr. Jones blinked at me and then closed his eyes.

"No. It's not your time. That's not why you came here. And I didn't come here for this." I flung the pouch against the wall.

I remembered Mrs. Dalworth saying, "He's an older dog, you know." I kneeled in the darkness and started to cry. If he died now, it would be too much for me to bear.

"You listen, Mr. Jones. I won't give up and neither can you."

I threw off my pack, opened my coat and put his damp body next to my warmth. He had trekked through the rain and mud, to get me to return to the cave. He'd risked his life for me. Why? For the stupid gold?

We needed a fire but it had to wait. I had to get him warm right away. I pulled my wool blanket and canvas out of my pack and wrapped the two of us in it like a cocoon. Mr. Jones grunted a little but didn't resist.

I thought of Papa and how he healed the horses back on the ranch. I could do it, too. I remembered working on my ankle here in the cave, how my hands had buzzed for days when I'd laid them over the injury. But with each day of healing, the buzzing diminished. By the time my foot was ready for the hike to the lighthouse, I could barely feel a tingle in my fingers.

I put my hands around Mr. Jones. My fingers ached, like I'd come in from the cold with icy hands, but I knew I could help him if I could remember how to do it. I closed my eyes. I saw Papa's hands guiding me over a horse's shoulder—he felt warmth where I felt tingles. There was something else I needed to picture, but I couldn't remember what it was. I kept trying, but it made me sleepy. I always got sleepy when Papa healed the horses.

I woke up in the dark, sweaty and hot. I threw back the blanket and canvas covering my head. Mr. Jones wasn't there. Shenoa was kneeling beside a fire, stoking it with pieces of dry cedar.

"You came back."

"So did you," she replied.

"Where is he?" I demanded.

"The little dog? He's gone out for a stretch. He is feeling much better," she said, expressionless.

"I don't believe you. You always say he's nearby."

"And was this not true?"

"Yes, but this time is different. He came here to die."

She laughed. "No, he did not. The trip was difficult for him and it is good you followed, but dying was not his purpose."

I untangled myself from the blanket. I wanted to believe her. I'd seen a lot of death. It was cruel and unpredictable. It seemed like it was coming for me again.

"Yes, you have seen a lot of death," she said, as if I'd spoken my thoughts out loud. "Did you not realize, that day in the clearing, that you are no longer afraid of it?"

I thought of Mr. Dalworth under the tree. Then I thought of Mrs. Dalworth and her sudden illness.

"Maybe death doesn't scare me anymore. But dying still does."

"All that live must take the journey. It's what you call... um, what is the word, logic of nature?"

I couldn't believe what I was hearing. "I think you mean law of nature."

"I prefer logic. One day, you will die and others who remain will mourn for you, just as you are here now mourning for those who have gone ahead of you. This is life. This is the journey."

I thought about everyone I'd lost. Science didn't enter into how I felt about it.

"Life hurts."

"Trying to hang on to it and realizing you can't is what hurts."

I had nothing else to say, no questions to ask, no snappy retort, nothing left but a strange emptiness where fear and anger had been.

After a long silence, I said, "I'm so tired of losing everything."

"Perhaps you should consider what you have gained. Some would say you have the luck of a horseshoe." I saw her smile as I closed my eyes.

I slumped back against the wall and put my hand on the ground where Mr. Jones had been. It was still warm. I felt him lick my hand.

48

i

I awoke to a hard jab in the ribs. I rolled over, my eyes squinting to adjust to bright daylight streaming into the cave.

"I appreciate you building a fire. Made it easy for us to find ya, squirreled away in this little hole."

I shot up and pressed my back against the wall of the cave. The brown-haired pirate had me cornered. He leaned into the cave and jabbed at me with a long stick.

"C'mon out o' there, boy," he said, "and don't make any sudden moves or I'm likely to lose my temper and beat you to an inch o' your sorry life with this here piece of wood. I should thank you for the nice map. I considered it an invitation."

He stepped back and hollered, "Found Mrs. Dalworth's little rat!"

I took tiny little breaths and tried to think. The end of the stick was pressing into my breastbone, pinning me against the wall like a stuck goose. He called me Mrs. Dalworth's rat.

"Now you get that rucksack o' yours an' crawl on out o' there real slow."

I obeyed without saying a word. The pouch of gold I'd thrown was lying on the cave floor only two feet out of his reach.

As I stepped down to the beach, he yanked my arm and I

stumbled. My knees stung as I hit the rocks.

"Get up," he growled, lifting me by the sleeve of my coat back onto my feet.

Before I could get my balance, he dropped me and I crashed to the ground in a crumpled heap. He picked up a rock next to me. I thought he was going to bash my head in with it. Instead, he straightened up and pegged it at the brush near the cave.

"Get the hell out o' here, you annoying mongrel," he yelled.

He picked up another rock, and threw it hard at the same spot. "Bull's-eye! Haha! That'll teach ya."

Mr. Jones? I looked for him but he wasn't there.

He dragged me to my feet. "Running for the hills, tail 'tween his legs, that mangy mutt o' yours," he said, spitting the words into my face. His breath smelled of dead fish and his eyes were like beads of black oil.

"Barking his fool head off and then running away! Some watchdog you got." He pushed me ahead of him and into the clutches of one of his burly mates. The sailor looked at the bush and back, bewildered.

Farther along the cove, three other men were drinking around a small fire. The beach above the waterline had been dug up and the three barrels from the *Salish Wind* had been loaded into their rowboat!

"Slippery little seal you caught there, Skulder," said the bald-headed pirate with the red beard whose name I couldn't recall. He laughed and slapped his thigh. "Scrawny boy, but maybe we can get a few salmon for him." Some of the other men snickered.

"Cut it out, Hample. You sorry bunch of seagoing sods wouldn't know an opportunity if it bit you on the nose." He turned to me. "Now empty that sack o' yours. Let's see what you got."

I unpacked my things, one by one. Impatient, the pirate tore the pack from my hands and dumped the contents onto the beach. My hand shovel clanked onto the rocks.

He poked at the pile with his long stick, finding nothing but overnight supplies.

"What are you doing over in this cove, boy? The old lady send you?"

"Yeah…"

My mind raced. Quick. Think of a story. You're good at stories. Think!

"Speak up."

"Yessir, she did. To, uh, dig for clams and oysters. For her chowder."

He licked his lips. I'd recalled she'd offered them some on their last visit.

"How'd you get here?"

"Trekked over the middle hill."

"When it's only ten minutes by water?"

"The lady lost her boat. You know, her husband…"

"… Right. She mentioned. Huh."

He pulled out my map.

"I see here you got 'shipwreck' marked off that point. I don't see any shipwreck out there. Do you fellas see a shipwreck?"

A dutiful chorus of "no" followed.

"So why'd you mark a shipwreck on that map?"

Even though I couldn't think fast since my accident, that question was telling. They didn't realize I'd been on the sunken ship.

"There was a storm. Say, a month ago? I come some days after for, uh, clams. Found bits of sail washed up. Uh, pieces of wood and such. Looked off that point. Tide was real low that day. Thought I saw the tip of a mast sticking out of the water."

"Don't see it now," said the brown-haired pirate called Skulder.

I shook my head. "Nope. Don't see any such thing."

"Must've been a deadhead," said the one called Hample.

"If there had been a shipwreck out there, we'd know about it, wouldn't we, boys?" Skulder said.

This time, a ragged round of "aye" followed.

"It's not a real map. It's just a drawing I made. Can I have it back?"

"No!" He knocked me backwards onto the beach. My head whipped when I hit the ground. Stunned, I couldn't get up.

"What're we going to do with him? Take 'im with us?" Hample asked.

"We aren't hauling him. I don't want no human cargo."

"What about the old lady?"

"You think she's going to come looking for some half-breed that run off on her?"

Half-breed.

He looked down at me and spit near my feet. "We'll get rid of him somewheres."

They were going to kill me and dump me. Anything I said would only get me another boot onto the rocks. I had to think of a way to escape, but my head was dull and my ears were ringing. I breathed into my hands, trying to think.

"Looky here. He's gonna cry like a girl," Skulder teased.

I lifted my head and glared at him, eyes burning like coals in a hot fire. If he gave me the slightest chance, I'd bury my pocket-knife into his neck and let him bleed to death.

"Oh, oh. We got company." Hample pointed at the bay.

A canoe rounded the point into the cove. Mrs. Dalworth's friends. The Lekwungen Chief stood up in the bow as they reached shallow water.

"Now what in creation does that sorry lot want?" Skulder said. "And how did that goldanged yapping dog get in the boat with them?"

I searched the canoe. Mr. Jones wasn't there.

"What dog, Skulder?" asked Hample, not seeing one either. There was an awkward silence as the canoe slid onto the sand.

The Chief and two men stepped out. The others stayed in the boat, pointed paddles held straight up and ready.

The Chief was dressed in a long brown topcoat and trousers. He wore the same top hat with the big feather sticking out of the band. Our eyes met. He caught my call for help in a glance.

The Chief pointed at me and spoke in his language, quiet and matter-of-fact.

"Well, I'll be danged. I think they want to buy him," Skulder said to his crew. Then, turning to the Chief, he rubbed his fingers together and said, "How much?"

The Chief took a small leather bag from his jacket pocket. He slowly untied the strings, looking up and down the beach as he worked.

Skulder shifted his weight from one foot to the other and back again. When the Chief worked the string into a knot, Skulder lost his temper.

"I haven't got all day! Show me your money! And shut that damn dog up before I knock him senseless!"

Everyone stared at him. The Chief smiled and continued picking away at his knot.

"Mate," Hample said quietly. "Are you all right? There ain't any dog here…"

Skulder was wild-eyed now. "What? He's right there, plain as day!" He pointed at the ground by my feet. "What's the matter with all of you?" he yelled. Hample looked over his shoulder at the rest of the men. They fidgeted and looked away.

The Chief emptied the contents of his bag into his palm. Pointing to me, he held up a nugget of gold for Skulder.

"Whadda ya know. Look what we got here," he said, laughing like a madman. He snatched the gold from the Chief's fingers.

"Sold!" He kicked a leg out into the air and spun around. "Get him off o' me, Hample! I swear I'm gonna beat him to a pulp." He swung his stick behind his heels, twirling around like a hornet's nest was after him.

The men threw furtive looks at each other.

"Skulder?" One of the other men dared to speak.

Color drained out of Skulder's face. He panted as if he'd just run the length of the beach. Sweat beaded on his forehead and upper lip.

"It's this island. I've got a sickness from this place." Alarmed, the men stood up and backed away from him.

"Load up, men," Hample ordered. He glanced at Skulder, who was frantically beating the sand with his stick, face as white as a brand-new sail. "I swear this island is cursed. We're getting out of here, once and for all!"

Luckily, I hadn't hit my head again when the pirate knocked me onto the beach. But the jarring fall hadn't been good. The familiar pressure, like a vice clamping down on the back of my head, made me nauseous.

The Chief helped me to my feet as the pirates launched their rowboat. We waited until they'd left the cove and pulled alongside their ship.

"Eagle Looking," he said to me. "We'll take you to Mrs. Dalworth."

He gestured for me to get in the canoe.

"I have to get something first." I pointed in the direction of the rock cave. "Can you wait a few minutes?"

"There is no hurry."

"You speak English."

"As do you. Go. We will wait."

I limped up the beach, bruised and cut from landing on the rocks. My whole body ached as I climbed into the cave. The pain was even worse in my heart as I returned to the place where I'd last seen Mr. Jones. Pressure on my cut knee made me wince as I crawled inside to retrieve the small pouch of gold. On the ground beside the pouch was his yellow bandana.

Tearfully, I tied it around my neck. He didn't make me come back to the cave to get the gold. He did it because I meant to leave and make him go, too. And then, the men who killed our friends and sunk the *Salish Wind* would get away with all of their crimes.

I closed my eyes. I didn't need shares in a gold company. I was glad Mrs. Dalworth had gotten rid of the worthless reminder. I didn't even need the gold I'd come back for. But I would keep my promise to Cook and get Mr. Miller's gold back to him. And I'd see that justice was done.

Mrs. Dalworth was on the beach when the Lekwungen canoe pulled ashore in Hidden Cove.

"Charlee! You're safe! I saw the black sloop sail past last night just before dark. I told myself, the lass is smart. She's a survivor, she'll come through. But I prayed all night anyway."

My balance was off as I stepped from the canoe. She caught me before I fell face first onto the beach.

"I've rattled my head again," I said, clutching her arms for balance. "I'm a little dizzy."

"Oh no. That is not good."

"I'm all right. But Mrs. Dalworth…"

A wave of grief choked off my words and she squeezed my hands.

"What is it, Charlee? What's happened?"

"It's Mr. Jones. He's gone."

"Why, whatever do you mean, lass? He's right behind you."

49

i

I spun around. Mr. Jones was perched on the rocks, sniffing the breeze, like nothing had happened.

"You're still here!" I crouched down to pick him up, but thought better of it when my vision blurred.

"Careful!" Mrs. Dalworth said, clutching my sleeve as I plopped down awkwardly on the beach. I took Kuno's yellow bandana from my neck and tied it back where it belonged on Mr. Jones.

"You helped me," I whispered, looking into his brown eyes, "and I can't explain how. But I understand more important things now. You are no ordinary dog."

Mr. Jones said he thought I was no ordinary girl, so that made us a very fine pair.

When our joyful reunion was over, the Chief spoke at length to Mrs. Dalworth. Her expression changed from concern to horror. I imagined he was giving her the full account of what had happened in Clamity Cove.

When she replied, I could tell she was thanking him for helping me and bringing me back. There were a lot of words, even as they pushed the canoe off the shore. Before they put paddles into the water, the Chief smiled at me. I nodded and smiled back. Then he spoke in his language to Mr. Jones, who sat beside me, listening intently.

We stood on the beach until the canoe slipped out of view around the north point of Hidden Cove. Mrs. Dalworth put her arm around me and helped me limp up to the house. By the time we got there, I could barely lift my feet to step onto the porch. I dumped my pack by the door and flopped into a kitchen chair.

"The weather is clear. The supply boat could come tomorrow…" I began. I had so much to tell her, so much to say.

"We'll discuss that later. Let's get you washed up and in some clean clothes first." She put a large pan of water on the stove. "You can have a nap when we're done."

"I don't want to sleep. I can't sleep."

"Then I'll put on the kettle for tea." I mustered a weak smile. In Mrs. Dalworth's eyes, a good cup of tea could fix almost anything. There was something to that, I thought.

"I'm sorry for running out on you the way I did." She had her back to me, busy at the stove.

"I managed fine, as I always do. Edgar put a railing on that staircase in the lighthouse for a reason."

"No, I mean I'm sorry I ran out on you after telling you about… about what happened to Edgar."

I couldn't look at her, I felt so awful about how I'd thrown it at her, with no consideration for her feelings, to ease my own pain.

"No point crying over spilled milk. But I would like to hear all you know. I hope you'll do that for me, so I have the truth."

I told her then about finding Edgar in the clearing, and how he'd obviously passed while sitting beneath a beautiful tree in the dappled shade, in a clearing where a majestic eagle lived. I told her he had tucked his notebook in his pocket, and although the weather had ruined it and the pages could no longer be read, I felt that he had written quite a lot there, while taking his final rest in that pretty place before he had passed. And the distinctive gold trim on his notebook was how I came to realize it was him. I told her I had a dream when I was alone and castaway, where I was asked to give him a decent burial and that's what I did. I told her all the details that mattered and left out the parts that were too awful to mention, the way Mizzy had always done with me.

"Edgar had a delicate constitution," Mrs. Dalworth said. "He'd catch a cold if he so much as got his socks wet."

"Hiking across this island is tough. It would have been impossible if he'd fallen in the water and had to tackle it soaking wet. Or if he got caught in poor weather. I'm certain he was trying to get home. He was facing southwest, facing the lighthouse."

"I always pictured him on land. I secretly hoped he'd be found on shore somewhere. But I saw the capsized boat. A man as strong as a mule can't survive those waters. To think he was on Deception Island the whole time."

The weight of her sadness slumped her shoulders, turned her lips down, made her breathing almost disappear, but she didn't cry.

"Thank you for telling me, dear. I can have peace now that I know where he is. Had you not been shipwrecked here, I'd never have known what'd become of him."

"I can't take you to see him."

"You're leaving, I know. There's no time."

"Not that. It's much too hard for you to get there."

After I'd washed and changed, Mrs. Dalworth bandaged my knee and smeared stinky salve on all my cuts and bruises. Satisfied that she'd mended me from head to toe, we had our tea by the fire and talked for the rest of the afternoon. I told her the story of Clamity Cove from beginning to end, with nothing left out. I told her about finding Mr. Jones in the cave and how Shenoa, the young Indian woman, had found me again. I told her about Mr.

Miller's gold, and how the pirates who had buried it returned to dig it up. She listened with her mouth hanging open.

I didn't stop there. I told her about the invisible dog that came with the Lekwungen and terrorized one of the pirates.

"That's very strange indeed," she said.

"It was Mr. Jones."

"That's what the Chief told me. He said Mr. Jones came to get them this morning. That's how they knew you were in trouble."

We looked at each other as if the secret was ours and we could never share it with another soul.

"That's a crazy story," I said.

"Yep, a real crazy story."

We grinned at each other.

"I've got some other bad news." I hung my head. I couldn't think of an easy way to tell her. "The Chief used your gold to buy me back from the pirates."

"Did he now?" she replied. "Well, I told you they were very good at business."

I looked up and she shrugged. "But that gold could have helped their whole village."

"Doesn't matter. As they see it, riches are in the giving, not in the taking. We could learn from that."

I got up from the table and dug into my pack. I pulled out the little pouch and emptied the three gold nuggets on the table in front of Mrs. Dalworth.

"Good heavens, lass. Where did you come by this?"

"It's gold from the *Salish Wind*. With my memory all mixed up after my accident, I forgot I'd kept a few nuggets to buy my way back to San Francisco. I figured Mr. Miller wouldn't mind since I'd be telling him how to find all the rest of it."

"Wait. I thought you said the pirates dug it up and took it."

"They did take the barrels. But I'd dug them up, taken the gold out and filled them with rocks. Me and Mr. Jones are the only ones who know where I put it."

"That's 'Mr. Jones and I,'" she corrected.

"Oh, I know. I still talk like my papa sometimes."

She smiled knowingly and then squinted at me. "Those traders will be in for quite a shock when they open those barrels."

"They believe the island is cursed. I'm hoping they'll think it turned the gold into stone. Because what other explanation is there?"

"You are one clever lass. I hope you're right about them. I hope they are superstitious enough to believe that," Mrs. Dalworth said.

I pushed the pieces of gold over to her.

"I want you to have these. Give some to our Lekwungen friends. I never meant to drag them into my trouble. Mr. Miller will understand. I'm not stealing from him. I'm making things right. There's a lot of gold. This is nothing compared to what's left out there."

Mrs. Dalworth nodded, speechless.

"I can't repay your kindness, but maybe it will also help cover my stay, and the cost of getting me off the island and on a ship heading back to San Francisco."

"I don't need payment. I've got enough," she said.

"Then keep it as insurance. My papa taught me to have a rainy day sock. Save it for that rainy day. You never know when some orphan might show up in your garden with a tale of pirates and a shipwreck."

50

i

Mrs. Dalworth and I were on the porch with our morning coffee when a ship poked into view just north of Hidden Cove.

"Well then, there they are," she said, pointing at the water. "That Brody chap keeps to his schedule. Could set your clock by him if it weren't for the weather."

I stood up and squinted into the glare of the morning light. The supply boat drifted into the deep waters of the cove. As they lowered their anchor, a creeping wave of dread washed over me.

"Are you sure this is what you want?" Mrs. Dalworth asked.

"I'm sure. How about you?"

"No time like the present."

The ship's crew lowered two rowboats to the water. The men set to work loading them with boxes and barrels. Half an hour later, they rowed the boats in unison toward the beach.

"Time to greet our visitors," said Mrs. Dalworth.

The two of us didn't speak as we walked from the lighthouse to the cliff overlooking the landing beach. We waited there while Mr. Jones ran down to the beach to supervise the arrival party. An officer wearing a navy and white uniform was lifted from the boat and deposited away from the water so the mucky sand would not foul his boots.

"That's our Captain Brody," said Mrs. Dalworth, waving as he started the climb up from the cove. She went to greet him at the top of the path. I followed, but hung back a little until proper introductions could be made.

"Good morning, sir!"

He removed his peaked cap. "Mrs. Dalworth! Good to see you again."

Captain Brody's dark brown hair was tied back from his handsome, clean-shaven face. She extended her hand to him and he took it in both of his, bowing deeply at the waist. I hadn't seen such a display of manners since I'd left Sonoma Valley.

"You're looking lovely this morning," he said.

"I've no complaints," she replied, smoothing her hair into place.

Before breakfast, she'd brushed her hair neatly back and used pins on each temple to keep it off her face. After the morning check of the lighthouse, she'd changed into a flowered housedress that reminded me of the beautiful rhododendron bushes in the Miller garden. Now I understood why she'd gone to all the trouble.

"I trust you and Edgar are well?"

"I'm afraid I have news about that," she said, steeling herself to inform him of Edgar's passing.

"But who have we here?"

Mrs. Dalworth looked at me for approval before continuing. I bit my lip and nodded.

"Allow me to introduce you to Miss Charlotte LeBeau, formerly of San Francisco."

"*Miss* LeBeau, you say. All the way from San Francisco!"

I knew I hardly looked like a young lady in Edgar's clothes.

"And most recently, on the crew of a lost merchant schooner called the *Salish Wind*," she added.

He straightened up. "I've heard of this ship."

"I'm sure you have. It went missing in August. I'm told the Royal Navy searched high and low for it, from Fort Victoria to the Pacific."

"Yes, we did. We had report of a vessel matching the description in distress off Cape Flattery. We searched the area, but never found a trace of her. She was presumed lost at sea."

"It wasn't lost at sea. It was shipwrecked here, and robbed," Mrs. Dalworth said.

"On Deception Island? And did you say robbed?"

"The lass has quite a story to tell. I have some tragic news of my own. Please. Come join us for refreshments up at the house while your men unload the supplies."

"I should be delighted."

Mrs. Dalworth began the tale of two tragedies, starting with Edgar's disappearance. She finally said the words, "Edgar has died." She explained the unfortunate accident, and my discovery of him, only as a consequence of my own horrifying ordeal as a castaway.

The Captain wanted to hear more about the shipwreck— where it was, what had caused the ship to sink, how we had come to run aground in the treacherous waters off Deception Island. He listened as I told him the basic facts.

Mrs. Dalworth and I had agreed it was wise to leave out the part about the gold shipment. We didn't want word to get out and have all manner of fortune seekers arrive on the island with their gold pans and shovels. We'd also agreed the parts about Shenoa helping me, and Mr. Jones disappearing and reappearing, might make the entire story seem false, so I didn't mention any of those things. Truth is, the story was outrageous enough without those details.

"At first, I'm ashamed to admit, I questioned her account myself," said Mrs. Dalworth. "The lass has been through considerable trauma. But the men responsible revealed themselves to me by recent actions. I bet if you look into who reported a ship in distress, you'll find out it was a black sloop belonging to some coastal merchants. Come to think of it, I never saw a name on that boat."

"British or American?"

"It didn't fly a flag either."

The Captain had been taking notes in a journal. He looked up from his book.

"The actions of this vessel are against maritime law. Providing a false report, if proven true, is also a crime. These are serious offenses, allegations of pursuit and robbery aside. Since the ship-wreck occurred in British waters, there must be an investigation into the matter forthwith."

"We assumed so," Mrs. Dalworth replied. "We've talked this over already. Although she'd planned to go with you to Victoria and return to San Francisco, she's decided to stay for the time being so she can provide all the details you'll need."

"Excellent. Since you are currently the sole witness, your account is vital, Miss LeBeau. That's French, isn't it?"

"Yessir. I'm from the Red River Valley. Originally," I said, for the first time in my life. I'd caught them both by surprise with that statement.

"You're a long way from home by all accounts. I will open a formal investigation as soon as I return to Victoria."

"I'd like to stay here on Deception Island. I can help Mrs. Dalworth with the lighthouse, now that she's all alone."

"A reasonable arrangement, under the circumstances. We'll need you here anyway when we conduct our preliminary search for the vessel. I gather this meets your approval, Mrs. Dalworth?"

"I'm delighted to have the lass stay on."

"Then consider it arranged. I'll return with a party to begin the investigation as soon as possible. At some point, Miss LeBeau, you may need to come to Fort Victoria. If we can track down the scoundrels responsible, the case will go before the courts."

The whole matter promised to be even more tedious and complicated than I imagined. But it was what I'd decided to do and I meant to stick with it.

"Sir, Mrs. Dalworth said you could mail letters for us. I need to send news home."

"Indeed, I can take your letters. You'll be seeing more of me in the coming months, weather permitting. I will bring any letters that arrive for you when I come out. If there is a silver lining to be found in all of this, your mail service will be almost as good as in the city."

"I'd be mighty grateful. Nobody back home knows I survived," I said.

"That is an extraordinary story in itself," Captain Brody said, shaking his head with dismay. "Mrs. Dalworth. I wonder if we might have a word in private."

"Certainly. Charlee, why don't you go see how the unloading is getting on?"

That was my polite cue to leave. I hesitated, then rose from the table. What did Captain Brody need to discuss without me present?

"Matters pertaining to lighthouse operation, Miss LeBeau," the Captain said reassuringly, as if he'd read my mind. "We shan't be long."

Mrs. Dalworth smiled, but her hands fidgeted with her teacup and saucer. The business had shifted away from my fate to hers.

51

i

The night before the supply boat arrived, after my return to the lighthouse with the Lekwungen, Mrs. Dalworth and I had talked for hours.

It began with a discussion on my departure. She'd barely gotten through the details of leaving on the supply boat when I announced I'd changed my mind. I told her I didn't want to leave with the criminals responsible for sinking the *Salish Wind* still running free. Mrs. Dalworth pointed out that my head injury was also a factor to consider, and I should not compromise my full recovery by undertaking difficult travel.

And so we decided it together. She would mail a letter of introduction to Mr. Miller outlining the situation and I would send one to Jake. We settled at the kitchen table with stationery and one of Edgar's finest writing pens.

"I'd appreciate it if you'd do the writing, lass. Penmanship was never my strong suit and these old glasses make it hard to keep my lines straight. Edgar had a beautiful hand, as I'm sure you noticed in his notes. By comparison, my writing looks like chicken scratches."

I dated the letter and Mrs. Dalworth began dictation.

"'Dear Mr. Miller. I am keeper at the remote Deception Island lighthouse in the Colony of Vancouver Island. I write bearing news of your vessel, *Salish Wind*.'"

"That's a strong opening."

Mrs. Dalworth beamed. "New paragraph. 'By now, you have likely received report that your vessel was lost at sea in August. This is not correct. I regret to inform you your vessel was indeed lost; however, it was the treacherous rocks guarding this untamed island that took her to her final resting place.'"

"A dramatic touch."

"Too much?"

"He's a man of letters. He'll appreciate it. What next?"

"'By now, you've been told all crew were lost; however, Miss Charlee LeBeau, along with the ship's dog, miraculously made it to the island. They are both here with me now at the lighthouse.' Do you want me to mention your injuries or not?"

"I don't think so. He'll just worry."

"Right. New paragraph. 'You should know that we will be asking the authorities to open an investigation into the loss of your ship. As Charlee will say...'"

"Attest?"

"'As Charlee will attest, the shipwreck also involved a daring pursuit and robbery.'"

She stopped to think.

"I should probably wrap it up, keep it to the point. What else needs to be said?"

"Just the part about me staying here."

"Oh yes. 'While the investigation is conducted, Charlee must remain here, as she is the sole witness to particularly heinous crimes. Since she has no legal guardian, she will remain under my care at the lighthouse until the facts of the shipwreck are reviewed and decided.'"

"I think he needs to know there's no need to rush up here. It would be like him to do that."

"Good point. New paragraph. 'I'm certain the authorities will be in touch with you regarding developments forthwith. As for Charlee, you need not worry for her well-being. I will see to her room and board as well as her schooling for the duration."

"My schooling?"

"You'll not stay under the Dalworth roof and neglect your education. You'll work on studies every day. Most of Edgar's books are out of my league but I can supervise like the best of them. I'll trade for some other books you might care to read. Where were we?"

I read back her last two lines.

"Good. 'In closing, I urge you to remain in San Francisco until they request your presence. Unfortunately, investigations like these can take some time. There is little point enduring the hardship of travel until there is something to be done.' Do you want me to mention the gold?"

"Too risky to put anything in writing about that. I don't trust anyone except you. Maybe say, Charlee would like you to tell Cook that she is still able to keep her midnight promise."

"Some kind of code, I presume? Write that down then. How should I end it?"

"Yours truly?"

"That has no flair. How about, 'With kind regards and wishes for a just resolution.'"

"Oh, that's perfect. He'll like that very much."

"Sign it, Mrs. Ellen Dalworth."

Her name was Ellen.

Pleased with her letter, Mrs. Dalworth stoked the fire and retired to her rocking chair to read her Bible. I wrote my letter to Jake, in the style we had always used for our secret and important correspondence. As always, he would read between the lines.

11:00 pm September 29, 1859

Dear Jake,

Greetings from Deception Island, from the lighthouse of the same name off the southern tip of Vancouver Island. This was an unexpected stop in my travels, to say the very least, but so it is that I find myself here instead of back in San Francisco.

As you have no doubt heard, my geological research party was unexpectedly disbanded and I'm no longer part of that great crew. I was deeply saddened by this as I had made some excellent friends. To make matters worse, I had an unfortunate fall while trekking in the wilderness. I assure you, I am doing quite well now that I'm able to rest and recover in a less hostile setting.

Since the sudden end of my internship, I have had considerable time to reflect on my life choices. It will come as quite a surprise to you that I have decided to change my field of study. While government studies are of no interest to me whatsoever (and I cannot be persuaded otherwise, dear fellow), I have found my geological studies, particularly with the recent emphasis on mineral extraction, to be equally unrewarding, and perhaps even detrimental. I have no passion for the subject any longer.

As I won't be back in time for school, and I'm unable to even say when I shall be able to return, home schooling has been arranged for me. A gentleman, late of the island, had a remarkable collection of mathematics and science books. The personal notebooks he left behind are a gold mine of information. I deeply regret the loss of such a brilliant mind, even though I'd met him only a few times in passing.

Math and science material aside, there is a tragic lack of literature available here. Fiction is extremely scarce on the frontier and I cannot bear to read the two titles I have on hand one more time. Since you have always upheld the value of a well-rounded education, please send me any literature you can lay your hands on, old or new. Recent works by any of the Brontës would be particularly delightful. Or perhaps even the latest poetry of a Mr. Walt Whitman.

I very much enjoyed our short time together when we met in Fort

Victoria last month. It reminded me of the old days, when we were very young and innocent in the world. While we can't turn back the clock, I'm confident we will enjoy more times like those in the near future. In the meantime, please write often, as we will receive special visits and deliveries over the coming months due to a pressing legal matter.

In closing, please give my love to the Jeffersons. I will see them both, and you as well, soon.

Until then, I remain,

Your loyal friend and sojourner,

C.L. Fitzquiddick

Formerly of the Salish Wind expedition.

PS Mr. B. Jones remains in my company. He sends his warm regards.

Mrs. Dalworth and I sent our letters off with Mr. Brody and the supply boat. As we turned in for bed after the midnight lighthouse check, I hoped that staying on the island had been the right decision. Mr. Jones curled up on his spot of my bunk and closed his eyes. Ever since I'd decided to stay, he had gone back to his old habits and happy routines.

I was reminded of something then.

"Mrs. Dalworth."

"Yes, lass?"

"What did the Lekwungen Chief say to Mr. Jones before he left?"

"Oh, let me think. It had to do with the schooner. Didn't make much sense, to be honest, although I recall the words were lovely. He said, 'She was carried here on the Salish wind. It is the Salish wind that will carry her home.' Something like that."

It wasn't about the boat at all. It was about my journey to find where I belonged.

I touched Mr. Jones's shoulder. He sighed, and I blew out my candle.

Author's Note

Much care has been taken in this novel to ensure the accuracy of people, places and events. While some historical figures appear, their roles within the story are entirely fictional.

With respect to historical records, the Deception Island lighthouse did not exist and there is no Deception Island in the Strait of Juan de Fuca. Nonetheless, the lighthouse is based on the first lighthouses built in the area around the time. Although its exact location is not specified, Deception Island's fictional location would have placed it within the traditional, ancestral and unceded territory of the Lekwungen First Nations.

Even though you won't find the island or the lighthouse on a map, if you sail west from Victoria, you might get a glimpse of Deception Island, emerging and then disappearing again in thick fog. Some sailors say the lighthouse blinks for those who look hard enough. Real or imagined, light always shines to guide our journeys if we look hard enough. It also marks the places of our ancestors, and the places where other brave souls have gone before.

Acknowledgments

To my bubble—Adua Porteous, Cita Airth, Cory and Walter. You keep me from disappearing entirely into my books and writing, and remind me that not all sweatpants should be seen outside of one's house. May the readers of this page one day wonder, "What's a bubble?"

To my family—Lisa, Carolynn, Susanne, Dennis, Don, as well as an extensive pack of in-laws, outlaws and relations. You are a diverse village of talents and personalities and you mean the world to me.

To my dear friends—I wish I could list all of you, because your endless support keeps me going. I promise I haven't stolen too many of your traits for my characters, or perhaps I should say, any resemblance to any of you is purely coincidental.

To Jan Carley, my writing partner, for being a voice of positive clarity when the work of self-publishing overwhelms; To Glenda McFarlane, my devoted editor, for guiding me through rewrites with so much insight, honesty and heart; To Joy Bruce, my diligent proof reader, for spotting the things all the rest of us still missed.

To Marty Dolan, my Art Director, for orchestrating the beautiful cover art and understanding my creative process; To Josephine Steeves, who imagined an island into existence, and rendered it exactly as Charlee would have done at Mrs.

Dalworth's kitchen table; To my sister Susanne Fauchon, whose sailing photograph graces the cover; To Cynthia Cui, for bringing the cover design elements together.

To my crew of beta readers, who endured early versions of the manuscript: Josie Steeves, Norm Root, Celine Kaufman, Marty Dolan, Jan Carley, Gayle McCaul, Jim McCaul, Sue Fauchon and Sam Steeves.

To my research and subject specialists: Barb Bluschke, mariner of wind and power, for designing the fictional *Salish Wind* and charting her historical sailing route; Norm Root, avid cruising sailor, for insights on sailing life and coastal journeys; Joanne Wendell, police forensic expert, for everything you'd wanted to know about forensics but were afraid to ask; Jeanie Yee and Colleen Yee, for subtleties of Cantonese in reference to good guys and bad guys.

To Cory, my Salishan Jack Russell Terrier, my angel in a dog suit, for teaching me about special dogs, and for making sure I got away from my desk for long walks in the fresh air.

Thank you all. I will always be grateful for your love and support.

About the Author

C.V. (Cindy) Gauthier has always lived on the west coast of British Columbia. She usually divides her time between the village of Steveston on the Fraser River and the old growth forest of the Sunshine Coast at Okeover Inlet.

Before turning to fiction writing, Cindy spent three decades as a secondary school educator in Vancouver. During that time, she was always writing something, from educational blogs and columns to open learning materials for the Commonwealth of Learning. The Charlee LeBeau Series is her first set of novels.

Although the series is classified under Young Adult and Historical Adventure, adult readers have found the novels resonate with their own personal histories, experiences and family stories. The series is ideal for junior high school students and is a particularly empowering read for young people. The books are written from a powerful place of hope and redemption, where no matter where you are from or what may happen in your life, it is possible to transcend and make the world a better place.

To purchase books, join the Reader's List, or find other news and information, please visit the author's website at cvgauthier. com. For author bookings or enquiries, please contact Tuann Andrews Publishing at tapublishing@shaw.ca or the author at cvgauthier@cvgauthier.com.

Charlee LeBeau & The Gambler's Promise, the first book in the series, won the 2020 Whistler Independent Book Award for fiction. The author judges who chose the winning title wrote the following:

> "*Charlee LeBeau & The Gambler's Promise* is a rollicking adventure of the wild west, packed with tall tales of treasure and romance, tragedy, and the dark deeds of villains. But it is also a deeper story about a young woman struggling with loss and finding, in her grief, the ability to not only cope, but to forge her own identity and independence, even in the face of cruel societal norms that force her to hide who she really is. Charlee is an engaging and spirited character that many young women will relate to as she refuses to allow circumstance or prejudice hold her back."
>
> —Gail Anderson-Dargatz

"...I suggest this be read, and then discussed, by whole families, not only for its evocation of time, place and character, but for the themes it fleshes out so well: the strength of girls, the nonsensical cruelty of racism, the human costs of greed, the redemptive power of friendship."

—Darcie Friesen Hossack

Charlee LeBeau & The Salish Wind is the second book in the Charlee LeBeau series. The third book is planned for release in the winter of 2021.

Printed in Canada